WATERFALL GLEN

Gold Imprint
Medallion Press, Inc.
Printed in USA

DEDICATION:
To mum and dad, for everything.

Published 2006 by Medallion Press, Inc.

The MEDALLION PRESS LOGO
is a registered tradmark of Medallion Press, Inc.

If you purchased this book without a cover, you should be aware that this book is stolen property. It was reported as "unsold and destroyed" to the publisher, and neither the author nor the publisher has received any payment from this "stripped book."

Copyright © 2006 by Davie Henderson
Cover Illustration by James Tampa

All rights reserved. No part of this book may be reproduced or transmitted in any form or by any electronic or mechanical means, including photocopying, recording, or by any information storage and retrieval system, without written permission of the publisher, except where permitted by law.

Names, characters, places, and incidents are the products of the author's imagination or are used fictionally. Any resemblance to actual events, locales, or persons, living or dead, is entirely coincidental.

Printed in the United States of America

Library of Congress Cataloging-in-Publication Data

Henderson, Davie.
 Waterfall Glen / Davie Henderson.
  p. cm.
 ISBN 1-932815-83-X
 1. Scotland--Fiction. 2. Americans--Scotland--Fiction. I. Title.
 PR6108.E56W38 2006
 813'.6--dc22

2005037120

10 9 8 7 6 5 4 3 2 1
First Edition

DAVIE HENDERSON

WATERFALL GLEN

CHAPTER 1

KATE BRODIE WAS WORKING ON A ROMANTIC SCULPTURE when the brass bell above her craft shop door gave a gentle tinkle. She looked up to see a Western Union messenger approaching the counter with a telegram in his hand.

"Miss Kate Brodie?" the man asked.

Kate nodded, curious. She'd never received a cable before, and had no idea who might have sent one now. She wiped her hands on her jeans, signed the messenger's clipboard, and had the cable ripped open before he'd even reached the door. It read:

FROM MESSRS ARCHIBALD CUNNINGHAM & CO,
SOLICITORS AND NOTARIES, INVERNESS,
SCOTLAND. TO MISS KATE BRODIE OF SAU-
SALITO, CALIFORNIA. IT IS OUR SAD
DUTY TO INFORM YOU OF THE DEATH OF MR
COLIN CHISHOLM OF GLEN CRANOCH. PLEASE
CALL US ON 44 145 3327 166 AS SOON
AS POSSIBLE REGARDING THE ESTATE.
SINCERELY — A. CUNNINGHAM.

Kate had never heard of a Colin Chisholm or Glen Cranoch, and knew there must have been a mix-up somewhere down the line. She headed over to the faux antique telephone on the counter to let Messrs Archibald Cunningham & Co know they had the wrong Kate Brodie.

Waiting for the international connection to be made, she looked at the telegram again and indulged in a flight of fancy. She'd been doing that a lot recently. Being the Kate in Kate's Crafts stopped life seeming empty but wasn't enough to make it full—not for someone who was 36 and still single—and there were days when the quaint, Victorian-fronted shop seemed as much of a prison as Alcatraz out in the bay. For a few moments Kate allowed herself to imagine the telegram actually was for her . . .

Then the phone started ringing in far-off Scotland. Kate caught sight of her reflection in a gilt-framed mirror and finger-combed her short blond hair, as if whoever answered would actually be able to see her. The face looking back at her had wide-apart silvery-blue eyes, a thinnish nose with just a hint of an upturn, and a mouth that she wished was a little fuller lipped and not quite so broad. The overall look was pixie cute, and she'd been told more than once that she had a Meg Ryan smile. She smiled wryly now at her flight of fancy, liking the sparkle in her eyes and the sweetness of her mouth—but not the little wrinkles that had recently started accompanying her smiles.

"Archibald Cunningham's office. How might we be of help?" The voice that rescued Kate from her wrinkles had a gentle Scottish lilt, and sounded like it belonged to a middle-aged woman.

"This is Kate Brodie in Sausalito. I've just received a cable asking if I would call this number, but I think there must have been some sort of mis—"

"Ah, Miss Brodie!" The woman sounded delighted. "We've been expecting your call. If you'll just be holding on for a moment."

After a succession of clicks a man's voice said, "Miss Brodie?"

"Yes, but not the Kate Brodie you're looking for, I'm afraid. I've never heard of this Glen Cranoch place before, and I didn't know any Colin Chisholm."

"Maybe not, but it seems that Mr. Chisholm knew you—or at least he knew about you."

"I don't understand."

"He developed an interest in his family tree, and discovered you at the end of the last remaining branch. Something to do with a Varri Chisholm who emigrated to America in the 1920s, I believe. Does *that* name ring any bells?"

"I'm sorry, no," Kate said. She truly was sorry. Even though she'd known it was all a mistake she was still strangely disappointed to have it confirmed. For a few wonderful moments she'd swapped the confines of her small souvenir shop for a far more exciting place. She wasn't able to keep the disappointment from her voice as she said, "My grandmother came from Scotland, but I'm afraid her name was Mary Millar."

Archibald Cunningham laughed. "Aye, but Chisholm was her maiden name, and 'Varri' is the Gaelic way of saying Mary. Your granny likely changed her name when she started afresh in the new world," he said. "It seems as if your name will be changing too," he added.

"What do you mean?" Kate asked, bewildered.

"How do you like the sound of Lady Kate of Glen Cranoch?"

Even if Kate had known what to say, she wouldn't have been able to get the words out because of the sudden hammering in her chest and tightness in her throat. Her hands were shaking, her legs ready to give way at any moment. She eased herself onto her high stool and rested her elbows on the counter, glad of the support.

"Hello? Still there?" Archibald Cunningham asked.

"Yes," Kate said quietly. "I'm just trying to take all this in."

"Aye, well I can see how it must come as something of a surprise, right enough."

Unable to hide the scepticism that followed her initial shock, Kate said, "Forgive me for sounding suspicious, but this all seems too good to be true. I feel sure there has to be a catch somewhere."

There was more than a hint of irony in Archibald Cunningham's laughter. "Oh, The Cranoch Estate has more than its share of problems, believe me," he said. "Some are very real, and others . . . Well, it's probably best not to go into that just now."

Kate had no idea what he meant by that. Before she could ask the lawyer to explain, he said, "Let's just say there's not much chance that you'll be able to hang on to The Cranoch unless you're an uncommonly wealthy or resourceful woman."

"I'm certainly not the first of those things."

"Well, there's a buyer who'll likely pay a good price for the estate if you want to sell it—and my professional advice would be to accept his offer. You'd save yourself quite a kerfuffle, and probably a fair amount of heartache, too."

"What do you mean, 'a fair amount of heartache'?"

"I couldn't really explain in words. You'd have to see Glen Cranoch and Greystane for yourself, then you'd understand exactly what I mean."

"Greystane?"

"Aye, the ancestral home of the Chisholms," he told her. "Anyway, if you do want to make the trip across the pond I can get Finlay to meet you at the airport in Inverness."

"Who's Finlay?"

"He's the handyman and ghillie."

Correctly interpreting the silence that followed, Archibald Cunningham said, "But of course you won't be knowing what a ghillie is, now, will you?"

"I haven't got a clue."

"It's a bit like a gamekeeper. Anyway, Finlay's an all-round good sort. He's at your service, along with Miss Weir—she's the cook and housekeeper—and a dozen crofters and their families."

"I'm sorry, you've lost me again. Crofters?"

"Aye, crofters. They're tenant farmers. But you can't afford to let them influence your decision about whether or not to sell the estate. Please bear that in mind if you do decide to pay a visit."

"Are these people depending on me in some way?"

"Well, let's just say that Finlay and Miss Weir are your employees; and as for the crofters, they hold their tenancies at your pleasure.

"Anyway, I can fax over the balance sheets and books if you'd like, and you can go over them with your accountant. Or, if you decide to come over here in person, I'd be happy to go through the accounts line by line with you myself. I'm afraid that whoever it is that explains them to you, though, they'll say the same thing."

"My head's spinning," Kate told him. "I don't know quite what to think about any of this, let alone what to say."

"Then don't say any more until you've had a chance for a wee think to yourself, Lady Kate. Meantime, if there's anything I can do to help, don't hesitate to call."

After thanking the lawyer Kate dialled her father's number, desperate for an answer. She was disappointed rather than surprised when she didn't get one. It was a nice morning and the chances were he'd be out sailing on *Lawman*, the small yacht that had been his second home since retiring from the Marin County Police Department. Unable to keep the excitement from her voice, she left a message on his answering machine: "Dad, something very strange has happened—please look into the shop as soon as you can."

Keith Brodie walked into the shop just after lunchtime, bringing some coffee, a couple of blueberry muffins, and a puzzled expression with him.

Kate did her best to explain the morning's events, but the words came out in a jumble because she was so excited.

Her father had to say, "Slow down, darling, and start from the beginning."

So she did.

When she reached the end, her father—who had talked his way out of confrontations with men carrying knives and guns and broken bottles in his time—was lost for words.

"Here's the cable," Kate said, handing him the flimsy piece of paper. It was dog-eared and almost torn in two because she'd spent most of the morning staring at it in a not entirely successful attempt to convince herself she hadn't imagined the whole thing.

Keith used his free hand to take a pair of half-moon reading glasses from the inside pocket of his vest. A bemused look crossed his face, and he shook his head as if barely able to believe what he was reading. "I knew that your mom's mother came from over there, but she never talked about the family she left behind. I got the idea there had been a bitter falling out over something because she never heard from her folks after she came to the States. Your mother and I never expected to hear from them, either. We certainly never expected anything like this."

"It's like some sort of fairytale, isn't it?" Kate said. "I keep expecting to wake up any moment and find out that it's all been just a dream."

"Well, if it is just a dream, I must be having the same one," Keith told her. Handing the cable back to his daughter, he said, "Have you thought about what you're going to do, Kate?"

"According to this Mr. Cunningham I don't really have much choice—I'll have to sell the place."

"How come?"

"I just gave you the good news. The bad news is that the house is very neglected, and the estate has running costs I wouldn't be able to meet." She hesitated, then added, "Besides, I have to think about what I'd be leaving behind here."

"If you're talking about me, don't make that a factor."

"You're the most important factor of all to me, Dad."

Keith moved closer to the high stool, so that he could put his arms around Kate and draw her head into his chest. "You're not trying to tell me you think your dad's so old and crumbly he needs looking after, are you?"

Kate drew back to look up at him, saying, "Of course not, Dad. I just like to think we're there for each other."

"However far apart, we'll always be there for each

other, Kate," he told her. "The important distance between two people isn't the one that's measured in miles."

"Dad, that's so sweet."

"It's just my way of saying I'd like a vacation in the Scottish Highlands every now and then. Just think, you could take me salmon fishing and deer hunting."

"What about this place?" Kate said, looking around the shop: at the hanging wall plates depicting Golden Gate Bridge, Fisherman's Wharf and Cathedral Grove; at the shelves stacked with hand-painted mugs and ashtrays; the trays of souvenir keyrings, and racks of tie-dyed T-shirts.

Watching her, Keith said, "Are you happy here, Kate?"

"I'm comfortable."

"Yes, I know, but that's not what I asked. Can you look me in the eye and tell me you're truly content?"

Kate sighed and looked around the shop again. Her gaze fell on a display cabinet of romantic sculptures—expressions of her unfulfilled desires and nameless longings. She'd once shaped such figures effortlessly with her long-fingered hands, but for some time now had struggled to visualize new poses or even recreate old ones. Her figures had gradually been taking on a cold, lifeless look, as if incapable of feeling love.

"I do feel stuck in a rut," she said finally. "Well, maybe 'rut' isn't the right word. It's more a daily routine that's not unpleasant, but doesn't really challenge me or let me grow. Like I said, my life is comfortable, Dad, but I sometimes feel as though there has to be a bit more to life than just being comfortable—and lately I've been wondering if I'm ever going to find it here."

"Then it sounds as if you have to at least go and see this place, Glen—"

"Cranoch—or, as Mr. Cunningham called it, 'Glen Crrranochh'," Kate said, putting on a comedy Scottish accent.

Her father laughed. "Anyway, the only way to find out if it's something you could make a fist of is by going there."

"What about the shop?"

"I'll look after it while you're away. I've been a bit thoughtless, Kate. You're long overdue a break."

"What if my stay turns into something more than a break? Would you be happy to turn Kate's Crafts into Keith's Crafts?"

"Somehow I can't really see it, can you?"

Kate shook her head.

"What I can see, however, is *Keith's Cabin*: a nautical supplies store, with me at the helm—and, if it did well enough, somebody else at the till so that I could still go out on *Lawman*. How does *that* sound?"

Kate smiled. "It sounds much more you than Keith's Crafts."

"I could buy you out or keep you as a silent partner," Keith told her. "Either way, the money would help you get on your feet."

"Thanks, Dad. From the sound of it, this Cranoch estate would be a bit of a money pit, though."

"I just want you to know that you have options. I'd

hate you to be held back in any way because of me; and your mother would have hated you to be tied up because of the shop."

"I don't want you to think I'm unhappy here, Dad. It's just that sometimes I feel the walls closing in."

"You should be feeling the wind in your hair, Kate, not the walls closing in. I have no idea what you'll find in this Glen Cranoch, but it sounds like a place where you'll at least feel the wind in your hair."

CHAPTER 2

A WEEK LATER KATE WAS ON A JUMBO JET BOUND FOR London, with an Inverness flight to follow. Butterflies fluttered crazily in her stomach as she thought about what awaited her in Glen Cranoch, and just how different the next few weeks were likely to be from any of the years that had gone before. All she knew for sure was that nothing she'd experienced was likely to have prepared her for what lay ahead.

She didn't know whether Greystane was little more than a barely habitable ruin, or somewhere she could turn into a home; whether the glen would be bleak and desolate moorland or wildly beautiful. She tried picturing the place in her mind, but didn't have nearly enough to go on; so instead she turned her thoughts to the people who lived there—Finlay, Miss Weir and the crofters. Would they be friendly and welcoming or regard her with suspicion, resentment and barely veiled hostility? Would the glen have the kind of isolation that drew people together and fostered a far greater sense of community than you got in a city, or would its people just feel plain isolated? She wondered if they wore tweed and tartan, ate porridge and drank whisky; or if those would turn out to be ridiculous stereotypes she'd look sheepishly back on after seeing them dressed in denims, Nike T shirts and baseball caps, drinking cans of Coke and eating slices of pizza.

Kate was still thinking about that when she fell asleep not long after the remnants of the in-flight meal had been cleared away.

The excitement of the previous few days had exhausted her, and when she woke up it was to the captain's cheery voice saying, "Good morning, ladies and gentlemen. The cabin crew are about to start serving a light breakfast, and shortly after that we'll be commencing our descent to Heathrow Airport in London."

They touched down ten minutes ahead of schedule and, with a couple of hours to kill before her connecting flight, Kate had a shower in the airport. She changed from jeans and black halter top into fawn slacks, a low-cut cream cashmere sweater, and a long Burberry coat and matching scarf she'd bought the day before because she thought they were what a Highland lady might wear. Finlay was meeting her at Inverness, and she wanted to make a good impression.

She spent the first part of the flight north trying to imagine what Finlay would look like, and the rest of it in a dreamy doze during which her imagination conjured up a convincingly detailed picture of a kilted Tom Hanks. He was tall, dark, and ruggedly handsome, reassuringly strong but comfortingly gentle. His voice was deep yet quiet, and his smile would make her heart skip a beat. So complete was the picture that, when the plane began its descent, Kate felt as if she was going to meet someone she already knew and loved rather than a complete stranger she'd never even seen before.

The butterflies Kate had felt on the other side of the Atlantic returned in force as she pushed her luggage-laden trolley towards the sign that said **MEETING AREA**. Pausing just before she turned the corner from partitioned corridor to rendezvous point, she took a compact from her handbag, finger-combed her hair, and gave herself a reassuring smile.

Maybe he'll be younger than Tom Hanks, with a roguish Ewan McGregor grin and unruly hair a sun-kissed shade between gold and ginger, she thought. Or perhaps he'll be older, more like Sean Connery, with irresistible charm and a voice you could listen to all day without hearing the words because you were so caught up in the accent.

But when she reached the rendezvous area there wasn't anyone remotely resembling Tom Hanks, Ewan McGregor or Sean Connery; just a slight old man in grey slacks, absently picking at a piece of fluff beside the regimental badge on his dark blazer. He looked at least 70, but his posture was ramrod straight. When he became aware of passengers filing into the meeting area he held up a piece of cardboard with **LADY KATE BRODIE** crayoned on it.

Kate tried to hide her disappointment. She could see he'd made every effort to look his best, from his Brylcreemed silver-grey hair and neatly trimmed David Niven moustache to the carefully folded white handkerchief peeping from the pocket of his blazer, the razor crease in his slacks, and the parade-ground polish of his shoes.

Their eyes met and Kate smiled. At first she thought his eyes were steely and cold, but she quickly changed her mind because they had more than a hint of mischief in them when he smiled back. He had an interesting face, Kate thought as she pushed her trolley towards him. His grooming meant he was too refined to be completely rugged, yet at the same time his weather-beaten complexion and the way the middle section of his nose was knocked slightly to one side made him too rugged to look refined.

"Are you Finlay McRae?" Kate asked, bringing her trolley to a halt in front of him.

"That I am," he said. "But you can't be Lady Kate Brodie, because Mr. Cunningham told me she was 36, not 26."

Kate laughed with delight, all her disappointment at not being met by a Ewan McGregor or Tom Hanks disappearing. She was charmed by his accent as well as his words. He had the same sort of singsong voice as Archibald Cunningham, but the words were slower and more measured, with some syllables shorter than she was used to hearing and others longer. "That's a nice way to welcome someone to your shores," Kate said.

"There's an even nicer welcome waiting for you at

Greystane: Miss Weir's making one of her stews, with a clootie dumpling to follow."

Kate was scared to ask what a "clootie" was in case it turned out to be a ruthlessly persecuted small furry animal, so instead she said, "How long is the drive?"

"It's about forty minutes by the quickest road, but I'm thinking you'd rather go by the scenic route. It's a wee bit longer, but well worth it for the view."

"I'm wiped out, but I'd like my first sight of the glen to be special."

"I'd like that very much, too," Finlay McRae said, and Kate remembered that this old man's future lay in her hands.

As soon as they walked out of the airport terminal Finlay switched places so that Kate was on the inside of the pavement. It was a little sign of manners that her father also displayed, but something that seemed to have died out among her own generation—much to her disappointment, none of her dates had ever done it, and each had immediately gone down in her estimation as a result.

"It's no limousine," Finlay said as they approached a beaten-up, dark green Land Rover, "but a fancy car wouldn't be very much use on the road up to The Cranoch."

"I can't wait to see this place," Kate said as Finlay opened the back door of the Land Rover and started loading the luggage. Kate made to help him but he stopped her, saying, "It's okay, Lady Kate, I'm not quite ready for the knacker's yard yet."

Kate pushed the empty trolley to a pick-up point. Finlay

held the passenger door open for her when she came back, and she said, "Thank you, Mr. McRae."

"Finlay," he said, "You can just call me Finlay."

"If you'll just call me Kate."

"Well, maybe when no one else is around," he said. "I wouldn't want to appear too familiar," he told her, then closed the door and walked around to the driver's side. "I'm sorry if it's not very comfortable," he apologized as they buckled up their seatbelts, "but Mr. Chisholm rarely left the estate, so a new car wouldn't have been a priority even if there had been money to spare."

"What was he like?"

"Mr. Chisholm? Do you know much about him?"

"I'd never even heard of him or Glen Cranoch until a week ago."

"So all this must have come as quite a surprise, then."

" 'Surprise' isn't even remotely ball-park close, Finlay, believe me. This whole thing still hasn't sunk in yet. I keep expecting to wake up at any moment and discover I've been dreaming."

"Aye," he said, "I can imagine. And where would you be waking up if you had just been dreaming?" he asked, and checked the mirrors before pulling out.

The question made Kate realize that the people of Glen Cranoch must be every bit as curious about her as she was about them. "I'd be in a small craft shop in a pretty little town just across the bay from San Francisco," she told him.

"Pretty enough to get homesick for?"

"Time will tell, I guess. How about Glen Cranoch, is it pretty enough to get homesick for?"

"I've only ever left it the once, and every day I was away I wished with all my heart that I was back home."

"Where did you leave it for?"

"A little jaunt to France and Germany. But that was a long time ago now."

"And you've never left the glen since?"

"Apart from trips to Glasgow, Edinburgh or Aberdeen—and Inverness, of course—for Mr. Chisholm, no."

"You must like the glen very much."

"It's partly that, and partly that the little I've seen of how the world has changed hasn't left me wanting to see any more of it. What, with traffic jams on the roads, litter on the streets and graffiti on the walls . . . Supermarkets where they sell food that doesn't have any more flavour than the plastic it's packed in and you don't even get a friendly smile when you hand over your money, instead of character-filled corner shops where your conversation was as valued as your custom . . . Children giving cheek to their parents, and teenagers walking about with rude words printed on their T-shirts . . . Young men with earrings and long hair, and young women with shaved heads and tattoos . . . No, I don't feel at all at home in that world, not the way I feel at home in Glen Cranoch.

"But sorry, there's me rambling on and I still haven't told you about your . . . would it be a second cousin?"

"From what I can make out, he was my grandmother's

sister's son."

Moving up through the gears, Finlay said, "I suppose there were two Colin Chisholms."

"What do you mean?"

"There was the Colin who went away to the war in 1940—a right handsome man, and something of a playboy, if I might say so; and then there was the Colin who came back in 1944."

"But the war didn't finish until 1945."

"For Colin Chisholm it finished in 1944. For Colin Chisholm a lot of things finished in 1944."

"I don't understand."

"Have you heard of The Few?"

Kate shook her head.

"When the war started we weren't ready for it," Finlay said. "We needed to buy some time, and the currency we bought it with was the raw courage of men like Colin Chisholm. He was a fighter pilot, and a damn good one at that. They were so heavily outnumbered they were known as The Few, and they helped hold back the tide.

"Then, just when the tide was turning—and it looked like maybe the family's run of bad luck had come to an end—Colin was shot down."

"What do you mean, the family's run of bad luck?"

Finlay went quiet, then told her, "I've maybe said more than I should . . . Certainly more than I meant to."

"Come on, Finlay, out with it."

"Well, I suppose it's okay to tell you, because I can't

imagine a sophisticated woman like you believes in superstitions and the like." All the same, he hesitated before carrying on, as if trying to find the easiest way to tackle a difficult subject. Finally he told her, "There are some people who say the Chisholms of Glen Cranoch have had more than their share of misfortune."

"What sort of misfortune?"

"The kind that breaks hearts and ends lives long before their time. Take the first war: two of the three serving sons died in the trenches—"

"That's horrible, but I suppose it wasn't all that uncommon."

"No, indeed, but the one who survived the slaughter went down on a troopship that sank within sight of the shore on the way home.

"I suppose every family has such stories; it's just that the Chisholms seem to have more to tell than most—at least one for every generation."

"You almost make it sound like a curse."

"There are some around here who'd use that word, but they're superstitious people who still live in the past—I mean even further in the past than me."

Before Kate could inquire as to the nature of the misdeeds that had led people to believe her family might be deserving of a curse, Finlay picked up the tale of Colin Chisholm: "Anyway, like I was telling you, just when the worst of the war was over, Mr. Chisholm's plane got hit. His canopy jammed and his face was badly burned before he managed to bail out. The doctors did what they could for him, with skin grafts and the like, but his mouth was left dragged down at one side in a permanent grimace."

"How awful," Kate said.

Finlay nodded. "He went from being the sort of person who turned heads because he was so good looking, to someone people either looked quickly away from or couldn't help staring at in horrified fascination." He took a sharp bend, then said, "You might have got to wondering why there isn't a mirror in Greystane, Lady Kate. Well, it's because Mr. Chisholm didn't even feel comfortable in the presence of his own reflection, let alone in the company of other people."

"He must have led a terribly lonely life, then."

Finlay nodded. "The only company he ever really had was mine. We shared a love of fishing, you see. We used to spend hours just enjoying the sound of the water, the feel of the breeze, the smell of the heather, and the walk there and back."

Kate thought for a few moments, then said, "I don't want to pry or appear insensitive, Finlay, but did Mr. Chisholm make any provision for you in his will? I'm only asking because you must have been far more like family to him than I was."

"He left me the Land Rover, Lady Kate. I hope you don't mind."

"Just Kate," she reminded him gently, sensing he didn't take anything for granted, and liking him all the more for it. "And no, I don't mind in the slightest. Quite the opposite—I was just worried in case you hadn't been left anything at all."

"You've nothing to worry about there. Colin Chisholm left me far more valuable things than the Land Rover. He left me memories of fish landed and ones that got away, of countless quiet conversations and companionable silences standing shoulder-to-shoulder with the sun at our backs and the breeze in our face and the sweet sound of lure breaking water and line running through reel. You can't put a price on any of that."

Kate thought about some of the people she'd known back home, the things they valued and talked about, and when she compared them with the old man sitting next to her the gulf couldn't have been any greater.

"Is there a river in the glen?" she asked to break the silence that followed.

"Not in the glen itself but in the little hanging valley above. It tumbles into the glen in a waterfall feeding a lochan that's mirror-flat on still days like this."

"A lochan?"

"It's a wee loch—a little lake, I suppose you would say if you weren't from these parts."

"I can't wait to see it."

"You soon will. We're almost at Glen Cranoch."

"I love the way you say Cranoch, all 'r's and 'ochs'."

"Its name is actually Corranoch. But that's a sad word in the Gaelic, so we shorten it and make it sound like something else."

"Corranoch," Kate said wistfully. "That sounds way too beautiful to mean something sad."

"Maybe so, but it does," Finlay told her. He turned left, onto a narrow, steep and bumpy road.

"What does it mean?"

"It's the Gaelic for wailing, for weeping in lament."

Before Kate could ask why Glen Cranoch was known as The Weeping Glen, Finlay said, "Close your eyes, Kate Brodie."

They were approaching the top of the grade and Kate guessed that Glen Cranoch lay on the other side. She closed her eyes as instructed. The engine beat grew increasingly strained, and the wheels spun furiously as the tyres struggled for traction. For a few heart-stopping moments the Land Rover seemed on the point of slipping backwards.

And then without warning Kate was pitched forward as the tyres got a grip, before being jolted up and down as the Land Rover crested the hill. She was aware of the ground flattening out, the engine being cut, and the handbrake going on.

"Just a moment longer, if you please," Finlay said.

The opening of the driver's door was followed by footsteps on gravel. Without knowing it, Kate held her breath. The door beside her squeaked open and Finlay said, "You can open your eyes, now, Lady Kate."

Kate had spent almost every waking moment since the arrival of Archie Cunningham's cable wondering what

Glen Cranoch would look like. Her imagination had conjured up everything from bleak moor to rocky mountain valley. But nothing prepared her for what she saw when she stepped out of the Land Rover now.

Stretching away below her was the narrow lochan, as mirror-calm as Finlay had described, but so dark that it seemed to reflect the depths below rather than the bright blue sky above or the steeply rising hills on either side. The grassy lower flanks of those hills gave way to the darker green of Caledonian mixed woodland, then the even darker green of coniferous forest. Above the treeline green was replaced by the purple and brown of heather and the grey of rugged granite peaks that were more mountain than hill.

However, breathtaking and beautiful as they were, lochan, hillsides, and rocky summits barely got more than a glance because her gaze was drawn to the far end of the glen, where two craggy granite outcrops were split by the foaming white of falling water tumbling into the stream that fed the lochan. A small cluster of white cottages lay at the foot of the crags, while a ruined cottage topped the crag on the right, and the other crag was crowned by an altogether more substantial structure: high walls enclosing a central square tower twice their height.

"This is your little kingdom, Lady Kate," Finlay told her, looking out across the glen.

"It's . . ." Kate couldn't find the words.

"Aye, it is," Finlay said, knowing exactly what she meant without having to hear it expressed in words. "And

I've seen it look bonnier than this, by far," he said.

"How could it look more beautiful than this?" Kate asked in a disbelieving whisper.

"I'm not a poet so I couldn't tell you that with words, Lady Kate. I'd have to bring you back here a dozen times so that you could see for yourself. I'd have to bring you here at dawn on a summer's morning when low mist hangs like angel's breath over the water and hides everything except for the crags, and they could be the tops of mountains ten thousand feet tall . . .

"And again at dusk in spring, maybe, when the sunsets are at their most spectacular and the things you see now in green and brown and grey are gold and bronze and copper instead, and the lochan shimmers like a pool of molten metal or a drop of amber.

"I'd have to bring you here on a cloudless night when watching moonlight rippling across the water is like seeing an ancient spell being cast by an invisible hand.

"I'd have to come back with you when the leaves are on the turn and their reflection makes the lochan look like the palette of an artist who's been mixing every shade of yellow, green, and brown and finds himself spoiled for choice because he's come up with so many beautiful colors.

"And I'd have to bring you back again a couple of months later, when there aren't any colors left at all, just a blanket of pure white, and the falls are frozen into fantastical shapes like something out of a fairy tale and we have a bonspiel on the lochan."

Finlay suddenly seemed embarrassed, and Kate guessed that he wasn't used to talking with anyone the way he'd just talked with her. "Forgive me, you must be tired," he said. "It was thoughtless of me to rant on like that."

She smiled at him. "Those were far from the words of a thoughtless man, Finlay." Turning back to the glen, she said, "I could stand here looking at this place all day."

"Aye, well, Miss Weir's anxious to meet you, so maybe we best be cracking on," he said.

Kate nodded, and reluctantly followed him back to the Land Rover.

As the they bumped down the untarred road and through the glen—with forested hillside rising on the left, the still waters of the lochan stretching away to the right, and the twin crags jutting up ahead—the splendour of the scenery led Kate to ask, "How can such a lovely place possibly have a name that's Gaelic for sorrow?"

"Look down by the lochan," Finlay told her, pointing out the window on his right until a bump threw the Land Rover to one side and forced him to grab the wheel again with the hand he'd just taken off.

Kate looked past the old Highlander at the water down below. For the first time she noticed small clusters of abandoned cottages every half-mile or so all around the lochan. Some were roofless and had badly scorched walls but were otherwise almost complete, while others were little more than lines and piles of stone.

"There used to be roofs on those cottages and fires

in their hearths," Finlay said. "There used to be women cooking around the fires and men herding cattle on the hillsides; little girls playing at their mother's feet and wee boys following in the footsteps of their fathers—not in my time, you understand, but I heard tell of how it was from my father, who heard from his father, whose father saw it for himself. That was in the days before the glen earned the name Corranoch."

"So what happened?" Kate asked.

Finlay didn't answer, and at first Kate thought he hadn't heard. Then finally he said, "When you have some time to spare, Lady Kate—later today if you feel like it, or maybe tomorrow—we'll have a walk around the glen and I'll tell you. You'll not thank me, but you'd doubtless hear it from others, anyway; and I think it would be better if you heard from me."

They were past the lochan now and, before Kate could press him on the matter, the sight of the waterfall and the crags up ahead made her forget all about the ruined houses.

"The cottages at the foot of Castle Crag belong to the crofters," Finlay said.

Kate barely heard his words or noticed the cluster of low, whitewashed cottages they referred to—she was too taken up by what lay beyond them. "The falls are so beautiful!" she exclaimed.

Finlay nodded and said, "Before this place was called Gleann Corranoch it was known as Waterfall Glen."

CHAPTER 3

THE ROAD WOUND UP AROUND THE BACK OF THE LEFT-hand crag but stopped some forty feet below the summit, at a place where the outcrop steepened abruptly.

"Welcome to Greystane, or Clach Glas as it's called in the Gaelic," Finlay said.

As Kate got out of the Land Rover and looked up at Greystane she found it hard to tell where crag stopped and building began. She guessed that the outer walls were a hundred feet long on each side and two storeys high where complete, but in places they'd crumbled to little more than half that height and were topped by ragged rubble rather than castellated battlements. As for the tower house itself, all she could make out from down below was one of its small, jutting corner turrets.

Hearing a grunt behind her, Kate turned to see Finlay unloading her cases from the Land Rover. Reluctantly she tore herself away from Greystane to give him a hand.

Once the cases were unloaded Finlay said, "I'm afraid the only way up is by those steps." He pointed to a narrow staircase chiselled out of the rock. A banister of chain links had been hammered into the face of the crag to the right of the steps.

When Kate set foot on the first step, suitcase in hand and daypack slung over one shoulder, Finlay said, "Mind how you go, Lady Kate. It can be a bit slippy. The chain's a last resort, though, because it's so manky."

Kate looked back at him quizzically. "Manky?"

"Aye, you know: barkit, clarty."

Kate laughed. "I love the sound of those words but I haven't the slightest idea what they mean."

"Right enough, I don't suppose you'd be hearing them very much in San Francisco," Finlay conceded. "Let's just say that your hands will be in need of a good wash if you have to grab hold of the chain."

"Thanks for the heads-up."

Non-plussed, Finlay said, "Now it's my turn to ask what you're talking about."

"Heads-up? It just means early warning."

"Heads-up," Finlay said. "I'll try to remember that."

Despite Finlay's warning, Kate soon had to reach for the chain with her free hand because she was so tired she needed all the help she could get to climb the steep stairway. Looking at the rusty imprint on her palm when she let go, she said, "I see what you mean, Finlay. I think I'm going to be a very 'clarty' lady by the time I get to the top."

Finlay chuckled away at that, before saying, "I think you've got far too much class to ever be called that, Kate Brodie."

Kate smiled. The smile soon wore off, though, and after a dozen more steps she had to pause for another break.

"If only I was a few years younger I could have carried you up these steps," Finlay said.

"If only I was a few younger I wouldn't need you to," Kate told him. "How do you manage to get furniture and things up here?" she asked.

"Mr. Chisholm never bought any. You'll notice that for yourself when you're looking around the house. Miss Weir got one of those Fridgedaire things for the kitchen about twenty years ago, and a machine that washes clothes. But, other than that, not much has changed inside Greystane since before the war."

"I suppose it would be a shame if it had been modernized and turned into just another house inside," Kate said.

"It would be a terrible, terrible shame," Finlay agreed. "That would be an awful thing to happen."

Smiling to herself at what was obviously Finlay's idea of a subtle hint, Kate picked up the suitcase and started up the rest of the steps. The next time she looked up, it was to see an arch in the outer wall, framing a door of rough planks bound top and bottom by rusty iron strapping.

"Just give it a shove, it's not locked," Finlay said when Kate reached the final step.

She pushed the heavy old door. It swung open slowly, and she caught her breath at what was revealed. Cracked stone flagging led to an ivy-covered tower house twenty feet on each side and four storeys high. It had an iron-studded door at its base, and a seemingly random scattering of tiny, deep-set four-paned windows on each floor.

To the right a long, single-storey building was attached to the side of the tower, running almost all the way to the outer wall. It, too, had only small, square-paned windows.

On either side of the path was a cobbled courtyard so overgrown that it was as much green as grey.

Likewise, the inside of the castle walls and the open stairways leading up to the ruined battlements were covered in moss and ivy.

"I don't suppose you'll have seen many places like this in California," Finlay said.

Kate shook her head, enchanted.

Near one of the open stairways that led up to the ramparts a ragged notch in the walls came down almost to the highest step. Kate walked towards the staircase, wanting to glory in the view.

"It's very much the worse for wear, there's no two ways about that," Finlay said, thinking Kate wanted a closer look at the damage to the walls. "But I don't think it's beyond repair if someone was to really set their heart on it."

Kate barely heard his voice, let alone his words. She put her suitcase down on the flagstones and started climbing the stairs. Half-way up she paused, because the ruined cottage on the crag opposite had come into view in the notch in the walls.

"I'm afraid the cottage doesn't belong to you," Finlay said, guessing what she was looking at. "Archie

Cunningham's had the devil of a job tracking down the man Mr. Chisholm left it to. There seems to be a bit of a mystery about him, which is quite appropriate given the history of the cottage. But that's another story..."

Again, Kate barely heard him. Her attention had been caught by the sound of rushing water. She hurried up the last few steps and gazed down at the whitewater river which flowed through the little hanging valley between the crags before tumbling into the glen below.

"Wait till you see the view from the top of the tower," Finlay called up to her.

"It can't be much better than this," Kate said, captivated.

"You can see a half a dozen other glens," Finlay told her.

"Are any of them half as beautiful as Glen Cranoch?"

"Maybe to other people, but not to me," Finlay said.

Kate reluctantly tore herself away and went back down the stairs. As Finlay led the way up the path he gestured towards the long building to the right of the tower and said, "That's the banquet hall. But before I show you that and the tower house we better stop off at the kitchen, if you don't mind, because Miss Weir can't wait to meet you. She'll have my guts for garters if she finds out I've been showing you around the place before introducing you."

"She sounds quite formidable."

"Plain-speaking, is how I think you'd best describe her if you were being polite—and if there was any chance she might be hearing you describe her, you'd definitely want to be polite. But under it all she's got a good heart. She's honest as the day is long, and she'll keep your house clean and your plate full."

Finlay turned left along the path, around the tower house. "This is what you might call Miss Weir's own little kingdom," he told Kate as they approached a stone-built lean-to abutting against the rear of the banquet hall.

Knocking timidly on the door, he said, "Miss Weir?"

A voice from inside said, "Don't tell me: her highness from across the water stood you up, and you all tarted up as if you were meeting royalty."

Kate had to work hard not to laugh out loud.

Drawing his head down and his shoulders up while he squirmed with embarrassment, Finlay said, "Miss Weir, I've got Lady Kate here with me now."

There was a long silence from the lean-to, and Kate could almost sense the mortified embarrassment within its walls.

The door finally opened and, accompanied by the smell of freshly-baked bread, Miss Weir appeared: a woman no taller than Finlay's five foot four but dwarfing him by virtue of a beehive dyed the sort of black that would make a lump of coal look pale in comparison. Whereas Finlay barely tipped the scales at ten stone Miss Weir weighed half as much again, with a fair bit of that in the chest that filled out the top of her white blouse and the hips that stretched her black skirt. She glowered briefly at Finlay before turning her attention to Kate. A smile as strained as the seams of her clothes crossed her heavily powdered face and she said, "I'm terribly sorry, I didn't realize you'd arrived, Lady Kate." She gave a half curtsy. Kate wasn't sure if it was just her imagination, but she thought she heard fabric tearing and stitches popping out one by one.

Turning to look at Finlay, but still speaking to Kate, Miss Weir said, "I didn't think that Mister McRae would bring the new lady of the house to the kitchen door like some hired help."

Addressing Finlay now, she said, "Have you not got a brain in that balding napper of yours, man! What on earth were you thinking about?"

"I'm sorry, Miss Weir," Finlay said, shrinking back like a chastened schoolboy.

"It's not me you should be apologising to, it's Lady Kate."

Before Kate could say that there was no need for an apology, or to keep calling her Lady Kate, Miss Weir said, "Now if you'll see to the suitcases and show Lady Kate through to the banquet hall, I'll rustle up a bite for her to eat. She must be half-starved after such a long journey."

"Actually, I'd quite like to see the kitchen," Kate said, fascinated by the little she could make out beyond the redoubtable figure in the doorway. "May I?"

Bemused, Miss Weir stepped aside. Her attention turned to Finlay—who was beating a hasty retreat with the cases—when she heard him muttering 'Awa' an bile yer heid, you auld dragon' under his breath. "The 'auld dragon'll' see you later, Mr. McRae," she said in a voice that could have cracked a roof slate, and one that made

Finlay McRae quicken his step and think of battle-hardened sergeant-majors as gentle souls in comparison.

Kate was barely aware of what was going on behind her because she was so taken up with the kitchen. It was unlike any she'd ever seen before. Apart from a fridge and washing machine, there wasn't a modern appliance in sight. The floor was covered in flagstones rather than tiles or textured vinyl, and the unplastered walls were lined with rough-hewn shelves crammed with jars of jam and honey, chutney and pickled preserves. The labels on each jar were hand-written, the tops sealed with wax paper held in place by elastic bands. Kate knew at a glance that nothing on the shelves had been bought in a supermarket. As well as freshly-baked bread she smelled a dozen other equally comforting aromas, from sweet to savoury, the latter coming from a large pot bubbling away on a vast, ancient, but lovingly cared for wood-burning stove.

"What can I get you to eat?" Miss Weir asked after closing the door.

"I don't want to put you out."

"I'd be much more put out at the thought of the lady of the house having to get food for herself while I stood back and watched. And besides," she added, "you wouldn't even know where anything is kept."

Realizing Miss Weir was desperate to show how indispensable she was, Kate smiled and said, "A sandwich would be fine, thanks. Cheese, ham—whatever's at hand."

"How about salmon and tomato?"

"Sounds great."

"And a cup of tea to go with it?"

Kate was about to ask for coffee, then thought, *When in Rome.* "That'd be lovely. I'll fill the kettle," she said, and started walking towards an antiquated, highly polished kettle that sat on the slate worktop beside the stove.

"You'll do no such thing," Miss Weir said, hurrying over to cut Kate off in action as well as word, then quickly added, "I mean, allow me, Lady Kate." She filled the kettle from a tap that groaned and shuddered before gurgling into life. "I'll just put this on the stove and then show you through to the banquet hall."

"Actually, I'd like to eat in here if that's okay—it's so cosy," Kate said, sitting on one of the two stools at the roughly-hewn pine table in the center of the kitchen.

"Aye, I suppose it is," Miss Weir said, looking around as if seeing a familiar place in a new light.

Kate looked on as Miss Weir used a knife the size of a cavalry sword to saw through the crust of a newly-baked loaf and then carve an inch-thick steak from a baked salmon that was still complete with head and tail.

"There you are," Miss Weir said, as she cut the resulting plate-sized sandwich in two and set it down in front of Kate. "That should keep you going until dinner."

Kate started to thank her but was drowned out by a rattling from the stove, followed by a high-pitched hooting. The room filled with steam, and for a moment Kate thought something was about to blow up. Then she realized that what sounded like a locomotive pulling into a station was just the old-fashioned kettle coming to the boil.

After making the tea Miss Weir said, "Would you be wanting a mug or the fancy porcelain stuff that Mr. Colin never bothered with?"

Knowing she'd just been shot point blank with a loaded question, Kate fought back a smile and said, "A mug will be fine, thanks."

Miss Weir put a large mug down beside Kate's sandwich and brought a jug of milk out from the fridge, saying, "I'm sorry we've none of that nonsensical half-fat milk that seems to be all the fashion these days, but I'm afraid we don't have any half-fat cows in Glen Cranoch."

This time Kate couldn't fight back her smile, so she used the sandwich to hide it. It was more than up to the job; she needed both hands just to get half of it up to her mouth. It was like a different kind of food altogether from the dainty, cellophane-wrapped sandwiches she was used to in the coffee shops of Sausalito and San Francisco, with their thin slices of bleached white bread or artificially colored "wholemeal", smears of margarine, and shavings of savoury filling. After taking her first bite, Kate realized Miss Weir was watching her intently, waiting for a verdict. "I had a salmon sandwich on the plane coming over, but it didn't taste anything like this," Kate told her.

"Aye, well, it wouldn't have been made with home-baked bread, salmon caught by Mr. McRae, and butter courtesy of Flora the cow from the crofts down below."

The sandwich was so much bigger than Kate was used to that she was full after eating half of it. She didn't want to offend Miss Weir by not finishing it, but simply didn't have room for any more.

Miss Weir read what was in Kate's mind from the look on her face and said, "Don't tell me you're full up already?"

Kate nodded, feeling like a little girl confronted by a fearsome nanny.

Miss Weir shook her head from side to side. Kate half-expected the beehive would stay where it was while the rest of her head swivelled, but it moved as one complete unit, not even a hair drifting out of place despite the vigorous head-shaking; testament to either the quality or quantity of her hairspray.

"You're not one of those dyslexia nervosics, are you?" Miss Weir asked.

Kate laughed and shook her head.

The denial didn't seem to convince the older woman, who said, "Well, we'll soon have you cured of that, don't you worry."

Kate knew there was no point protesting any further, and instead said, "Wouldn't you like some tea yourself?"

"Well, now that you mention it." Miss Weir whipped out a mug, filled it with tea and milk, and perched herself on the stool opposite Kate. "I'm just hoping you're not going to suggest that I try one of the scones I made for you this morning, because I might be tempted and I should really be watching my weight."

"Go on, be a devil."

"Well, I'll maybe just take a little one. Can I be getting one for yourself as well?"

"I won't have room for dinner if you do, and it smells too good to miss," Kate said diplomatically.

With surprising agility, Miss Weir flew off the stool and over to a big platter of scones on the worktop next to the bread. "I'm just looking for the smallest one," she said, a predatory hand hovering over the scones.

Kate suspected Miss Weir was thinking aloud, but that her words weren't a perfect match for her thoughts.

This suspicion was confirmed when the housekeeper returned with a scone that wasn't much smaller than the teaplate it was sitting on. She cut it open and spread a thin layer of butter on it. After taking a bite she said, "Hmm, a bit dry. It needs a wee spot of jam to moisten it." Again she seemed to be thinking aloud when she said, "I suppose there's no harm if I just have the one spoonful." She dismounted from her stool once more, and when she came back she had a jar of strawberry jam in one hand and a tablespoon in the other. After rolling off the elastic band and peeling back the wax paper she dug the spoon into the jar in agricultural fashion and brought out a mountainous, wobbling heap of jam. Upending the spoon over the bottom half of the scone, she scraped every last trace of jam from it with a knife, which she then meticulously wiped on the top half.

"That looks good," Kate said as Miss Weir set about

devouring the scone.

"Aye, but it could do with a bit more jam. I just wish I didn't have to think about my figure," Miss Weir lamented. "Are you sure I can't get you one?"

Kate shook her head. "I really am stuffed, thanks."

"I'll just leave the rest of the sandwich on the table if you don't mind," Miss Weir said. "It'll do for Finlay. There'll be a timid, mouselike knock at the door any minute now, mark my words, and a wheedling little voice saying, 'Miss Weir, I wonder if I might trouble you for just the smallest bite to eat'."

Kate laughed at the perfect imitation of Finlay's sing-song lilt. "Something tells me that, underneath it all, you're quite fond of him," she said.

"I suppose I am, at that," Miss Weir conceded. "He must have been quite a man," she said thoughtfully, and for once in a quiet voice. "You might have noticed a wee ribbon on his blazer. Well, I once asked him what it was for, but he changed the subject and wouldn't tell me. I'm a nosy besom, I have to admit, so I asked Auld Davie about it—he's one of the crofters who served with Finlay during the war. He said that the pretty little ribbon is for the Military Medal. He also said it's second only to the Victoria Cross."

"How did Finlay win it?" Kate asked, impressed even before hearing the details.

"The hard way."

"I can't imagine there's an easy way to win a medal

like that."

"No, indeed. Anyway, he didn't win it charging forward with a blazing gun and all-consuming rage, blinded by the heat of battle to the risks he was taking, but with an altogether more uncommon kind of courage. It turns out Finlay McRae was one of the first men—well, he can't have been much more than a boy—to set foot on the beaches during D-Day. While the bombs and bullets were flying all around and other men dived for cover he stayed on his feet to pipe the commandoes ashore to the tune of *Highland Laddie*."

Kate had taken to Finlay from the start, and now felt admiration for him as well as affection.

Miss Weir started washing up the plates and knives. Before she'd finished there was a barely audible knock at the door, followed by a timid, "Miss Weir—"

Kate couldn't hear the rest of what Finlay said for the sound of her own laughter.

"Come in, Finlay. We've been expecting you," the housekeeper announced smugly.

The door opened and in came Finlay, taken aback to see Kate sitting quite the thing at the kitchen table.

"It's okay," Miss Weir told Finlay. "It seems that Lady Kate is quite at home taking a mug of tea with the likes of us."

As Finlay sat down, Miss Weir said, "You'll be wanting a sandwich, I take it."

"Just if there's one already made," Finlay said, looking

at the leftover half of Kate's sandwich sitting in the middle of the table.

Miss Weir shook her head. "Men," she said to Kate. "They're so predictable."

"I'd prefer to say 'reliable'," Finlay said.

"I can rely on you wanting a mug of tea and a scone as well, I suppose."

"That you can, but I'll see to it myself."

"That means he wants to pick his own scone," Miss Weir told Kate.

Finlay polished off his sandwich in short order and got up to help himself to a scone. "I see that someone's already taken the 'smallest' one," he said, peeved.

Once more, Kate had to work hard not to burst out laughing.

Finlay took a bite of his scone and said, "It's very nice, Miss Weir. Yes, very nice indeed. But maybe just the littlest bit dry, if I might be so bold as to say so."

Without a word Miss Weir brought him the jam jar.

"It only needs a spoonful," he said.

"Aye, well, just remember what happened with your wallies the last time you took more than that."

Kate knew it was probably better not to ask, but couldn't keep her curiosity at bay: "Wallies?"

"Aye, falsers—you know, false teeth."

"Miss Weir!" Finlay said indignantly. "I'm sure Lady Kate doesn't want to know about such things."

Miss Weir carried on regardless. "Greedy guts here

overdid it with the strawberry jam one afternoon and got his wallies stuck fast in a scone. Not a pretty sight, I can assure you. In fact, I'm still having nightmares about it yet. It was a month before I could bring myself to even think about baking another tray of scones or making a pot of jam."

"Miss Weir, please! A man's entitled to a bit of dignity in his senior years," Finlay protested, so embarrassed that his face had turned almost the same color as the jam on his scone.

"Not if he gets his wallies stuck in a scone, he's not," Mrs. Weir said.

Finlay shook his head sadly and said, "Old age is a terrible, terrible thing."

Kate laughed. "I'm sorry, Finlay, but your accent cracks me up," she told him. "You only said terrible twice but I heard way more than two words' worth of 'r's."

"You're not going to be tricking me into saying words with lots of 'r's in them just so you can laugh at me, are you?"

"It's a distinct possibility once I've had enough sleep to be able to think straight."

"You must be exhausted, right enough. Would you like to get some rest now, and I'll show you around after?" he asked.

Kate shook her head. "There's no way I could sleep until I've looked around this place, Finlay—I'm way too curious and excited."

CHAPTER 4

"After you," Finlay said, opening the door at the foot of the tower house.

The windows were so small and high that little light was let in, and at first Kate had no idea what sort of space she was walking in to. As her eyes adapted she discerned different shades of shadow, and gradually the shades took on shape and form. Rows of wooden pews flanked a central passage leading to a dais with a simple altar. The ceiling was braced with thick wooden beams, and the walls were lined with dark oak panelling.

"This is the chapel," Finlay said in a reverential whisper.

Kate understood why Finlay's tone had changed. She'd always thought it seemed more likely that man had created God rather than the other way around, but even so she experienced an almost religious sense of awe as she stood there. Grand churches and cathedrals distracted a congregation with the glories of their architecture and artistry; this plain, dimly-lit little place left a person with nothing to think about but God, and seemed far more holy as a result. Pointing to a double door on the right, barely distinguishable from the panelling it was set in, Finlay said, "The banquet hall's through there, if you want a look."

Kate followed him through a slender, slanting shaft of sunlight, their footsteps echoing on the flagstones as they made their way along the rear of the chapel and up the narrow passage between the end of the pews and the panelled wall.

Finlay opened the double doors to the banquet hall and stood aside to let Kate enter. She hesitated before doing so, as enchanted by what lay in front of her as she had been when she opened the door in the outer wall and caught her first sight of Greystane. "Finlay," she whispered, "it's amazing!"

The ceiling was dominated by a chandelier which wouldn't have looked out of place in the ballroom of a grand hotel. It hung over a long table, which had at least thirty antique chairs around it. Their legs were elegantly bowed, their upholstery a plummy velvet. The far wall was taken up by a tall fireplace, above which hung a round leather shield crossed by two rusty old basket-hilted broadswords. Sunlight streamed through the deep-set windows in the long wall to the right, while the opposite wall was lined with oil portraits in ornate gilt frames.

One picture in particular caught Kate's attention. It hung the wrong way around, so that only the blank canvas backing was on display.

"That's Jamie's picture," Finlay said, following Kate's gaze. "He was sent off to fight with Bonnie Prince Charlie in 1745 while his older brother stayed at home. Landed families often hedged their bets and backed both sides in those days. Anyway, Charlie's men were slaughtered at Culloden, a bleak moor not far from here. Jamie was spotted running away from the enemy, not at them, and was never seen again. The story goes that he was too ashamed to show his face in the glen. His portrait was turned to face the wall, and it's hung that way ever since."

"You mentioned a run of misfortune in the family—is the 'curse', or whatever you might want to call it, down to Jamie?"

Finlay shook his head. "Jamie brought shame on himself and disgrace to his family, but not the sort of bitter hatred that lies behind a curse."

"If Jamie's not to blame, then who is?"

Finlay moved on to the next painting and said, "Him . . ."

The portrait showed a weak-jawed man with shifty eyes and strands of ginger hair combed over a balding pate.

"And especially her."

Kate looked at the man's portrait with little more than passing interest, but caught her breath when she saw the picture hanging next to it. It showed a young woman with shoulder-length blond hair, cold blue bedroom eyes, and a seductive smile. Kate stood rooted to the spot as she stared at the old oil painting because there was something disconcertingly familiar about the woman it portrayed. The longer she looked at the face, the more it unsettled her. How could someone she'd never seen or even heard of before be so hauntingly familiar? She stared at the painting as if mesmerized.

Not noticing Kate's distraction, Finlay carried on with his commentary. "Malcolm and Lady Carolyn," he said, with no attempt to hide his disgust.

"What did they do to earn such hatred?" Kate asked.

"I'll tell you when I give you a tour of the glen, Lady Kate, because it'd be better explained in the places where it happened."

"Come on, Finlay—you've got me intrigued."

"I couldn't do the telling of the tale justice with words alone," Finlay told her. "And, believe me, there's enough injustice in this story as it is."

Before Kate could press the old ghillie any further he'd moved along the line of portraits, stopping near the far end at the picture of a sophisticated blonde with her hair pinned up and just a hint of the look of Lady Carolyn about her. She was shown with a silk-gloved hand draped around the shoulder of a handsome, high-cheekboned man. "This is Janette Chisholm. She would be your grandmother's sister, if I'm not mistaken," Finlay said. "The two of them never got on at all, from what I heard. I'm not surprised, because Janette was what you might call a bit of a madam. Anyway, they fell out over Struan." He gestured to the man in the painting. "As you can see, Janette got her man—like she got most of the things she set her sights on."

"And my grandmother left the country to start a new life in America," Kate said.

Finlay nodded. Still looking at Janette and Struan, he

said, "These two belonged to what I think was politely referred to as the 'Lost Generation', giving themselves over to the pursuit of pleasure after the horrors of the Great War, and burned themselves out while they were still young as a result. They partied like there was no tomorrow, turning Greystane into a northern outpost for their fancy friends from Edinburgh and London."

Kate imagined the banquet hall filled with jazz from a gramophone horn and smoke from a dozen cigars; with perfume and laughter and loud conversation; the clicking of fingers to summon servants, the popping of champagne corks and the clink of crystal decanters. She imagined handsome, brandy-clutching men in bow ties and dinner jackets, and beautiful women in fishtailed, sequined evening dresses, with silk gloves that came up to their elbows, and foot-long cigarette holders. She could almost see them doing the *Foxtrot* and *Charleston*, like a Jack Vettriano painting come to life. "Do you remember any of those parties?" she asked.

Finlay smiled. "Like they were yesterday," he told her. "I've been playing the pipes since I had enough breath in me to fill a bag, and I used to be invited here to do a turn during the grand bashes. The Chisholms even had a special wee kiltie outfit made up for me with a dress sporran, white lace shirt, and black velvet waistcoat. I suppose I was comic relief for their sophisticated friends. I must have been a funny sight, right enough—an earnest-faced, skinny wee scrap of a boy dressed up to the nines—but

I can remember being pleased as punch with myself, full of my own importance when I marched around the table, playing my heart out." He smiled at the thought, and the sparkle in his eyes told Kate that as he looked down the banquet hall he was seeing down the years.

Finally coming back to the present, he said, "The table's on trestles, so that after a banquet it could be cleared away to make room for dancing—Highland or waltz or whatever the fashion of the day. That's why this floor is wood and not stone," he added, tapping the polished floorboards with the tip of a burnished brogue. "It's far easier on the feet."

"Sounds like you've done quite a bit of dancing yourself."

"Not since the war. No one's danced in here since the war," he said, with more than a hint of sadness. "I never did any of that fancy nonsense, you understand, just the Highland dances. Have you ever done any Highland dancing yourself, Lady Kate?"

Kate shook her head. "What's it like?"

"Oh, it's fun," Finlay said, his eyes sparkling again. "During a fling or a reel the floor would shake and the paintings would seem set to jump off the walls as if the people in them wanted to join in. The windows rattled like the glass was ready to fall out of the frames, and the chandelier swung like it might come crashing down on our heads at any moment—and nobody gave a damn, because we were so caught up in the music and the moment." He let out a wistful sigh and said, "There hasn't been a night like that here for more than fifty years. That's far too long, Lady Kate. But sorry, there's me ranting on again."

"Finlay, I love listening to your 'rants'," she told him.

He looked away shyly, and in that moment Kate thought he was more like a little boy than an old man.

Kate's eyes were drawn back to the portraits, and she said, "What happened to them—Janette and Struan?"

"It caught up with them—the curse or their lifestyle, depending on how you want to look at things. Struan's liver packed up, and Janette didn't last too much longer. She went grey overnight after he died, and within a year she was dead herself. A heart attack, the doctor said. A broken heart seemed more like it, if you ask me—broken by losing Struan, and by the shock of what happened to her son, Colin."

Finlay walked to the last portrait in the line and said, "I've told you about what Mr. Colin was like when he came back from the war—this is what he was like before he went away."

The picture showed a dark-haired, dashingly handsome man with clean-cut, well-co-ordinated features, bright blue eyes, and a boyish smile.

"A damn shame," Finlay said. "Aye, a damn shame."

Looking at the painting and thinking of the terrible thing that had happened to the man it depicted, Kate said, "Finlay, do you believe there's some sort of curse on my family?"

The old Highlander pretended not to hear. "You'll be

wanting to see the rest of the house, now."

"Finlay!"

"If you'll just follow me, I'll show you the lounge and bedrooms," he said, hurrying past Kate so that he didn't have to meet her eye or answer her question.

Kate followed him back to the chapel, then through a doorway in its left-hand wall and up a narrow, steeply pitched wooden staircase.

Opening the nearest door when they got to the first-floor landing, Finlay said, "This is the sitting room."

The room had a 1920s art deco feel to it, and a musty atmosphere of faded, slightly tatty grandeur. It was dominated by a wrought-iron fireplace with an insert of cream ceramic tiles painted in a rosebud pattern. The maroon-toned Oriental rug that covered most of the floor and took the place of a carpet was threadbare; the ivory-colored chaise longue was frayed and grubby, and the matching chairs by the fireside had badly worn armrests. Kate sensed that the room had been furnished by someone with good—and expensive—taste, but had been sorely neglected over the years.

"It's seen better days," Finlay said. "A bit like myself."

Kate smiled, then turned her attention to the pictures on the oak-panelled walls. She took her time to walk around and study each painting in turn. They ranged from idyllic rustic scenes to vivid depictions of battles at sea, with dismasted, smoke-shrouded men-of-war firing broadsides at each other from point-blank range.

"I'm afraid they're not originals," Finlay said, confirming what Kate's practised eye had already discerned.

"Once they were, every one of them, but Mr. Chisholm had to sell them off one by one over the years. He replaced them with prints of the exact same pictures. I didn't notice the difference, but Mr. Chisholm did."

"He must have been heartbroken at having to part with them," Kate said.

"It must be heartbreaking for you thinking about it. Maybe I shouldn't have told you that he once had the originals."

"It comes down to whether you take the approach that the glass is half full or half empty, Finlay, and right now my glass seems a lot more than just half full."

Finlay smiled. "I like that attitude," he told her. Opening a door to the left of the tall fireplace, he said, "Through here is the study."

Kate walked into a room whose walls were lined from floor to ceiling with books bound in brown and maroon and dark green leather. There was just room for a rickety old step-ladder, a mahogany escritoire with a computer sitting on it, and a matching chair. "The computer looks so out of place," Kate said, thinking that a blotter and inkwell would have been much more in keeping with the surroundings than the monitor and keyboard.

"Mr. Chisholm got interested in gene research in his last few years," Finlay informed her.

Kate couldn't imagine that as a hobby. Seeing her puzzlement the old ghillie added, "You know, family trees and things."

Kate suppressed a smile.

Looking at the packed shelves, Finlay said, "When it was too dreich—sorry, when it was too wet and miserable—to go fishing, this was where Mr. Chisholm came. He must have spent hours looking through atlases and old history books. Armchair travelling and living in the past, I suppose you could say."

Suddenly claustrophobic, Kate was glad to leave the little room. After they'd climbed another set of stairs Finlay opened the nearest door and said, "This is the master bedroom; there's a smaller one next door for guests."

The room contained a four-poster bed in dark wood, with a cream-colored quilt. At the foot of the bed was an ornate French dresser with bowed legs, serpentine front, and a large oval mirror turned so that the silvered side faced the wall. The room's only window was two panes wide and two high, deeply set and framed by tiny chintz curtains held in place by matching tie-backs. Kate walked towards it, stopping when she was barely half-way there, and said, "Oh, Finlay, the view!"

"Aye, it's really something. Miss Weir and myself sleep in the attic bedrooms on the next floor—not in the same room, of course," he added quickly, as if horrified by the thought. "There're three bedrooms up there, and a small privy, too, and although there's not much space they each have a little turret with a window seat, and when you're sitting there you feel like you're in an eagle's nest."

Kate was too taken by the view from her own room to pay much attention to a description of Finlay's. The window faced directly down the length of the glen. The dark blue ribbon of the lochan stretched out below her, with the forested hillsides rising steeply on either side of it. Other glens were visible in the distance but Kate barely gave them a second glance. She only had eyes for Glen Cranoch.

"—suit you better?"

Kate was so caught up with the view that she only heard the tail end of the question, so she said, "I'm sorry, Finlay, I didn't quite catch that."

"I was wondering if you'd like me to show you around the glen this afternoon, or if tomorrow would suit you better."

"I can't wait to see it, Finlay, but I'm ready to crash out. As for tomorrow, I'm afraid I have a meeting with Mr. Cunningham in the afternoon. I've nothing planned for the day after that, though."

Finlay looked more than a little put out. "What about tomorrow morning?"

Kate was about to say that she wanted to sleep late, but the look on Finlay's face made it clear that he'd be terribly disappointed if she didn't take up his offer. At first she couldn't work out why it was so important to him—and then she realized he must be wanting to sell her on the attractions of the glen before she met Archibald Cunningham to discuss its fate. "Tomorrow morning would be fine," she told him.

She turned back to the window for one last look at the

panoramic view.

When she tore her gaze away from the glen, Finlay was gone and she was alone with the four-poster bed. All at once everything caught up with her—the long journey, the uncertainty of what lay at the end of it, and the excitement of seeing Glen Cranoch and Greystane. She kicked off her shoes, lay on top of the quilt, and was asleep the moment her head touched the pillow.

Kate woke up just before 5 p.m. after something longer than a nap but shorter than a slumber. The first thing she saw when she opened her eyes was the frilly fringe around the top of the four-poster, and for a moment she felt like she was in a doll's house. She blinked and looked around. The unfamiliar surroundings added to the notion that she must be dreaming. Even after she remembered about the transatlantic flight and Finlay McRae, the climb up the staircase cut into the crag, and her first sight of the tower house that topped it, she still had to get up and look out of the window to convince herself it was all real.

The sun was setting beyond the hills at the far end of the glen, and Kate bathed in the light and gloried in the view. Before her eyes the craggy summits changed color and seemed to soften, as if granite was being transformed to amber. Bewitched, she watched as the green of hillside forest was swallowed up by shadow, and the lochan turned from a shimmering pool of liquid gold to a bottomless well that plumbed the depths of night. It was all so enchanting that at one point she actually pinched her arm in a bid to convince herself it wasn't just a dream.

After a soak in the old enamel en-suite bath she put on jeans and a white cotton sweater—happy to dress casually now that she'd met Finlay and Miss Weir and knew they had no airs or graces—before going downstairs for something to eat.

Kate wanted to take her evening meal in the kitchen but Finlay led her to the banquet hall instead, where a place was set for her.

Sitting alone at the head of a table that would have seated thirty—and faced by a mountainous helping of stew and dumplings that would have fed half a dozen of them—Kate got the feeling that, while she'd been sleeping, Finlay and Miss Weir had formed a little conspiracy with the intention of doing all they could to impress her with Greystane's grandeur.

She smiled at the idea. The smile didn't last long, however, for as she unfolded her napkin and looked around the empty hall her gaze was drawn instinctively to the picture of Lady Carolyn, and again she was unsettled by that strange, unaccountable sense of recognition. For a moment she actually considered turning the painting around to face the wall, like Jamie's picture. All that stopped her was the knowledge that she couldn't comfortably explain away such an action to Finlay and Miss Weir.

She tried shifting herself rather than the painting so that the wall of portraits was at her back. However that only made things worse because it wasn't a case of "out of sight, out of mind", but rather "IT'S BEHIND YOU!"

Moving back to the head of the table, Kate did her best to concentrate on her food and forget about the painting. It took all her willpower but, with the help of a healthy appetite and the perfectly cooked meal, she managed.

She was more unsettled than she'd realized, however, because when the polished brass handle of the door that led to the lean-to began to turn fifteen minutes later, it gave her such a fright that the fork fell out of her fingers and clattered on the plate. Powerless to move, Kate made no attempt to pick it up. She just sat there as the door swung open and the clash of silver on china echoed from the old walls.

Finlay appeared and said, "Sorry, Lady Kate, did I give you a fleg?"

Kate was able to muster a smile at the funny word. "A what?" she asked.

"A fleg—a fright."

Her smile turned to a laugh. "Yes, Finlay," she told him, "you gave me a wee fleg."

Finlay chuckled at hearing the Scottish words spoken in an American accent. "Do you want a little longer to finish your meal?" he asked when he saw how much food was left on her plate.

"No," Kate said, a little too quickly, not wanting to be left alone again with the portrait of Lady Carolyn. "No," she repeated again more calmly. "I'm full, thanks."

Finlay grimaced. "Miss Weir likes to see an empty plate, Lady Kate. It's not quite 'finish your greens or you won't get any desert', but not far off it."

"You'll have to help me out, then," Kate said, sliding the plate across to him and handing over her knife and fork.

Finlay took a seat, gave Kate a conspiratorial grin, and set to work.

"I better leave something or the auld boot'll get suspicious," he said several minutes later, reluctantly sparing a morsel of dumpling and a few token chunks of beef.

Kate laughed, then accompanied him through to the kitchen to thank Miss Weir for the meal.

The "auld boot" inspected the remains of the meal, smiled at Kate and said, "You've done better than I expected, lass."

Kate smiled back, but lies and deceit didn't come easily to her and there was enough guilt in her expression to arouse Miss Weir's suspicions. Looking from Kate to Finlay, the housekeeper said, "That wouldn't be gravy on your moustache, now, would it, Finlay McRae?"

Finlay's hand quickly shot up to his neatly trimmed moustache, the panic in his gesture and the alarm on his face an eloquent admission of guilt.

Kate did her best to come to Finlay's rescue, saying, "It's just that there was enough for two, Miss Weir, and it seemed much too good to waste. Besides, I felt silly sitting there all alone. How about if we eat in the kitchen from now on, or you two join me in the banquet hall for meals?"

"That's very kind, but it just wouldn't seem right," Miss Weir said.

"It can't be more wrong than one person eating alone at a table that seats thirty," Kate said, made uncharacteristically assertive by the fresh memory of eating dinner alone with the portrait of Lady Carolyn.

Miss Weir still looked unconvinced.

"I'll tell you what—how about if we eat breakfast and lunch here in the kitchen, and dinner together in the hall—how does that sound?"

"Aye, well—"

"Good." Kate smiled. Turning to Finlay, she said, "There's a lot of ground to cover tomorrow morning, so I imagine you'll want an early start. How does eight o'clock sound?"

"It sounds just fine," Finlay told her.

"Eight o'clock it is, then—I'll set my alarm." She was about to leave, but stopped and said, "Finlay, Miss Weir, thanks for making me so welcome. I can't tell you how much I appreciate it."

With that she walked through the door that led back to the banquet hall, smiling when she heard Finlay say to Miss Weir, "And to think you were worried she was going to be some stuck-up besom who'd be looking down her nose at us."

Kate was still smiling a few minutes later when she curled up under the covers and drifted off to sleep to the sound of the waterfall far below.

CHAPTER 5

"Do you mind if Hamish joins us on our wee jaunt around the glen?" Finlay asked after breakfast the next morning.

Kate had no idea who Hamish was, but again her mind conjured up images of a kilted Tom Hanks.

They were quickly dispelled when Miss Weir explained: "That's his wee West Highland Terrier."

Kate smiled at how wrong she'd been once more, and said, "No, of course not."

"Good," Finlay said. "If you'll excuse me, then, I'll just nip upstairs and see if he's awake yet."

"He spoils that dog something terrible," Miss Weir said after Finlay left. "He even made a little bed for him out of the bottom drawer of his chest, and lined it with a blanket."

"That's so sweet."

"Aye, he's a loveable wee beast, right enough."

"Hamish or Finlay?"

Miss Weir laughed.

A few minutes later Kate heard yelping from the other

side of the serving door that separated lean-to from banquet hall.

"Don't you dare bring that dog in the kitchen!" Miss Weir shouted.

The door opened and Finlay stood there, meticulously careful not to set foot over the threshold. He was cradling a little white terrier with black button eyes and a red tartan collar.

"Oh, Finlay, he's such a little cutie!" Kate said, getting off her stool to pat the dog.

"Aye, he's a bonnie wee thing, right enough," Finlay agreed. "We're ready when you are, Lady Kate."

Hamish led the way, scrambling down the crag at the side of the staircase ahead of Kate and Finlay. When they reached the Land Rover, Finlay said, "It's such a nice day you'd maybe rather take a walk than a drive."

Kate nodded. "Much rather."

"Good. I'll be able to show you some places not even a Land Rover can go. Like this one," he said, turning not left down the track they'd driven up the day before but instead right, along what was little more than a dirt path that led towards the hanging valley and the opposite crag. As they made their way along the trail, with Hamish bounding happily in front of them, the thunder of the falls grew louder with every step.

"I love that sound," Kate said. "I left my window open last night and drifted off to sleep with it, and it was the first thing I heard when I woke up this morning—well, once I'd switched off my alarm clock. It's a beautiful sound to start and end the day with, isn't it?"

"Aye. You might not think quite the same when there's been a storm, though, because there's so much water going over that it can be deafening even with your window closed."

Kate tried picturing Greystane in a storm. She couldn't imagine a place she'd rather be curled up in on a night of howling gales and flashing lightning—or a place she'd rather walk around than Glen Cranoch on a sunny summer morning such as this.

As they drew nearer the falls and lost height, so the crag opposite loomed ever higher. Kate paused while they could still see the derelict cottage on top of it.

"It's supposed to be haunted," Finlay told her. There was nothing mocking or derisory about they way he said the words.

"That's all the glen was missing—a haunted house," Kate said.

"Oh, it's got far more than its share of them," the old Highlander told her. "I'll show you some of them later."

"Is this to do with the 'curse' and the ruins down by the lochan?"

"It is indeed. But the ghost in the cottage up there has nothing to do with the curse," he said, pointing to the crag. "That was Jamie's Cottage, and no one's lived in it since. A few have tried, but even the least superstitious haven't stayed."

"Have you ever seen anything spooky up there?"

"No, but that's probably just because I've never got

close enough."

"I can't believe you've lived here all your life and haven't at least had a peek."

"Aye, well, if you'd been with me and Mr. Chisholm when we were just boys and he was just plain Colin and you'd heard what we heard, then you'd find it easier to believe."

Intrigued, Kate said, "What did you hear?"

Finlay didn't answer. Studying him as he gazed up at the ruined cottage, Kate guessed that he hadn't heard her question. Instead, he was hearing whatever it was that had frightened him all those years ago. "Finlay?" she prompted.

He was startled by her voice, as if he'd forgotten she was even there.

"What did you hear?" she repeated.

"I think we heard the ghost of Jamie Chisholm," he told her.

Kate was about to laugh, but the old man's expression stopped her. Even sixty or seventy years later, he was obviously still deeply disconcerted by the incident. "What happened?" she asked.

"Mr. Colin and I were climbing up Jamie's Crag..." he nodded to the rocky outcrop on the other side of the tiny hanging valley. "We got almost to the top, and that's when we heard it."

Again the memory seemed to have overtaken him, and Kate had to prompt him with, "Heard what?"

"It sounded like a pibroch—a bagpipe lament—coming from Jamie's Cottage."

"Couldn't it just have been the wind whistling through the ruins—I'm sure that can make an eerie sound."

"It can indeed. But the thing is that there was barely enough breeze to ruffle our hair that day, let alone enough wind to make music. I thought I might have been imagining things, but then I looked at Colin and he was looking back at me from a face that was white as a sheet. We scrambled back down the crag like a couple of startled rabbits and never climbed it again, or even talked about it."

"Now I've got to go up there," Kate said.

"Unfortunately we don't have time today," Finlay told her, not sounding in the slightest sorry.

"Maybe we can go there another day," Kate said, looking up at the ruin.

"Aye, maybe," Finlay said without conviction.

"You said something yesterday about the cottage not belonging to me—who does it belong to?" Kate asked.

"A man by the name of Cameron Fraser, apparently. I got the impression that Archie Cunningham had found out more about this Mr. Fraser than just his name, but for some reason he wouldn't let on what it was. He just said: 'I'd rather have you make your own mind up about the gentleman, and not be influenced by anything I say,' whatever that might mean."

"I can't begin to imagine what it means," Kate said thoughtfully, looking up at the cottage.

"You should have a word with Miss Weir, then—she's been doing enough imagining about it for two people."

Kate smiled.

"Anyway, never mind about Jamie's Cottage and Cameron Fraser, whoever he might be; I want to show you my favourite place in the world." He led Kate to the end of the path, where they were level with the tops of the trees lining the banks of the hanging valley. She followed him down a wooden-sleepered staircase that wound through the trees and led to an old stone bridge spanning the river just before it plunged into the glen below. An enormous rock sat in the middle of the fast-flowing water, dividing it into two forks and forming the foundation for the central pillar of the small, twin-arched bridge.

Kate walked to the center of the bridge, speechless, and leaned on the stone parapet. Castle Crag towered high above the trees to her right, with Greystane just visible atop it . . .

Jamie's Crag, with its ruined cottage, rose to her left . . .

And the river thundered beneath her feet, running from the hanging valley at her back to cascade over the falls just ahead. The dark lochan fed by the waterfall stretched away into the distance in the glen below.

"Finlay, this is beautiful," Kate told him when she was finally able to speak. "It's just perfect."

"It's the secret weapon in my little campaign to persuade you to hang on to Greystane and not sell it to those English carpetbaggers."

"Who?"

"I'll leave it to Mr. Cunningham to explain it to you this

afternoon. When he does, and you think about whether or not to sell, Lady Kate, just remember this place."

"I couldn't forget it if I tried," she told him.

"I wish we could stay here longer but there's a lot more to show you, and you said you were wanting to know about the story behind the 'curse'."

"Yes, I am."

Finlay led her back up the sleepered staircase, along the path at the back of the rocky summit of Castle Crag, and then down the track they'd driven up in the Land Rover the day before. They paused at a gentle flapping above them and looked up to see an osprey leave its cragside ledge and circle with deceptive laziness high above the lochan, its broad wings barely beating. Kate caught her breath even before the osprey broke off into a swooping dive and skimmed the surface of the still water, rising moments later with a big fish squirming in its talons. "I can't believe that just a couple of days ago I was in San Francisco," she said, watching the majestic bird of prey fly off with its prize. "This isn't just like a different country, it's like a different world, a different time."

"I've really nothing to compare it with," Finlay said. "Sometimes I wish I'd seen a bit of the wider world, but then I stand on Waterfall Bridge and I can't really wish for anything more than I have around me here." The quiet contentment vanished from his voice when he said, "The people who lived in the places I'm about to show you must have felt the same way, I imagine. That's why it broke their hearts to leave. It was their tears that christened Gleann Corranoch."

"The glen's not completely empty, though, is it?" Kate asked, seeing wisps of smoke rising towards them from the whitewashed cottages clustered at the foot of Castle Crag.

"That's the crofters," Finlay said. "You're only talking about a dozen families, though, whereas there used to be hundreds living here before Lady Carolyn's 'improvements'."

"You say 'improvements' as though they made things worse, not better."

"I'll leave you to make your own mind up about that."

They continued their descent of Castle Crag in companionable silence. After passing the crofts they made their way down to the lochan, and the nearest of the clusters of cottages Kate had glimpsed from the Land Rover the day before. They were very different to the neat, whitewashed crofts at the foot of the crag. Some were little more than piles of rubble, with only four corners to suggest the shape of what had once stood there; others had crumbling gables and looked close to collapse. A few were almost complete apart from the absence of a roof, but they looked just as derelict as the others because their windowless drystane walls were cracked and blackened by fire.

Finlay led Kate over to one of the more complete cottages, Hamish trotting along at his side. "Every half mile or so around the lochan there were little farm townships, each made up of cottages like these," he told her. The doorless doorway was so low he had to stoop to pass through it.

Kate had formed the impression that Hamish followed Finlay everywhere, but the little Westie whimpered now and shied away, preferring to hang back outside. She understood why when she followed Finlay into the shell of the ruined dwelling. Even without a roof the windowless interior was dark, and a shiver ran down her spine despite the fact that it was a warm, sunny morning.

Looking down at some scorched flagstones, Finlay said, "This is where the fire would have been—just an open hearth that they'd burn squares of dried peat on, with a hole above it in the divots of the roof to let some of the smoke out."

"There wasn't even a proper chimney, or any windows?"

"No."

"It seems so primitive."

"Aye, but well thought-out, none the less. An open fire heats a house better than one that's set against a wall, and the soot you get without a proper chimney helps make the roof waterproof and kills off any creepy crawlies. It's a better fire for cooking on, too. They'd hang a big cauldron from the rafters and use it to make porridge or broth or clapshot."

"Clap-what?"

"Clapshot—a mash of cabbage and potatoes."

"Is that all they lived on?"

"Not if they'd been on a *creach*—a cattle raid."

"They ate the evidence, did they?"

"Aye," Finlay laughed. Looking around, he said, "They sat on creepies—low stools that kept their heads below the smoke—and slept in a sort of big, open box filled with heather for a mattress."

Pointing to the far end of the cottage, he said, "Over there would be the byre."

"The what?"

"Byre. A place for animals—a few cows, goats, sheep, and some hens."

Kate tried to imagine the sights, smells, and sounds that would have resulted from such a primitive arrangement. "It must have been very 'atmospheric'," she said.

"If it was what you were used to, it would seem like home," Finlay told her.

Kate was glad to get outside. She'd felt something like claustrophobia in the ruined cottage, but knew there had been more to it than that because she'd been in smaller places before without experiencing any such discomfort.

Finlay reached down to muss Hamish's white coat, saying, "You're a wee fairdy, aren't you? Can't say I blame you, though. These old houses give me the willies, too." Then he straightened and started walking again, resuming his little history lesson. "This flat ground around the lochan would have been used for growing oats and barley and potatoes."

Looking a little further afield, he said, "Highland cattle would roam the lower hillsides in winter.

"In the better weather they'd be driven up to the sheilings—the high pastures where the deer forest is now—so they didn't trample the crops.

"On a fair day like this the people would repair the roofs, get the harvest in and cut peat for the winter. They did those things for the clan chief as well as themselves, because they didn't pay their rent with money. There was nothing money could buy in this part of the world back then, so there wasn't any use for coin of the realm.

"As well as providing their labor and a share of whatever the land and animals produced, the clansmen would answer the chief's call when he lit the fiery cross; when he needed men to protect his land or just his honor. Their loyalty gave him status and security—things that were worth far more than money to a man of means in a lawless land."

"That all sounds quite onerous."

"Aye, I suppose it does, but in return they got much more from the chief than just the use of the land."

"Such as?"

"The knowledge that they could turn to him for food if they were hungry, for justice if they were wronged, and protection if they were threatened. He'd provide all those things if he could because he thought of himself as their father, and it was a matter of pride to a man that he looked after his children. Often the chief's help must have meant the difference between life and death in the days when there was no social security to protect the poor and sick, no police force to protect the old and weak and threatened."

Looking around the glen, Finlay said, "It can't have been an easy life, but I can see how a person would be content living it, in a way that people don't seem to be content now. They might not have had many possessions back then, but they had the freedom and joy of living in a wild and beautiful land."

Turning back to Kate, he said, "Maybe that doesn't sound like very much, but that's only because people have become so far-removed from the land that they've forgotten the powerful beauty of being close to it. People have got so used to looking out for number-one in pursuit of trivial luxuries which can't bring lasting happiness that they've forgotten what it means to be part of a community that shares the burden of the bad times as well as the bounty of the good."

"I can see your point, Finlay, but I think you're maybe romanticising things more than a little, the way people do when they look back at the past from a present that seems less than perfect." Recalling the inside of the ruined cottage, she said, "It must have been a squalid, miserable life at times—most of the time, I guess. I can't see how there would be any chance to improve your lot or make things better for your family. That's not living, just existence. I'm not trying to defend whatever it is my family did in the past—I don't even know the what of it yet, let alone the why—but I think they can at least be forgiven for imagining there was room for improvement."

"Maybe over time they might have been forgiven for the what and why, but there are a lot of people who'd say they've been damned by the how."

"Damned is a pretty strong word—was what they did

really that terrible?" Kate asked.

"To be fair, what they did was little different from what most of the other landed families were doing at the time. It was the way they went about it that led to talk of a curse."

"What *were* the landed families doing?"

"Getting rid of the people who lived on their land. I don't mean with a bullet in the head, though in some cases that would have been a kinder way to go about it. No, it was more of a knife in the back, an abdication of ancient responsibilities, a betrayal of time-honored traditions."

"Why would they suddenly start acting so badly?"

"After Culloden the Highlanders were stopped from wearing tartan, speaking the Gaelic and carrying arms, so that a 'rebellion' might never be allowed to happen again. Law and order was brought to what had been lawless lands—"

"I'd have thought that was a good thing," Kate said as they walked beside the lochan, Hamish splashing happily in the cool, clear water.

"In a way it was, but it meant that the chiefs no longer relied on their clansmen for protection from warring neighbours, and their prestige no longer depended on how many fighting men they could put in the field. In other words, they didn't need their 'children' for status or security any more.

"No longer able to play the part of warlords, or forced to play the part of benevolent fathers, they sought new roles. They looked to the growing cities in the south:

Glasgow and Edinburgh and London; to town houses and ballrooms, gaming parlours and gentlemen's clubs, boardrooms and stock exchanges. They were exposed to a different way of life that was based on cold, hard cash and not a warm heart: where a man's worth was determined by his bank balance rather than his benevolence; where honor and responsibility didn't count for nearly as much as the cut of a man's clothes, the cutlery on his table, the art collection on his walls and the bottles of wine in his cellar. One by one they succumbed to the temptation to sell their souls for coin of gold."

"In what way?"

"They soon found out their lavish new lifestyles couldn't be funded by the old clan system, so they brought in factors to manage their estates as commercial enterprises, to evict the Highlanders and give sheep the run of the land after renting it out to the highest bidder.

"Later, after the wool boom had gone bust, they planted forest for deer—" he gestured to the trees on the hillside above them "— groomed the moors for grouse and hired out their Highland homes as hunting lodges. Glens like this one that had once been the home of little communities were turned into playgrounds for handfuls of privileged men who hunted animals for fun rather than to feed their families."

"I think I'm starting to understand," Kate said quietly.

"You can call these changes 'improvements' rather than clearances, 'removals' rather than evictions . . . You can argue that there had been more cattle and people than the land could comfortably support, and that without what happened there wouldn't have been any hope of progress, just recurring poverty and famine . . .

"But you can also argue that land is held in trust rather than owned outright, that it should be cared for to support the many and not just exploited to benefit a few. You can question whether this is progress, Lady Kate," he said, pointing to the next cluster of ruined cottages up ahead.

"There had been famines and poverty before the clearances, but there had also been trust and loyalty and kinship, and that should have counted for something," Finlay told her.

Kate sensed his quiet outrage, and in a strange way found herself sharing it. But she also felt some things that Finlay McRae would never feel as he wandered around Glen Cranoch: responsibility, guilt, and a humbling shame. "What happened to the people who were cleared off the land?" she asked, with a sense of dread.

"The 'lucky' ones were sent to the edge of the estates and given little parcels of land so barren that it broke their ploughshares as well as their hearts. They had to turn to the sea for a living and learn how to build and sail boats, make and mend nets—all on coastlines with few places to launch or land a boat or shelter from a storm," he told her. "Imagine living on land so poor that in spring the wind blew seeds from the soil before they could take root . . .

"Mildew and sea spray rotted the harvest in summer . . .

"And in winter, if you didn't want to watch your family starve in front of your eyes, you had to put to sea in an open boat in storms that drove down from the Arctic or all the way across the Atlantic. A hundred boats were lost in a single year on the thirty-mile stretch of coastline just north of here," he said. "In this one county the Government and landowners spent a million pounds to accommodate sheep, and just £500 to house the people who'd been 'removed' to make way for them. People who'd lived and worked on almost 800,000 acres were 'relocated' on just 6,000.

"If you weren't 'lucky' enough to get a plot of barren land on the coast, but had a little money to fall back on, you could try making a new life over the water, booking passage on one of the coffin ships bound for America—"

"I know I'm going to be sorry I asked, but why were they called coffin ships?"

"Because the conditions were so bad that many passengers ended up in a different promised land from the one that was advertised at the harbor gates.

"As for the survivors, they arrived in a strange land with only the clothes on their back and homesickness in their hearts.

"Of course if you were a young man and didn't fancy the fishing boats or the coffin ships, you could always join the army and fight for 'your' country. A prime minister of the day said that besides ensuring even the bloodiest of battles would be won, sending in the Highlanders had the advantage that not many of them would return home to cause trouble; while an English general who commanded them declared that it was 'no great mischief if they fall'.

"And as for the people who had no plot of land on the coast, no passage on a coffin ship or place in the army, all they could do was head for the cities to the south, where they were forced to swap their 'primitive' cottages for tenement slums and their Highland glens for rat-infested alleys, coal mines, and factories."

Looking from the ruined cottages to the woman at his side, he said, "I'm well aware that there are two sides to every story, Lady Kate, and I don't know enough about history to tell you what the other side of this one is. All I can speak of is the side that the people who once lived here would tell you if they had a voice you could hear."

"I understand, Finlay," Kate said quietly, shocked by what he'd told her and by the contrast between the idyllic setting and the terrible images his words conjured up. "And this was happening all across the Highlands?" she asked.

"Aye, all across the Highlands."

"You said something about it being worse here than in other places, though," Kate said as they continued towards the far end of the lochan. "That's hard to believe, because it sounds as if it was terrible everywhere."

"I don't think there could be a kind way to evict people from their homes and exile them from their glens, but some ways were crueller than others. Lady Carolyn's way was the cruellest of all."

"What exactly did she do?"

"First of all she talked her husband Malcolm into clearing that side of the glen—" he pointed to the opposite hillside "— to make way for sheep. In his heart he must have known it was wrong, but what he felt for Carolyn was stronger than what he felt for his 'children'. Still, at least he arranged for them to have plots on the coast—a faraway part of the estate that his wastrel son Alisdair would later sell to pay off gambling debts."

"If the Highland clansmen were such fierce warriors why didn't they put up any sort of a fight?" Kate asked, looking across the lochan at the forlorn remains of an abandoned little community.

"They did as their chief told them, Lady Kate, the way children should always do what their father tells them."

The sight of an old church up ahead, at the end of the lochan, prompted Finlay to add, "And they did what their ministers told them, too—not realizing that the ministers weren't giving voice to the word of God, but were acting as mouthpieces for the lairds and ladies."

"Why would men of God do that?"

"Because it wasn't God who gave them money for manses and for churches like that one up ahead." He pointed to the old stone church. "It wasn't God who put them in a pulpit or had the power to remove them from it. So the ministers told their flock that the exodus was the act of a vengeful Almighty angered at their sins, and that they should be grateful for the chance of redemption.

"In the last little township to be cleared on the other

side of the lochan, though, an old woman called Jessie McDowell refused to leave her cottage. She said she'd lived there all her days, and that was where she'd die.

"When Lady Carolyn heard that, she told the sheriff's officers who were charged with enforcing the eviction orders, 'The old witch has lived long enough as it is. Burn the cottage and grant her wish to die in it.'

"The sheriff's officers went back to Jessie's cottage with torch in hand. Some neighbours dragged Jessie from her home just before it was burned to the ground. They put her on a cart and took her to the coast. She died as soon as she got there, and her last words were a curse on Lady Carolyn and her issue."

Kate shivered again, despite the summer sun.

"As for the other clansmen who'd been moved to the coast, they could barely feed themselves, let alone pay rent. When the winter came they had to beg Malcolm for help. Full of guilt, he gave it to them.

"Lady Carolyn was furious when she found out; she saw them as a liability rather than a responsibility. She told Malcolm the clansmen had to learn to stand on their own two feet . . . or fall.

"Not long after that, Malcolm found out that Lady Carolyn was having an affair with the factor who'd been hired to oversee the leasing of the land. No doubt brokenhearted by his wife's betrayal, and guilt-ridden by what he'd done to his clansmen, Malcolm took his own life."

"The first victim of the curse?"

"So it was said."

"Given a free reign, now, Lady Carolyn set about clearing the rest of the glen with a vengeance. The Highlanders didn't feel the same sort of loyalty to her that they'd felt to Malcolm, however, and she guessed they might resist. She waited until they were in the church up ahead one Sunday and had some sheep farmers who'd been made special constables—a law unto themselves, in other words—put their houses to the torch.

"When the clansmen came out of the church it was to find their homes were in flames. They didn't even have a chance to salvage their belongings, which was just as Lady Carolyn intended because she didn't want them going to the coast and becoming a burden on the estate like the families Malcolm had evicted."

"What happened to them?" Kate asked, shocked.

"She got the minister to gather them here." They'd reached the church. "Right here in the churchyard they gathered, and were told that passage had been booked for them on a ship bound for America. The minister assured them that a new life awaited them, that God's will was being done, and things would work out for the best.

"When they got to the port they found there was indeed a ship waiting for them. They boarded it without realizing that Lady Carolyn hadn't just bought their tickets, she'd also sold their labor. They'd been indentured, bound to work for five years to pay for their passage.

"After they were gone Lady Carolyn got the minister

to hold a service of thanks in here," Finlay said, reaching for the church's wrought-iron door handle. As he pulled on the rusty handle the door shuddered slowly towards him inch by inch, for wind and rain had warped the wood, and lack of use had stiffened the hinges. It made a grating sound that set nerves on edge, like a nail being scratched across a blackboard.

When the door swung fully open a blast of cold, stale air swept out, carrying with it the smells of mould and damp, neglect and decay. Any thoughts Kate had that she was imagining the odours were dispelled by the little dog at her feet: Hamish wrinkled his nose, let out a whimper, and shrank away.

Inside, the church was criss-crossed by slanting shafts of daylight. Again, Kate thought it might have been her imagination, but it seemed to her that the areas between those beams of light were darker than they should have been. There was no soft diffusion of the daylight, just brilliant shafts of almost solid light cutting through an even more solid darkness, like spotlights falling on an otherwise unlit stage. She was so caught up by the striking scene in front of her that she didn't notice Hamish backing away another half dozen steps. She felt as though the interior of the church was exerting a visual gravity on her, with its pools of shadow so dark as to be devoid of all detail, and circles of light that fell on empty pews. A faint rustling from deep inside the church startled her as much as a sudden clap of thunder, and she jumped as you do in a dream where you're falling and you wake up just before you hit the ground. Her eyes were drawn to the source of the sound—the pulpit at the far end of the aisle. There, the brightest shaft of light fell on a large old book, which she took to be a Bible. The book was lying open on top of the lectern, and a breeze that seemed to come from within the church rather than without gently tugged at its pages without ever quite managing to turn them over.

The rustling was followed by a faint whispering from among the pews. Moments later some dried up old leaves drifted out from between the seats—a possible explanation for the sound in any other place, but not a wholly convincing once in a place such as this.

When Finlay started speaking his voice startled her because she'd forgotten he was there. "That service of 'thanksgiving' was the last time the church was used," he said. "Half a dozen southern sheep farmers sat in pews that once held over a hundred Highlanders," he told her, looking around the desolate, empty church. "Despite the holy setting it must have been the unholiest of affairs, because when they came to sing the first hymn the sheepdogs apparently got up on the seats and drowned out the words with their howling.

"That's why it came to be called the Weeping Glen, Lady Kate."

When Kate was finally able to speak, she said, "I thought you were trying to convince me to hang on to the estate, Finlay, not frighten me away from it."

"Believe me, I am trying to convince you, Lady Kate—with all my heart I am. From what I hear of the vultures who're circling the Cranoch you're the only hope for the people who live in it and love it, and before I met you I was thinking I would just show you the good things in Glen Cranoch and not mention any notions of a curse and what had led up to it . . . But when I saw the sort of person you are . . . Well, I couldn't live with myself if I didn't give you an idea of what you might be letting yourself in for if you try to make Glen Cranoch your home."

CHAPTER 6

Kate's first impression of Archibald Cunningham was of a shining pate surrounded by a neatly trimmed fringe of silvery-grey hair, because he was looking down at some papers on his desk when she was shown into his office.

As the lawyer looked up, Kate's next impression was of a soft mouth that smiled easily, and calculating eyes that gave something of a lie to the ease of the smile. A man of no little wit and wisdom, she decided, though she suspected there would be a slightly sardonic turn to his wit and a calculating shrewdness about his wisdom.

He got up to shake her hand, saying, "Sorry to keep you waiting, Lady Kate. I was taking a call about The Cranoch, but I'll get to that later. Please, have a seat." He gestured to the two Regency elbow chairs set at neat angles in front of his desk.

"This whole thing came right out of the blue, then?" he asked as Kate sat down.

Kate nodded. "One minute I'm running a small craft shop near San Francisco; the next, a Highland estate."

"And have you had a chance to see around The Cranoch yet?"

"Yes. Finlay gave me a guided tour and some history this morning."

"I can imagine the highly colored version of history he would give you, but that's by the by. It's not the past I'm concerned with, Lady Kate, it's the present—and the future. I thought I'd give you a different kind of tour of The Cranoch: an overview of its financial situation. Then maybe we could run through the options. Unless, that is, you've already made up your mind what you want to do . . ."

"Actually, I have," Kate said. She was thinking about her first sight of the glen the day before, with Finlay standing at her side describing its many different moods . . .

About Greystane rising from Castle Crag almost like it was a part of the rock . . .

The breathtaking view from the bedroom window, *her* bedroom window . . .

The little stone bridge and the sound of the water flowing under it before plunging into the glen . . .

The osprey swooping towards the lochan . . .

And the kindness of Finlay and Miss Weir.

"I know what I want to do," Kate said. "I just don't know whether it's a realistic option."

"Well, hopefully I can be of some help in clarifying things for you."

Knowing she couldn't fool the man in front of her into thinking she was any kind of expert in estate affairs, but wanting to let him know she wasn't just some ditzy blonde he could string along, she said, "If you don't mind me asking, do you stand to gain significantly more if I sell the estate, or if I hang on to it?"

"You mean, can you trust me?"

"I didn't want to put it so bluntly but . . . yes."

"Let's put it like this: if you want to sell and use me as your agent I stand to gain a tidy lump sum; if you hang on to the estate, and to me as the factor, then over time I'll also make a pretty penny. But if you're not happy with how I handle things today, you won't choose me as either your selling agent or your factor and I won't make anything at all. So, quite apart from the ethics of it all, it's in my best interests to look after your best interests."

Kate blushed, feeling like a naive little girl if not a ditzy blonde, and realizing just how far out of her depth she was.

"I won't presume to tell you what to do or what not to do. I'll just do my best to make sure you're in possession of all the facts and understand their implications before you make your mind up," the lawyer said. "Fair enough?"

Kate nodded.

"Good. Now, from what you've said—and, if you'll forgive me saying so, the slightly dreamy look in your eyes as you said it—I take it that you'd prefer not to sell?"

Kate nodded again.

"I can't say I blame you, because it's a lovely little part of the world. But I have to caution you against letting The

Cranoch's beauty blind you to its problems. Don't get me wrong, the estate has a lot going for it; but it's also got an awful lot working against it."

"After walking around it this morning, I find that hard to believe."

"I'm afraid I have to look at it in terms of balance sheets rather than scenic beauty, Lady Kate. You said you run a small business?"

"Yes, but nothing on this scale."

"The scale might be different but the principles are exactly the same. In a nutshell, The Cranoch is like a shop that's been losing money for about 50 years. It was highly profitable as a sheep run in the early 1800s; then as a hunting estate up to the 1930s.

"But once Colin Chisholm took over . . . Well, he wanted his privacy, for reasons Finlay has no doubt explained. He wasn't prepared to share Greystane with paying guests and so, as factors, our hands were somewhat tied. We did our best to market The Cranoch as a holiday venue to the huntin' shootin' fishin' set, but we could only offer accommodation in the crofters' cottages. The people who follow those pursuits want to be waited on hand and foot in the big house; they're not prepared to put up with bed-and-breakfast in a crofter's cottage."

"Didn't you explain all that to Mr. Chisholm?"

"At every opportunity. But, rather than follow our advice, he chose to keep the estate afloat by literally selling off the family silver piece by piece. Not just the silver, but the *objet d'art* that had been collected over the years when the family's finances had been in a somewhat sounder state.

"Unfortunately, I have to inform you that we're now at the stage where there's no family silver left to sell."

"Your hands wouldn't be tied with me, Mr. Cunningham," Kate said, smiling because she felt the problems weren't as insurmountable as his earlier words had led her to fear. "I wouldn't mind sharing Greystane with guests if they were helping make the estate a going concern. In fact, I might even enjoy the company," she told him, having visions of meeting and maybe mingling with actors, sports stars, and minor royalty.

"I'm afraid it's not that simple," Archibald Cunningham said. "Take Greystane: it's four hundred years old and in the most exposed location imaginable, so it needs constant care and repair. Unfortunately, Mr. Chisholm could barely afford to do the little jobs, let alone the big ones.

"Then there's the estate itself. It's a common misconception that a sporting estate is basically an area of unspoiled wilderness, and that looking after it is just a matter of letting nature run its course. In fact a good sporting estate might look wild but it's anything but a wilderness. It doesn't happen by itself, and doesn't just look after itself. In its way it's as manufactured and manicured as a golf course, with the natural balance distorted to favour one or two target species and a single predator."

"The paying guest."

"Indeed, the paying guest. To maintain that artificial

balance you've got to juggle dozens of different factors, each of them affecting the others, all of them needing to be constantly kept in check."

"And at the moment the balance of The Cranoch isn't quite what it should be for a sporting estate?"

"To carry on with the golfing analogy, if you'll forgive me—the game's a passion of mine, if not an obsession—The Cranoch is closer to a pitch-and-putt course than to Pebble Beach, and Greystane House is closer to a caddyshack than the clubhouse at Augusta. I hope I'm not overstepping the mark by speaking so bluntly, but I'd be remiss not to."

"I understand," Kate said, trying hard to keep the disappointment from her voice and the tears from welling up in her eyes.

"In short, it's sorely neglected, Lady Kate: not just Greystane but the whole estate. You'd have to spend a considerable amount of time and money on them to attract the sort of people who pay top dollar," the lawyer told her.

"Even if you can afford to meet all those one-off costs and get Greystane and the estate into first-class shape, you'd then be faced with increased running costs to maintain them in that condition."

"But it was profitable in the past," Kate said, clutching at straws.

"It's a different world now," Archibald Cunningham said. "The extra hired hands you'd need would expect to be paid far more than the estate workers and domestics who worked for a pittance back in the 'good old days'. In other words, your income would go up, but I don't think it would go up nearly as much as your expenses. You'd still have a crippling revenue gap, Lady Kate."

"Are you effectively saying that my only realistic option is to sell?"

"I'm saying that if you want to avoid selling you have to come up with a way to close the revenue gap, or else subsidize The Cranoch's constant loss-making from a source of income outside the estate. I don't know if perhaps your shop near San Francisco would be able to do that?"

Kate laughed, but with irony rather than humor.

Picking up on the irony, the lawyer said, "I take it that's a 'no'."

"The shop makes enough to support me and my father, but that's about it. Anyway, I get the feeling from what you've said that I'd have to sell my share in the shop just to pay for the immediate repairs Greystane's going to need."

"Quite possibly. There's a rather long list of things Mr. Chisholm put off that can't be ignored for much longer.

"As I said, if you want to hold on to The Cranoch you'll have to come up with some way to boost its income. I'm afraid it's a bit beyond my remit—not to mention imagination—to make any suggestions in that respect. It's really more of a job for a business consultant, but it's a Catch 22 situation."

"How do you mean?"

"The good consultants don't come cheap, so the times when you need their services the most are the times when you're least able to afford them."

Kate felt all her romantic notions crumbling to dust as Archibald Cunningham explained the harsh realities of the situation. She knew that if worse came to worse she'd still leave Scotland a relatively wealthy woman, yet somehow she also knew that she'd be unhappier than before she'd ever heard of Greystane and The Cranoch. Suddenly Kate was no longer worried whether the man sitting across the desk from her thought she was a ditzy blonde, a dreamy romantic or a dumb American, and the tears were running down her cheeks.

She expected Archibald Cunningham would barely be able to keep the mockery from his face, given that he had a somewhat sardonic expression at the best of times. However, the solicitor reached into the breast pocket of his pinstriped jacket and brought out a linen handkerchief for her, and there was genuine sympathy in his voice when he said, "I'm sorry I can't be more positive, Lady Kate, but I wouldn't be doing you any favours if I wasn't brutally honest. You've been presented with something that must be like a bit of a dream come true; I have the unpleasant task of making you face the reality of it."

Kate wiped her eyes with the handkerchief, feeling even more like a little girl now as she said, "I'm just so disappointed. It was better than a dream, Mr. Cunningham. When I looked out of my bedroom window in the tower I felt like I was a princess in my own little fairytale castle. I'm sorry, I know that must sound so stupid."

"No need to apologize—I understand. I'm not saying you have no choice other than to give up Greystane and walk away from Glen Cranoch; all I'm saying is that it'll take no little imagination to think of a way to keep it."

Trying to get her act together, Kate said, "What other sources of income does the estate have?"

"Not many, I'm afraid. There are a dozen crofts—little mixed farms run by the tenants to feed their families and the laird or lady, earn a little spending money and pay a token rent—but that's all it is, a token rent. There's no real money in it for the crofters or the estate. The crofts are really just a way for people who love the land to be able to live on it, and for the estate to employ at least a handful of essential workers it couldn't afford to pay in cash. They're almost like a last remnant of the old days, when people paid rent by giving service and a share of their produce to the clan chief," he said. "You could always try raising their rents but, realistically, they couldn't afford to pay. They barely get by as it is."

Kate wiped away the last of her tears and, thinking about the terrible events Finlay had related that morning, said, "Raising the rents isn't an option, Mr. Cunningham."

The lawyer nodded. Looking at some notes he'd made on a yellow legal pad, he said, "There's some revenue from timber, supplying a few specialist local markets—quality furniture-makers and the like—on a small scale."

"Couldn't we make more by supplying bigger markets further afield?" Kate asked, more in hope than expectation because she guessed there must be some reason why such a course of action wasn't already being followed.

Sure enough, the lawyer said, "The Cranoch's hillsides are too steep, the forest not really extensive enough, the roads in and out too poor to make it a real money-earner. You can't supply the big buyers with the bulk they need and, even if you could, you can't compete on price."

"Have you not got any good news for me, Mr. Cunningham?" Kate asked.

"There is a silver lining to all the clouds," he said. "I know you'd rather not sell, but if you decide you have to, there's a buyer who's expressed the sort of interest that's likely to translate into an offer it would be difficult to refuse."

"No matter how much money I was offered for The Cranoch, I wouldn't find it difficult to refuse."

"I understand that, Lady Kate, but you have to face up to the fact that you won't have a choice unless you can come up with a way of turning the estate around.

"Anyway, this party has been interested in The Cranoch for some time. They wanted to meet Colin Chisholm to make an offer but he had no use for money—he was too old to spend it. They must have been keeping an eye on the situation, though."

"Why do you say that?"

"The day after Mr. Chisholm's death notice appeared in the local newspaper they were in touch with me, as executor of the estate, asking to arrange a meeting; and then Finlay reported seeing a stranger 'snooping around', taking lots of photographs of Greystane and the glen and obviously out for more than a walk. He turned up again the next day, and Finlay confronted him—rather angrily, by all accounts—because he guessed the man was checking out the estate, circling like a vulture.

"Anyway, I didn't want to meet with the prospective buyer until I'd had this talk with you.

"As luck would have it they called just before you arrived, saying they're in the area at the moment and asking if they could meet me to discuss the estate. I suggested a business dinner at five o'clock in The Caledonian Thistle Hotel, just around the corner, so that if you'd like to hear what they have to say it won't involve you in another trip into town. If you've got other plans, though, or would rather let me act as intermediary and give you the lowdown later, that's fine."

Kate sighed heavily. Fighting back the urge to dismiss the offer of a meeting out of hand, as Colin Chisholm had done, she said, "I suppose there's no harm at least hearing what they have to say."

"Indeed not. I don't have to be present other than to introduce you, but I would strongly recommend that you let me sit in. These people have a thousand little tricks for pressuring you into making on-the-spot decisions you might regret later. They might well say there's a time limit on their offer, come up with some apparently plausible reason why the deal has to be done tonight or by noon tomorrow or 5 p.m. on Friday, when in truth that'll almost certainly not be the case. They've been interested in the estate for over a year, by my reckoning, so the chances are they'll still be interested in it a few weeks or months from now."

Kate nodded to show she understood.

"But I wouldn't wait too long," the lawyer cautioned.

"Why not?"

"While it's not a good idea to accept an opening offer, if you leave the unpalatable decision until you can't hang on any longer they'll take you to the cleaners because they'll be the ones bargaining from a position of strength. They'll sense your desperation, because that's part of what they do, and they'll move in for the kill without mercy, because that's another part of what they do."

"Just exactly who are *they*, Mr. Cunningham, and why are they so interested in Glen Cranoch?"

"*They* are Yeoman Holdings, a London-based development company. As for why they're so interested in Glen Cranoch in particular, that's a little harder to say because their portfolio is so wide. From what I can make out, it seems to cover everything from residential developments through to commercial and leisure interests." Archibald Cunningham looked at his watch and said, "It's just coming up to four o'clock now; how about if I meet you in the hotel bar about ten to five and we'll go into the restaurant together?"

Kate nodded.

"I have another client at four, but you're most welcome to pass the time in the waiting room, and I'll get Mrs. Cunningham at the desk there to bring you a coffee."

"Thanks, but Finlay's waiting to drive me back to The Cranoch. I better let him know what's happening."

"On the subject of Finlay—and Miss Weir, for that matter—they're likeable souls, but you can't let the tail wag the dog."

"What do you mean?"

"This has to be about what's best for you, Lady Kate, not what's best for them."

"You're right, Mr. Cunningham, they're likeable souls," Kate said. She was about to get up to leave but the lawyer stopped her, saying, "There's one more thing. I almost forgot, because it's literally a peripheral matter."

Kate settled back in her seat.

"It concerns the ruins of a small cottage on the estate."

"Jamie's Cottage?" Kate had intended asking him about the derelict cottage and its new owner, but the matter had slipped her mind after hearing just how dire the estate's financial position was.

"Yes, Jamie's Cottage. I take it Finlay's mentioned it to you?"

"Briefly."

"And you'll have seen Jamie's portrait and know why it's turned to face the wall?"

Kate nodded.

"Well, being the youngest son, instead of inheriting the estate he was just given the cottage to live in, and the right to collect a little rent in kind from some of the clansmen.

"After his flight from Culloden and fall from grace

his wife and son left the glen. I suppose she didn't want her child to be brought up in a place where he'd hear his father's name being blackened. They never returned, and that line of the family was conveniently forgotten . . .

"At least until a little while ago. In his later years Colin Chisholm got interested in genealogy, possibly so he could find out if he had anyone to leave the estate to. He bought a computer and seems to have got quite clued-up about using it. He even set up a little business on the Internet, tracing Scottish family trees. He wasn't making more than pocket money, but it probably helped him feel he was doing something productive with his time.

"As well as tracing your line, which is how we knew roughly where to look for you, he traced Jamie Chisholm's. Colin never found any trace of Jamie himself—what happened to him is a complete mystery—but he managed to trace the black sheep's issue down the years. Almost without exception Jamie's male descendants seem to have served in the army. Maybe they felt they had a point to prove when it came to courage, or maybe they were never told about Jamie, and the army connection is just a coincidence.

"Whatever, just before Colin Chisholm died he traced the sole surviving member of Jamie's branch of the family, and called me to put a codicil in the will regarding the cottage."

"Why would he want to do that?" Kate asked. "I'm not asking because I resent it," she added quickly. "I'm just curious, since this Jamie seems to still be held in contempt two and a half centuries after Culloden."

"I can only guess about that, but perhaps there's a clue in what Jamie's living descendant does, or did: his name's Cameron Fraser and he saw active service in the Balkans with The Black Watch—that's a Highland regiment. At a guess, something about that might have struck a chord with Colin Chisholm, a man who was so badly wounded in the service of his country.

"Also, it's been my experience that when people get to the age Mr. Chisholm had reached, their mind often turns to unfinished business. He maybe saw Jamie's Cottage as just that. Whatever Jamie's disgrace, the cottage had still belonged to his wife and child—and so, by extension, Colin Chisholm maybe felt it rightfully belonged to Jamie's heirs."

"Do you know anything about this Cameron Fraser?" Kate asked.

Archibald Cunningham hesitated, as if considering a delicate matter, then said, "All I know is that he recently left the army under something of a cloud."

"What sort of a cloud?"

"The kind that doesn't have a silver lining, I would venture to suggest."

"What makes you say that?"

"He resigned his commission just before his term of enlistment was up."

"So?"

"That's a most peculiar thing to do, given that his pension benefits would be determined by the rank he held on leaving. He could have left as a lieutenant; instead he left as a private."

"That does seem strange. Why would someone do that?"

"All I can imagine is that it was either a matter of conscience or of necessity. It's as if he felt the army had done something so dishonorable that he had to register a protest, or he'd done something so dishonorable the army insisted he do the honorable thing."

"Did he fall or was he pushed, in other words."

"Yes, quite."

Archibald Cunningham's phone rang. "Excuse me," he said to Kate. He picked up the phone, listened for a few moments, then glanced at his watch and said, "Thanks, dear. I'll be with him in a minute."

He hung up and said to Kate, "My four o'clock client's here. Probably just as well—we were holding a bit of a board of inquiry into Mr. Cameron Fraser, which was rather naughty of us given that the man's not even here to defend himself." He pulled back his chair and got to his feet.

Kate did likewise.

"So, I'll see you at ten to five in the bar of the Caledonian Thistle, then?" Archibald Cunningham asked.

Kate nodded and shook his hand.

"I'm sorry I didn't have better news, but the day might yet have a happy ending."

Kate tried to force a smile but didn't come close to pulling it off.

A few minutes later she was settling down on a bar

stool beside Finlay in The Piper's Arms, the bar she'd arranged to meet him in.

"It's a sare fecht to be surrounded by that . . ." Finlay said, looking at all the bottles of Scotch behind the bar, ". . . and reduced to drinking this," he said, holding up a glass of fresh orange.

"I'm sorry, Finlay, but I don't even trust myself to drive on the roads back home, let alone over here."

Finlay sighed, looked into his drink and said, "So here isn't going to be home, then, I take it?"

"I wish with all my heart that it could be, Finlay, believe me."

"But . . ."

"From what Mr. Cunningham told me, it doesn't look like I can afford to keep Glen Cranoch, however much I want to."

"I understand."

"I hope this doesn't seem like I'm rubbing salt into a wound, Finlay, but I'm having dinner with someone who wants to buy the estate."

"That'll be the English 'gentleman' I saw snooping around the other day, I take it."

"Yes, I think so. Anyway, I wonder if you'd mind hanging on to give me a lift back to the glen afterwards." She reached into her handbag and brought out her purse. "I'd like to buy you a meal while you wait," she said, offering him a £20 note.

"It's all right, Lady Kate, I'll wait without the money."

"Please," she said, feeling like she was trying to salve her conscience in some small way, and that perhaps Finlay didn't want to let her.

Finlay's next words, and the way he spoke them, told Kate she'd been right. "Thank you, but that's quite all right, Lady Kate," the ghillie said. "Miss Weir has a meal waiting for us back at Greystane, and I'm sure it'll be far nicer than anything I could be buying with £20 in any fancy restaurant.

"Now if you'll excuse me, I'll call and let her know we'll be late and that only one of us will be eating." With that he got up and walked over to the payphone at the far end of the bar.

Kate watched him as he stood with his back to her. He rummaged in the pockets of his tweed jacket for change, then just stood there for a moment, leaning against the phone, and she thought his shoulders slumped ever so slightly. Finally he put a coin in the box, punched in a number and, moments later, started talking into the headset.

He talked for two or three minutes, and Kate guessed that he was informing Miss Weir of much more than just their late return.

Finlay went to the toilet after hanging up, and was gone for so long that Kate was starting to get concerned.

When at last he came back, she said, "Finlay, are you all right?"

"Aye, I'm fine," he told her. "I'm just feeling I owe you an apology, Lady Kate. I was terribly, terribly short with you and I'd no right to be. It's just been a difficult time for myself and Miss Weir, what with the uncertainty of it all. We'd been prepared for the worst, but then we finally met you and saw what you were like and how much you seemed to like Greystane and Glen Cranoch—"

"I do, Finlay, and not just Greystane and Glen Cranoch, but you and Miss Weir. If there was any way . . ."

She was about to tell him that in any case nothing had been decided yet, but stopped because she knew that, whatever she felt in her heart, the decision had effectively been made.

CHAPTER 7

KATE ARRIVED AT THE CALEDONIAN THISTLE AT QUARTER to five. There was no sign of Archibald Cunningham, so she ordered a sloe gin to calm her nerves while she waited. Before she could get her purse out to pay for the drink a man of about her own age walked up to the bar, held out a £5 note, and said to the barman, "I'll get that."

"It's all right, thank you," Kate told him, uncomfortable at the idea of accepting a drink from a man who hadn't even introduced himself.

However, the barman had already turned away with the money in his hand.

The man who'd bought the drink was more than a head taller than Kate. He strained the seams of his charcoal grey suit at chest and shoulder, and the collar of his white shirt. He had a thick head of coal-black hair and eyes that were almost as dark. His face was heavy featured, and there was a deep dimple in his ample jaw.

It was a description that Kate might have found appealing if she'd been reading it in a book, yet she didn't find the man standing next to her attractive in the slightest. She liked self-assurance in a man, but loathed over-confidence of the kind she saw in this man's expression and sensed in his body language. "Thank you, but I don't accept drinks from strangers," she told him, making no move to reach for the cocktail.

Other men might have called it quits and walked away with an attempt at a couldn't-care-less shrug of the shoulders, or mumbled an embarrassed apology. But this man smiled and said, "Tony Carling, pleased to meet you. Now we're not strangers, so you can accept the drink."

His accent was English, and Kate decided she didn't like it. She wasn't sure what to do, but just then the cavalry arrived, albeit in a form as unlike John Wayne as possible—the portly figure of Archibald Cunningham. "I hope you've not been waiting long," the lawyer said to Kate. His smile died away when he sensed the tension between Kate and the big man next to her.

Kate shook her head. "Nice to see you," she said pointedly. Then she turned from Archibald Cunningham to Tony Carling and said, "I'm sorry, I have an appointment."

The solicitor took his cue and called across to the barman, "Charlie, I have a table booked for five o'clock."

"Ah, yes, Mr. Cunningham. Table six should be ready for you now, if you want to be going through."

"Excuse us," Archie said firmly but politely to Tony Carling. Putting an arm around Kate's shoulders in fatherly fashion he guided her towards a dimly-lit room dominated by a log-burning fire.

Kate's relief was short-lived. She had the feeling they were being followed, and looked back to see the big man walking just a few paces behind her.

Archibald Cunningham turned to see what was wrong. He stiffened, and Kate sensed that physical confrontations weren't his strongest suit. She guessed that not many people would relish a confrontation with Tony Carling—and that Carling knew it, and enjoyed moments such as this. "I've told you we have an appointment," Kate said, making no effort to hide her irritation.

"Yes," the man said, "but if you're the Cunningham party, then your appointment is with me."

Turning from Kate to Archibald Campbell, the big Englishman reached out a hand and said, "Tony Carling, Yeoman Holdings."

Archibald Cunningham smiled with barely disguised relief as he shook the outstretched hand. "Archie Cunningham, agent for Lady Kate Brodie," he said, indicating Kate with his free hand.

"A pleasant surprise in every way," Carling said, looking at Kate.

"Come on through, man," Archie said to Carling.

They'd no sooner sat down at the fire—Kate barely had time to take off her Burberry raincoat and scarf—when a waiter came over with three menus and said, "Can I get you something to drink?"

Before Kate or Archie could reply, Tony Carling said,

"A sloe gin for the lady, a Bacardi and Coke with ice for myself, and the usual for Mr. Cunningham."

Archie looked taken aback.

Carling smiled. "The barman knew you by name, so I'm guessing the waiters know you, too."

The tone of Carling's voice and the smug expression on his face did nothing to change Kate's opinion that he had considerably more than his share of confidence.

"I don't know if you'd prefer to eat first and talk business after, or the other way around," Archie said, addressing both Kate and Carling.

Before Carling could say anything, Kate said, "I'd like to get straight down to business."

"Fair enough," Carling said. "I'm chairman and chief exec of Yeoman, and as such I have full financial authority to act as I see fit on the firm's behalf. To all intents and purposes I am the firm. The reason I've asked for this meeting is that Yeoman would like to make an offer—a very generous offer—for the Cranock Estate."

Archibald Cunningham winced at the mispronunciation but let it pass, saying only, "We're listening."

Kate knew that Carling was about to quote a figure, but hadn't the slightest idea what it would be. Her heartbeat quickened and a slight sweat broke out on her brow. She hoped Carling wouldn't notice, but knew deep down that he must because he was studying her so intently. Just as she'd sensed that Carling enjoyed watching Archibald Cunningham suffer in the moments before introducing himself—that he'd deliberately let those moments drag on a little longer than was necessary—so she knew that he was doing the same thing now with her, and was deriving a similar enjoyment.

Finally Tony Carling said, "A quarter of a million pounds."

Kate was glad she was sitting down. She had a little under twelve thousand dollars in her checking account, and it was the most money she'd ever had in her life. It took every ounce of composure she possessed to keep her face expressionless, but she couldn't help from swallowing. She knew Tony Carling would have noticed, and that he'd know what it meant.

Just then the waiter came over with their drinks, but the three people sitting around the table barely noticed him.

Archie said to Tony Carling, "Quite frankly, I'd hoped your interest was going to be more serious than that."

"Just how much more 'serious' were you *hoping* it was going to be?"

"Considerably more."

"Well, quite frankly, perhaps you'd like to consider this: the estate can't possibly be making money—"

Archibald Cunningham made as if to interrupt, but Carling stopped him with a dismissive gesture and the words, "You did say you wanted to be serious about this. Now, as I said, the estate can't be making money and, frankly, I don't see how it ever can in anything like its present form."

"How do you know we don't have plans to change it from its present form," Kate said, but was sorry almost as soon as she'd spoken because she was aware of how lame and unconvincing she sounded.

Tony Carling gave a patronising smile that made Kate want to slap him, then said, "Call it an educated guess. The kind that's let me build Yeoman Holdings up from scratch into a business that can buy a country estate that's dying on its feet and provide the investment needed to give it new life."

Kate had promised herself she wouldn't say another word unless she had to, but she was too concerned about the fate of Finlay and Miss Weir, the crofters she'd never met, and the glen she'd fallen in love with to stop herself from asking, "What sort of 'new life' did you have in mind?"

"The good life."

"Care to be more specific?"

"Care to give me a reason why I should be?"

"Because I care about more than making money, Mr. Carling. I care about Glen Cranoch and the people who've lived in it all their lives and love it even more than I do. Is that a good enough reason?"

Carling took a drink of his Bacardi and Coke, then said, "We plan to turn the glen into a ski resort in winter, the lake into a water sports center in summer, and the little castle thing on top of the hill—"

"Greystane," Kate said through gritted teeth.

"Whatever," Carling said. "We want to run a chairlift

up to it and turn it into a visitor center with a restaurant, a tartan tat souvenir shop, and a token attempt at a museum.

"There are other glens we could do it in—let's face it, they're ten-a-penny in this part of the world—so there's no point playing hardball with me because it's my ball and I'll just go and play with it somewhere else. But I imagine you don't like messing around any more than I do, so I'm not going to pretend that Glen Cranock is anything other than our first choice. The slope and snowfall are right for winter sports; the depth and size of the lake are good for water skiing; and the little castle is pretty much straight out of a storybook."

"I'd say all of that adds up to more than quarter of a million pounds," Archibald Cunningham said frostily, trying to keep a professional calm in the face of the Englishman's dismissive description of Glen Cranock.

"It might have done if the estate was viable and you could make a go of it yourself," Carling said. "But as it stands it's a financial black hole, and I'm willing to bet that people won't exactly be queuing up to pour money into it."

"You don't believe in beating around the bush, do you?" Kate said.

"Life's too short. Too many other deals to make, places to go, people to meet."

"What about the people who work in Greystane just now?"

Carling swirled the ice around in his drink, then said, "We'd be prepared to offer them positions appropriate to their abilities."

Kate thought about what sort of positions a man like Tony Carling would consider appropriate for Miss Weir and Finlay, and how long their pride would let them work for him. Not wanting to pursue that train of thought for too long, she addressed her next concern: "And what about the crofters and their families?"

"They'd have to move, of course," Carling said without any trace of regret. "I'd be prepared to accommodate a handful of your people as a goodwill gesture, but the bottom line is that I'm running a business, not a charitable foundation, and I can't run it around people who're in the way."

"All of this is purely academic as long as we're talking about a figure in the region of the one you mentioned as an opening gambit," Archibald Cunningham said quickly, before Kate had a chance to say anything.

By way of reply, Tony Carling took a checkbook and gold pen from the inside pocket of his jacket. He wrote out a figure on the first blank page before holding the checkbook up in front of Kate and then Archibald Cunningham. "No bargaining, no horse trading," he said. "That's as high as I'll go."

The figure on the check was £275,000.

"The offer's good for ten days. If you haven't asked me to sign the check by then I'll tear it up, and when you do finally ask me to write out a check—and I think deep down we all know it's a matter of 'when' and not 'if'—the number I write on it won't be as big as that one. In fact, it won't even be as big as the first offer I made you."

His point made, Carling put the checkbook back in his pocket, picked up one of the menus and said, "Now, why don't we order?"

"Actually, I'd rather eat back at Greystane," Kate said. She picked up her coat and scarf and walked out without even putting them on.

Behind her she heard Archibald Cunningham saying, "If you'll excuse me one moment, Mr. Carling . . ."

Moments later the solicitor was at her side, saying, "Lady Kate, that was a little rude."

"Are you talking about his behaviour or mine?" Kate said as she pulled on her raincoat.

"Lady Kate—" Archie said, making a token attempt to help her with the sleeves.

"He started it," Kate said. She knew she sounded like a child, but couldn't help herself.

"It's nothing personal. It's just how he does business."

"Then how he does business sucks. He's talking about spoiling somewhere unspoiled, not to mention turning people's lives upside down."

"I know you're upset—"

"You're damn right I am."

"I understand why, but you have to think about yourself, not Finlay and Miss Weir and the crofters, however likeable they might be."

"I won't be able to think about myself in quite the same way in the future if I only think of myself right now, Mr.

Cunningham. I'm not sure that any amount of money would make up for that."

"I understand, believe me I do, but you have to be realistic. What we'd like to do and what we're actually able to do aren't always the same thing, are they—and this is one of the times when they're definitely different. Tony Carling might be unconscionably rude but, if you put that aside, I think he's right. It is a matter of 'when' you sell, not 'if'. It's just a matter of time until your money runs out. It's a question of whether you get a reasonable sum for the estate in the next week or so; or whether you have to sell it at a bargain-basement price a few months down the line—all the while prolonging the uncertainty of the very people you're trying to protect, falsely raising their hopes of having a future in the glen.

"Selling now is a case of being cruel to be kind," he told her. "I know that can't be easy for you, because I think you're too kind to be cruel for any reason, but that's where I earn my money. You can say your goodbyes and fly back to America and I'll handle the rest. My conscience will be clear, and yours should be, too, because there's nothing else we can realistically do in the circumstances."

Kate didn't say anything.

"I have to tell him something, Lady Kate," the lawyer prompted.

"Tell him I'll sell . . . When I'm sure there's no way I can turn the estate around and stop the crofters being thrown out of their homes; when there's no way I can stop the glen being turned into a tacky resort and Greystane being turned into a 'tartan tat' shop."

"That was a most unfortunate turn of phrase," Archibald Cunningham conceded.

"I'll only sell to him when I'm absolutely sure there isn't anything else I can do," Kate said.

"By then you'll be in no position to drive any sort of bargain."

"I don't care about the money, Mr. Cunningham. I've never had that sort of money before, so I won't miss it."

"But there's no sense in throwing it away. The Cranoch is indeed a black hole, just like Carling said. There's no point pouring good money into it after bad, Lady Kate."

"I don't think an unspoilt glen, a house that's stood for four hundred years, and people like Finlay McRae and Miss Weir are a bad cause to spend my money on. And even if I don't manage to turn things around, at least the money I've spent will have bought the satisfaction of knowing I did my best, and that's priceless."

"I almost hope for your sake that your money runs out soon, otherwise Yeoman really might lose interest."

"No, Mr. Cunningham, Yoeman won't."

"How you can be so sure?"

"For the same reason I'm sure about not selling unless and until I absolutely have to: because, whatever he might say, deep down Tony Carling knows what I know—glens like The Cranoch aren't ten-a-penny. In fact, I don't think there's anywhere else quite like it," she told him, then turned on her heel and walked away to find Finlay McRae.

Dawn the next day found Kate dozing fitfully in the back pew of Greystane's chapel.

After lying awake for hours in the four-poster bed she'd slept so soundly in the night before, she'd finally dropped off into the most disconcerting nightmare. She dreamed she was in the banquet hall, looking at the row of gilt-framed pictures hanging on the wall. A portrait of herself hung in place of Lady Carolyn's picture.

From behind her she heard derisive laughter and turned to see Tony Carling sitting at the head of the table, raising a tumbler of Bacardi and Coke in a mock toast.

The door to the chapel swung open and the sound of howling dogs issued forth, taking up where Tony Carling's laughter left off.

Stumbling through to the chapel she saw Finlay dressed as a minister standing behind the pulpit. "This is what they call progress!" he shouted to a congregation of sheep dogs sitting up in the pews.

The canine congregation started whimpering and cowering, and when Kate turned back to the pulpit it was no longer occupied by Finlay but by a grotesquely aged parody of Miss Weir. Their eyes met, and Miss Weir screamed, "Damn you for what you're about to do, Lady Kate Brodie! May you never know another moment of love in your godforsaken life."

In the moments after waking from the frightful dream Kate was so convinced she heard howling in the chapel two storeys below that she got out of bed and padded down the narrow staircase in her oversize T-shirt to check that there weren't any dogs sitting on the pews. She'd taken a seat in the empty chapel for a few moments, suddenly feeling the need to say a prayer to a God she barely believed in . . .

And the next thing she knew, someone was shaking her awake. Raising her head slowly, her neck stiff, she saw in the weak dawn light that the someone was Miss Weir.

"What are you doing down here at this time, lass?" the housekeeper asked. "It's only just gone six o'clock."

Kate rubbed her eyes and sat up, her body cramping in a dozen places as she did so. "I'm sorry, Miss Weir," she said sleepily.

Miss Weir laughed. "It's your house, Lady Kate. You can sleep on the table in the banquet hall, if you want. I was on my way to the kitchen to get breakfast started when I saw you slumped forward and was just concerned—aye, and curious too, about why a person would want to sleep on a hard bench when they've got a four-poster to lay their head down in."

"I didn't come to sleep," Kate said. "I came to pray for inspiration. And, if I couldn't get that, for forgiveness."

Miss Weir put an arm around Kate and, in an uncharacteristically gentle voice, said, "I thought Finlay and I convinced you last night that you've nothing to feel guilty about."

On the drive back to the glen the night before Kate had told Finlay the gist of her meeting with Archibald Cunningham and Tony Carling.

She'd repeated it all again to Miss Weir when the three of them sat down for a late dinner in the banquet hall—Kate at the head of the big table, Finlay on her right, Miss Weir on her left, the dinner going cold on the plates in front of them. Finlay and Miss Weir put a brave face on it, but Kate was barely able to hold back her tears. She wanted to console them, but when she tried to find the words she finally started crying. The two of them ended up consoling Kate, and she'd suddenly been deeply ashamed. Wiping away her tears, she'd said, "Finlay, Miss Weir, please forgive me. I've just been offered more money than I ever dreamed I could have, for a place I hadn't even heard of a couple of weeks ago. You must think I'm terrible crying like this. It's just that . . . It's just that what I would be giving up seems worth so much more than the money I'd be gaining . . . Worth so much more than any sum of money . . . And, more than that, it's what I'd be doing to you and the crofters and the glen that bothers me."

"You'll just be doing what anyone in your situation would do," Finlay said.

"And most people wouldn't even shed a tear," Miss Weir added.

"You must think it unforgivable that I'm feeling sorry for myself when I stand to gain something, and you and

Finlay stand to lose your jobs and home."

"We'd think less of you if you didn't cry at all, Kate Brodie," Miss Weir told her, "or if the tears were just for yourself."

Kate had reached for Miss Weir's hand, and for Finlay's. Clasping them in her own, she'd said, "I meant every one of the words I said to Mr. Cunningham, about how I'll hang on to Glen Cranoch unless I can't keep it any longer. I want the two of you to start thinking about ways to turn this place around, to make it pay. I'm not even talking about making a profit; I'm not interested in making money, just making the estate break even.

"But I want you to think about something else, too—about where you'd go and what you'd do if I am forced to sell The Cranoch. Archibald Cunningham told me it would be a case of 'when', not 'if'. Deep down, I know that he's almost certainly right." She paused after that, as if needing time to gather her thoughts, or just her composure, then said, "I'll go around to the crofters tomorrow and ask them to attend a meeting so I can say to them what I've said to you: ask for ideas—and tell them to start thinking about a future outside the glen in case we can't come up with any."

"Between us I'm sure we'll think of something," Miss Weir had said. She'd squeezed Kate's hand and, at exactly the same moment, Finlay did the same thing. They'd all smiled at each other unconvincingly before turning their attention without enthusiasm to the lovely meal Miss Weir had prepared. For once even Finlay just picked at his food.

Now, in the chapel the next morning, Miss Weir said, "You can't take the weight of the world on your shoulders, lass, or it'll crush you."

"But I'm the Lady of The Cranoch, so I have to take the weight of this little part of the world on my shoulders."

"If I was you, I'd just take the money."

"If I do, I'm going to feel like a second Lady Carolyn."

"Lass, I don't think you could possibly be any less like Lady Carolyn."

"I'd be responsible for a second clearance, just the same."

"No, not just the same. Somehow I couldn't see you burning crofters' cottages around them and selling them into servitude."

"Still, the bottom line is that the crofters will have to leave their homes and the glen and face an unknown future."

"The future'll take care of itself," Miss Weir said. "As for the present, the best thing you can do is go back upstairs and lay your head down in that four-poster bed.

"Then, when you wake up, you can go around the crofts like you said last night." Miss Weir put a reassuring hand on Kate's shoulder and said, "We'll all work together, everyone in the glen, like we always do and see what we can come up with, okay?"

Kate nodded. On an impulse she hugged Miss Weir before doing what she was told: going back upstairs to bed.

CHAPTER 8

It was almost noon when Kate woke up, and Finlay and Miss Weir were having lunch by the time she made it down to the kitchen.

Finlay offered to go around the crofts with her, but there was a rod and bait box outside the kitchen and she guessed he'd been about to set off on a fishing trip. She didn't know how much longer Finlay would have the chance to enjoy an afternoon casting in the still waters of the lochan or the fast-flowing little river in the hanging valley above it, so she smiled her thanks and said she'd manage on her own.

After a cup of tea, some small talk, and a big salmon sandwich, Kate set off down the steps and the stony track that wound around Castle Crag to the glen below.

She was halfway down the crag when she noticed something from the corner of her eye: a little cloud of dust blossoming on the dirt track at the far end of the glen. Seconds later the more substantial shape of an approaching vehicle appeared in its midst. The dust cloud died away as the driver parked near the old church—still too far away for Kate to make out what kind of vehicle it was, let alone tell anything about the person who got out. Rather than visiting the cluster of whitewashed cottages at the foot of the crag as she'd intended, Kate kept on walking. She was curious about who had just driven into the glen and why. Besides, she was glad of an excuse to delay knocking on the crofters' doors with bad news.

By the time Kate reached the first abandoned farm township she could tell that the parked vehicle was some kind of little van.

A little further on, she saw that it was a fawn-colored camper and the driver, who was looking at the old church now, was a man. Even from a distance there was something unmistakably masculine about his build and bearing—tall and broad-shouldered, with a long-legged gait and no roll of the narrow hips.

As Kate walked and watched, she saw the man hesitate at the door of the church, then turn his back on it and walk towards the first cluster of ruined cottages. He stood perfectly still for a very long time when he got there. Kate sensed he was trying to decide whether to enter the nearest cottage, but that something was stopping him.

Finally turning away from the blackened building, he walked down to the lochan and along the water's edge. Every so often he crouched down, reached for something around his neck and raised it to his face. He seemed to be taking pictures: the Yeoman Holdings snooper Finlay had seen the other day, Kate guessed. Her curiosity turned to a mix of disgust and anger. At first she wondered if it was Tony Carling himself, but as she drew nearer she saw that this man was slimmer, and that his walk didn't have any suggestion of an aggressive swagger about it. One of Carling's minions, she decided.

The man crouched on one knee again, not just pointing and shooting as Kate did when snapping a picture, but obviously taking great care with the composition. He hesitated, and Kate thought he'd spotted her. But when he lowered the camera it was to look up at the sky. Kate looked up to see what was of such great interest, but all she saw were clouds. Then she realized that he must be waiting for the clouds to move in or out of the shot.

He stayed crouched like that for at least a minute, camera cradled in his left hand, right elbow braced on his knee, before finally firing off a shot and getting to his feet.

Kate was close enough now to see that the man was about the same height as Tony Carling, but lean and rangy. He wore stonewashed jeans and a faded blue plaid shirt with the sleeves rolled up and the buttons undone, over a plain white T-shirt. He was so caught up in taking photographs that Kate sensed he wasn't aware of her approach.

The man seemed a little startled when he finally noticed Kate. He acknowledged her with a nod of the head, but Kate didn't nod back. She prided herself on being able to turn strangers into friends with just a smile, but the memory of her last meeting with a representative of

Yeoman Holdings was still fresh in her mind, and she didn't feel like giving this one a smile. She was close enough now to see that the man's thick, dark brown hair was neither straight nor tightly curled. His tanned face had high, hard cheekbones planing into a clean jawline that couldn't be called weak or heavy, below a mouth that was a little closer to broad than narrow. As Kate looked into his hazel brown eyes her heart skipped a beat and she had to work hard not to return the smile he gave her. He was like a sort of less rugged version of Tom Berenger, she thought. She had to remind herself that this man worked for Tony Carling, that he wanted to turn the crofters out of their home, and Glen Cranoch into a—

She couldn't bring herself to think about it any more, so instead she just said, "Can I help you?" in the most unhelpful of voices.

"I'm looking for Glen Cranoch," he said. He had less of an accent than Finlay, but was unmistakably Scottish all the same.

"You can't wait, can you?" Kate said.

The man's friendly smile gave way to one of bemusement, and he said, "I'm sorry?"

"You can't even wait until you actually own the place, can you? What are you taking pictures of: where the ski-lifts will go, or some sort of fast-food concession, maybe? Wouldn't a McDonalds or a Pizza Hut look great over there?" She pointed to the shingle beach at the end of the lochan, beside the abandoned church.

"I'm afraid—"

"How can you look at all this," Kate said, turning away from him to take in the hills rising up on either side, and the two crags in the distance, "and not feel ashamed at what you're going to do to it?"

Pointing to the cottages at the foot of Castle Crag she said, "Because of you and your friend Tony Carling, the people in those little white houses are going to be forced out of homes their families have lived in for generations. I hope you're proud of yourself."

"I'm sorry—"

"I'll bet you're just broken-hearted." Kate shook her head in disgust. "How can you sleep at night?" she asked him. "If I was a man I would throw that camera of yours into the water and run you right out of the glen."

"So much for Highland hospitality," he said.

"You're going to destroy the place I love and dispossess the people who've become my friends: what do you expect me to do, throw my arms around you and welcome you with a hug?"

"A hug would be nice."

For a moment Kate seriously considered slapping him, but settled for saying, "I'm glad you find this funny."

"Funny peculiar, not comedy funny. I think there's been some sort of misunderstanding."

Kate had calmed down, but not enough to stop herself from saying, "The misunderstanding is if you and Tony Carling think I'm just going to give you the glen on a plate.

I'm no Lady Carolyn."

The man was about to say something, but seemed to think better of it.

Guessing what had gone through his mind, Kate said, "Go on, at least have the guts to say what you were just thinking: Tell me that I'm no lady, right out."

"At least give me credit for having the good manners not to say it."

"I'll credit you with a cold heart, or at best a callous indifference," Kate told him.

The man looked a little thoughtful at that, perhaps even a little hurt, as if her words had hit home.

Kate was puzzled by that. A man with a cold heart or a callous indifference wouldn't have been hurt by what she'd said.

"I think I've maybe come to the wrong glen," the man told her.

"You're damn right you have. Still, it's an easy mistake to make," Kate said bitterly. "They're ten-a-penny, as your bully-boy buddy said. Why don't the two of you go and find another one to trash."

"Are you from Greenpeace or something?"

"What?" now it was Kate's turn to look confused.

"You know, Greenpeace. Don't kill the whale, the Rainbow Warrior, that sort of stuff."

"Why do you say that?"

"From your accent you're obviously not from these parts, but it's also obvious that you care pretty passionately about them. I wondered if you were maybe some sort of activist."

"No, I'm not some kind of loony activist."

"I never said 'loony'."

"No, but it's what you were thinking, right?"

He smiled. "It's quite funny, you seem to have an uncanny knack of knowing what I'm thinking, but you obviously don't have the slightest clue who I am."

"I might not know who you are, but I know exactly what you are. Finlay's told me all about your little meeting the other day."

"Finlay?"

"Yeah, you know the little old guy you probably laughed at when he stood up to you. The guy who played the bagpipes on the beaches at Normandy. It's the only time he's ever left this glen, and now he's going to have to leave it for good because of you."

"Look, I think you've got me—"

"You're not fit to lace up his boots," Kate said angrily.

This time her words really seemed to hit home, because the man said, "You're wrong about everything else, but you're probably right about that."

Kate thought that the man suddenly seemed much older. The boyish smile was gone so completely now that she found it hard to imagine she'd ever see it again. Moments earlier he'd joked about Kate knowing exactly what he was thinking, but now she didn't have the slightest idea what lay behind the troubled look in his hazel-colored eyes. Suddenly she found it a little harder to be angry with him.

"I'm sorry," she said, "but I feel strongly about this. I don't know if there's a law of trespass in this part of the world, but I really think you should leave."

"You sound like you own the place."

"For the moment, I do."

He looked taken aback. "You're not what I expected."

"What did you expect? What did Tony Carling tell you about me? No, wait, don't tell me. I'd rather not know."

"I've never met this Tony Carling or even heard of him, and I'm sorry if I've strayed somewhere I shouldn't have, into the middle of a feud between neighbours or something, but I couldn't see any other way to get where I wanted to go." Looking around, he added, "And even if I could have seen another way, I'd have wanted to come this way. It's the most beautiful place I've ever seen, and I thought it looked like the most tranquil, too."

"Until you met me."

Finally the man did smile again. "I don't have to say what I'm thinking with you, do I? Am I really that transparent?"

"Quite the opposite, in fact you've suddenly got me all confused. How can you be working for Yeoman Holdings and yet not know who Tony Carling is or what he's got planned for the glen? Are you some kind of freelance photographer on contract to him?"

"I'm a freelance photographer, but not on a contract to this firm Yeoman Holdings or anybody else. I was just taking photos for the love of it. That's something I've not done for a long time, and I'd forgotten how good it could be."

"You have nothing to do with the plans to buy the glen?" Kate asked.

He shook his head.

"You're not the man with a camera Finlay confronted earlier this week, then?"

Again he shook his head.

"I've made a bit of a fool of myself, haven't I?"

He nodded.

Suddenly they were both laughing.

"Kate Brodie," she said, reaching out her hand. "I don't have the nerve to say 'Lady Kate' after the way I've just behaved. In my defense, though, I've only been a lady for a couple of days."

Kate saw his boyish smile again. It was wider this time, and accompanied by a sparkle in his eyes. Her heart skipped more than one beat and her chest tightened at the thought that she didn't have to hate him.

As the tall man shook her hand, he said, "I'm sorry I didn't introduce myself earlier, but—"

"I just got wired into you and didn't give you a chance, did I?" She covered her face with her free hand and said, "I feel so embarrassed. Goodness knows what you must think of me."

He gently prised Kate's hand away from her eyes. Looking straight into those eyes, he said, "You read my mind a couple of times before; let's see if you can do it again and guess what I think of you."

Kate blushed, and the man didn't just smile this time, he laughed. It was a quiet sound that made Kate happy, and suddenly the two of them were laughing together.

When they'd stopped, Kate said, "I did it again, too, didn't I?"

"What?"

"Interrupted you before you had a chance to introduce yourself."

He nodded. "Now that I do have a chance, I better take it. I'm Cameron Fraser, and I was looking for a place called Jamie's Crag. It's on The Cranoch Estate, so we must be neighbours."

Kate smiled with a happiness she hadn't felt since before the meeting with Archie Cunningham. Then she remembered that meeting. Her smile faded, and she said, "We're neighbours for now, at least."

"I take it this is where Tony Carling and company come in?"

Kate nodded. "Yes, this is where Tony Carling and company come in." She turned from Cameron to look around the glen, and said, "Can you believe, they want to turn this into a ski resort, and Greystane into a glorified souvenir stall selling 'tartan tat'. He actually had the nerve to say that to my face."

"But they can't do any of that if they don't own it."

"I own it, but not for much longer."

Cameron's puzzlement at why she'd give up a place she obviously loved was clear on his face.

"I can't afford to keep the estate," Kate explained. "I feel obliged to tell you, in case you had any ideas of maybe rebuilding Jamie's Cottage. The chances are you won't be looking out on this view for much longer but on a ski resort instead. Maybe that'll make your property worth more. I hope so. I hope you're not another of the many people I seem destined to let down."

Cameron Fraser reached for her hand again, this time not to shake it, just to hold it. "If you've got to sell, you've got to sell. It's not the end of the world."

"It'll be the end of this little part of it, though."

"No other offers on the table?"

Kate shook her head. "I can't afford to keep it on the market for long, either. Apparently the estate's dead on its feet. It would take a small fortune to get it back in working order as a sporting estate, and even then it would need to be subsidized to keep it going."

"What about running it as something other than a sporting estate?"

"I'm open to ideas, believe me. I'm going to have a meeting with the crofters—Carling wants to turn them out, of course—to see if they've got any ideas. You're welcome to come along. I could do with all the support I can get."

"Just let me know where and when."

"It'll be in the hall at Greystane—that's the little castle on the crag opposite your cottage," she told him, pointing to the far end of the glen. "I'm sorry, I don't know the when, yet. I'm just about to go around and see the crofters now, see what time suits them. Do you have a phone number I can call when I've fixed a time?"

He shook his head.

"How can I get in touch with you? You can't be staying at Jamie's Cottage; it's a bit of a ruin from what I've seen."

"I'll be around there for a few days in the camper, seeing how much work needs done and getting an idea if I can afford to do it," he told her. "I might well be in the same boat as you, but without even a buyer. This firm Yeoman hasn't made any approach to me."

"If it did, would you sell?"

"Not unless I had to, after what you've told me about their plans for the glen."

"What would you do if you were me?"

"Same answer, I suppose. Sometimes you've got to just bite the bullet, though. Looking on the bright side, at least you'd get enough money from selling this place to set you up in style somewhere else," he said.

"I'm sure it would, but no amount of money could buy me a clear conscience."

The man stiffened at those words and a troubled look flitted across his eyes. Again Kate experienced the strange mix of knowing what he was thinking one moment, and the next moment feeling like he was looking at something she couldn't see, something from a profoundly troubled past. She remembered what Archibald Cunningham had said about the man standing in front of her: that he'd resigned his commission in the army at considerable personal cost, and how that probably meant he was either a bit of a saint or some sort of sinner. Cameron's expressions, and the words that had triggered them, suggested it was the latter. However, Kate found it difficult to reconcile that notion with his quiet, gentle manner. She found herself wanting to do something to ease the hurt he was obviously feeling and make him forget whatever it was that troubled him. Before she'd even thought about what she was doing, she said, "I'll show you mine if you show me yours."

Suddenly all his attention was on her again, his eyes were smiling, and one eyebrow was slightly raised.

She playfully punched him on the arm and said, "Houses. I'll show you mine if you show me yours."

He laughed. "Deal," he said. "I've got a feeling I'm about to be embarrassed, though."

"How come?"

"Yours will be much bigger than mine."

"What if I promise I won't laugh at you?"

"Like you're not laughing at me now?"

"I'm not laughing at you. I'm just laughing because I'd forgotten how good it feels to flirt with a man." She'd said what was on her mind without thinking what the words would sound like when they were spoken aloud. Putting a hand over her mouth, she mumbled through it, "Whoops! Told you more than you needed to know there, didn't I? Nice one, Kate. Now *you're* laughing at *me*."

"I'm not laughing at you. I'm laughing because I'd forgotten how much fun it is to flirt with a woman . . . And how sweet and pretty a woman can be."

"Wow," Kate said, feeling a kind of happiness she hadn't known for far too long. "I can't imagine I did too much to remind you when I was winding up to slap you a little while ago."

"You didn't remind me then of sweet, but you reminded me of pretty, even when you were angry."

Not believing she was going to do what she was about to do, but not able to stop herself from doing it, Kate got on her tiptoes, put her arms on his shoulders and kissed him lightly on the cheek. The kiss lasted barely a heartbeat, and then she took her arms from his shoulders, settled back on her heels and stepped away from him. "Now do you consider yourself welcomed to Glen Cranoch?" she asked.

"So warmly I don't think I'll ever want to leave."

"You might change your mind when you see your cottage."

"Looks a bit like these, does it?" Cameron asked, his mood changing again as he pointed to the blackened clusters of cottages scattered around the edge of the lochan.

Kate nodded. "At least, that's what it looks like from a distance. I haven't had a closer look yet."

"You talked earlier as though you had."

"I've just heard a bit about it. Have you?"

"I don't know anything about it at all. I got a telegram out of the blue saying I'd fallen heir to a derelict cottage, thanks to some relative I'd never even heard of. It came at a time when I wasn't sure what direction to go in next, just that I wanted to go in a different direction. So here I am. Talking of directions, what's the best way to get up to the cottage?"

"I think if you follow the track you were on, then turn right at the foot of the crags, there's a place where the stream that runs into the lockhan—"

He smiled, and Kate asked him why with her eyes.

"It's just funny to hear a Scottish word spoken in an American accent," he told her. "Are you going native?"

"Yes, I think I am. I don't think I got that word quite right, though. How would you say it?"

"Lochan."

She laughed and asked, "How do you do that?"

"Do what?"

"Get the 'och' in your lochan."

"You managed it there yourself."

"That's just because I was doing a comedy impersonation of you."

"You should hear me say 'sporran', that would really give you a laugh."

"It just did. What an earth is a sporran?"

"It's the dangly purse a Scotsman wears over his kilt."

"You know what question's coming next, don't you?" Kate said, a mischievous smile on her face.

"I think I can guess."

"Well, what's the answer?"

"I'll leave it to your imagination."

Kate threw her head back and laughed, then said, "So,

have you got a kilt, then, Mr. Fraser?"

"Not any more, but I find myself wishing I still had."

"Was it part of your uniform?"

His smile slowly faded, and again Kate got the sense of someone who wanted to leave the past behind, not be reminded of it.

For a moment Cameron said nothing, and then he asked, "How did you know I used to wear a uniform?"

"Archibald Cunningham mentioned it when he told me who my neighbour was going to be."

"And what else did Archibald Cunningham happen to 'mention'?"

"Just that you were a soldier, or had been. He maybe got that wrong, though, because you said you're a photographer."

"Not all soldiers carry guns."

When he didn't elaborate, Kate said, "I'm sorry, I didn't mean to sound like I was prying." Guessing that a change of subject—or, rather, a return to the one she'd sidetracked him from—was in order, she said, "Back to the lochan—"

"You're a quick learner: you got more 'och' in your lochan that time."

"Aye, I did, didn't I?" she said in a passable impersonation of Finlay's lilt.

Cameron had to laugh.

"Anyway," Kate turned back to face the far end of the glen, "there's a place at the bottom of the two crags, where the stream—"

"The burn. A wee stream is known as a burn in this

part of the world."

"I've got to learn a whole new vocabulary, don't I, as well as just a comedy accent."

"At this rate, just give it a week and nobody'll be able to tell you weren't born here."

"Aye, well," she said, doing another Finlay McRae. "There's a place where the burn looks shallow enough to ford, and I think you can follow the track around the front of Jamie's Crag, and up around the back of it to your cottage at the top."

"When you asked if I'd heard anything about the cottage . . . There was something in your voice: just what exactly have *you* heard about it?"

"How can I put this?" Kate said, pondering out loud. Finally she settled on, "Do you believe in ghosts, Mr. Fraser?"

"You're kidding me . . . a haunted house?"

She nodded. "Apparently so. Do you know anything about the man the cottage is named after . . . Jamie Chisholm?"

"Just that he's a very, very distant relative."

"Maybe it's not my place to tell you."

"As if you could help yourself," Cameron said.

Kate laughed. "Now it's your turn to read me like a book, huh?"

"It's pretty obvious you've got a story you can't wait to tell."

"Apparently he fled the field in disgrace at some old battle—Cullodeon or something."

"Culloden," Cameron said quietly.

"Yeah, that's it. Anyway, he was spotted fleeing from the battlefield, and never seen again. His portrait hangs facing the wall in Greystane, and his old cottage is supposed to be haunted."

Cameron looked thoughtfully up at Jamie's Crag, and Kate got the feeling he'd almost forgotten she was even there. Wanting to remind him, she said, "So, do you believe in ghosts?"

"Not that kind."

"What other kind is there?"

Cameron didn't answer, just kept looking at the crag. Kate didn't know if he hadn't heard her question or just chose not to reply. She didn't push it because, although she was more intrigued by him with every moment, she didn't want to intrude. She just watched him, studying his profile, liking the slight curl of his hair and wanting to run her fingers through it, liking the straightness of his nose, the smooth plane of his cheeks, wanting to trace his clean jawline with her fingertips.

"I've never seen a haunted house," she said finally.

He turned from the crag back to her and said, "Would you like to see mine now?"

"I'd love to, but I have to go around to the crofters and arrange that meeting I mentioned." As she said it she realized with surprise that for the last few minutes she'd forgotten all about the meeting and why she had to hold it—things she hadn't been able to get off her mind for the last day or so, no matter hard how she tried.

"How about tomorrow?" he asked.

"Definitely. Now, if you're showing me yours tomorrow, how about if I show you mine tonight?"

"Now there's an offer I can't refuse."

"We're still talking about houses here, remember?"

"For a moment I almost forgot."

"Have you any plans for dinner?"

"Actually I do: a couple of sandwiches and a Mars bar in my camper, with LeeAnn Womack and Matraca Berg for company."

"I'm almost being deafened by the sounds of violins, and I'm not just talking about your choice of music."

"At least you didn't make fun of my choice of music."

"I'm a bit of a closet C&W fan myself. When it's bad it's awful, but when it's good it strikes a symphony of chords . . . And I don't think it gets any better than LeeAnn Womack's voice or Matraca Berg's songs. Ever heard *Strawberry—*"

"*Wine*," he said, answering her question by completing the title of the song. "It's my favourite country and western song," he told her, "along with *I Hope—*"

"*You Dance*," Kate said, doing to him what he'd done to her a moment earlier.

They both laughed. "Sounds like we could do a duet," Cameron said.

And then they weren't laughing quite so hard because there had been a nameless longing in his voice and in her eyes. For a moment neither of them spoke, then Kate said, "Seven o'clock at my place okay for you?"

"Seven is fine. Meantime, can I give you a lift to the crofters' cottages?"

"It's okay, thanks. I love walking through the glen. I don't know how many more chances I'll get, so I want to make the most of every one."

"I understand. It's that kind of place, isn't it?" he said, looking around.

"Yeah," Kate agreed, "it's that kind of place."

She walked with him to the camper and said, "See you at seven, then."

He smiled and hesitated for a moment before nodding and getting in the van.

Kate was smiling, too, as she watched the van disappear in a cloud of dust.

Cameron Fraser hadn't kissed her, but she knew that he wanted to.

CHAPTER 9

THE WINDING TRACK FLATTENED OUT JUST AS CAMERON was wondering if his camper van would make it to the summit of Jamie's Crag, and the old cottage came into view.

His first sight of the ruined house gave him second thoughts about wanting to stay there. He'd expected dilapidation, but not that it would bring back sights and sounds and smells so vividly that he could almost be in another country, several thousand miles away, and at another time, several months ago. The walls here were plain stone rather than whitewashed, and the roof was grey-slated rather than red-tiled, but the cottage had the same ghastly, desolate air as the houses in that other country.

Walking around the outside of the cottage, Cameron saw all the little details that had given the overall impression of neglect: gaping black holes in the roof where slates were missing; the old wooden door hanging off its hinges; cracks in the tiny, dirty windows sunk into the thick stone walls.

Going over to the nearest of the two windows, he peered through an empty square where the glass was missing altogether. It was like looking into a bottomless well or the darkest of midnight shadows. He moved to one side so he wasn't blocking the daylight, but it made no difference. The inside of the house seemed to swallow the light and give nothing back. Even as his eyes became dark-adapted he couldn't make out any distinction of shape or shade.

All he could see was why people might think the cottage was haunted.

He didn't get such a sensation himself, however. His disquiet came from the presence of a different type of ghost, the kind that haunts the memory and torments the mind, a product of conscience that lingers in the shadows of consciousness.

When details finally started emerging they came from the darkness inside him rather than the blackness within the cottage. He saw an old woman with a gaudy headscarf, clutching a framed photograph to her chest . . .

A cattle truck filled with frightened people instead of cowed beasts . . .

Bodies hurriedly buried in forest clearings and unploughed fields.

When Cameron took a step back he wasn't recoiling from Jamie's Cottage but from his own past. The derelict cottage reminded him of that past so graphically that his first reaction was to drive flat out to Archibald Cunningham's office in Inverness and instruct the lawyer to sell the place if he could. The impulse was so strong that he reached for the handle of the camper door.

But he stopped without opening the door. He knew he'd have nowhere to go after leaving the lawyer's office. He knew that this place was as remote as he could get. He couldn't run away any further. He couldn't run away forever. Jamie's Cottage was at least a place to go, with a reason for going there. He could rebuild it, and with it maybe something of his life. He could make the outside weathertight and the inside habitable, a place he wouldn't want to run away from, a door he could open without being overwhelmed by brooding darkness from within.

Then there was Glen Cranoch itself. Turning from the cottage to look at the glen spread out below he saw a chance to start afresh. It was everything he could hope for: a place where there weren't many people, and the few he met would know little or nothing about him; where he could pretend to be a decent human being and maybe fool them.

In time he could maybe even fool himself.

Movement caught his eye from down in the glen. A slender figure with short blond hair. Kate Brodie. She'd almost reached the cluster of crofters' cottages and was looking up at Jamie's Crag and waving.

Before he knew it, he was waving back.

Long after Kate had disappeared inside one of the whitewashed cottages Cameron was still thinking about her; about the sparkle in her eyes when she smiled, the way she tilted her head back a little when she laughed. Suddenly he wanted to see her smile and hear her laugh again, whereas before he met her he hadn't wanted anything to do with anyone.

For a little while Cameron Fraser forgot about the things he'd remembered when he looked into the blackness of the cottage. He forgot about the things he'd seen the previous winter, during the months he'd spent shooting people dead.

It had been a long and bitter winter, and Cameron had shot a lot of people. Men and women, old and young, innocent and guilty alike. He shot them point-blank, so that he could see each harrowing detail on every single face.

He could still see those faces now. They stared at him when he daydreamed, filling his empty moments with waking nightmares . . .

They peered at him from the blackness when he switched out the light at the end of the day . . .

And when he closed his eyes they were still there, staring at him sightlessly—part of the darkness that had become a part of him.

He hadn't shot them with the Browning automatic pistol holstered on his hip, but with the Leica R6 camera hanging around his neck, loading up with 35mm film cartridges instead of 9mm bullets.

He was what the army called a technical specialist, and his specialty was photography. They thought of him as a soldier who just happened to know how to take photos, but he thought of himself as a photographer who just happened to wear a uniform. No matter how much time he spent on firing ranges he still felt clumsy and awkward with the Browning in his hands, like he was missing a couple of fingers or had too many thumbs. He trembled ever so slightly when he took aim, and had never learned to squeeze the trigger smoothly. He always hesitated and then snatched at it, and, each time he fired, he recoiled a little before the gun did. He never felt like a soldier, even with the Browning in his hands—especially with the Browning in his hands—but he always felt like a photographer. When he'd had the Leica in his hands it felt like part of him and he'd felt quietly confident about getting the job done.

Until the job was shooting people dead.

Before that winter his assignments had comprised portraits at passing-out parades and stunted action shots for Press releases and posters—photos of fit young people doing adventurous things in exotic places.

Then one day, out of the blue, he was asked how he'd feel about being seconded to a United Nations special investigation unit in Kosovo. The fact that he'd been asked rather than ordered gave him an idea that the assignment would be pretty rough. The thought filled him with dread, but alongside the dread was the knowledge that he'd had a free ride and now it was time to earn his keep; there was the feeling that he was a phoney, wearing a uniform but only playing at being a soldier; a desire to prove something to his father—and himself—by swapping easy street for a combat zone; and the urge to actually do something that truly mattered, to earn the pride and satisfaction that came from taking on a difficult job that had to be done.

He'd been warned that it would be harrowing, and thought he had a rough idea what to expect . . . But there are some things that other people's words and your own imagination can't prepare you for, however stark their words and however vivid your imagination. The sort of things he saw in a forest outside Blace on his first sortie with the unit.

He'd always loved forests, felt at peace whenever he set foot in them. It was something to do with the way it was always a little cooler than the surrounding area on a hot day and hotter on a cool day, stiller when it was windy, and drier when it was raining . . .

It was the welcoming give of the ground that makes up a forest floor . . .

The half-heard, half-imagined sounds of countless unseen little creatures as they went about their lives; the gentle whispering of branches overhead, as if the trees were talking to each other in a language he couldn't understand but could listen to forever just for the lyrical sound of it, and the perfect peacefulness of the silence that punctuated the words and sentences . . .

And it was the quality of light, subtly transformed in ways more magical than any filter on a lens could achieve: soft in some places, hard in others; falling in bright tiger-striping or enchanted, slanting beams and shafts with little universes suspended in them; or hanging in ethereal, pearlescent mists.

Maybe it was instinct, maybe it was just an overwrought imagination, but the forest outside Blace had seemed strangely different. He'd felt that from the moment he set foot in it. There were no slanting shafts of daylight, just bone-chilling tendrils of mist. The trees were gnarled and twisted, more dead than alive. The branches lacked leaves and the wind didn't whisper through them, it howled and wailed and moaned. Raindrops gathered on the bare branches like tears on eyelashes before falling to the ground in a ceaseless sobbing, and he had the feeling that if you drank from the little hollows where the water pooled it would be as bitter as bile. It seemed like a place that spring would never reach, let alone summer; where sweet-scented flowers would never blossom and butterflies would never flutter their brightly-colored wings. It was a place where you could feel lonely even when surrounded by other people, and lost even when you had a map in one hand and a compass in the other. It was a place that held shadows where there shouldn't be any; where the silences could be uncomfortably long, and far more disturbing than any sound.

It was a place where rumour had it the inhabitants of a village had been taken after being rounded up in the middle of the night.

The rumour said that the villagers had been herded into a

clearing in the trees, and never came out of the forest again.

Even before Cameron's unit came across the forest clearing, with its tell-tale dark swath of recently disturbed earth, he'd known instinctively that the rumour was true.

Cameron thought he'd seen the worst things a person could see at the bottom of that hastily covered pit . . .

But a few days later, in another forest, he realized he'd been wrong. It wasn't just that there were twice as many bodies this time, it was the fact that they were ethnic Serbs, not Albanians. It was the shocking realisation that there were no good guys or bad guys or righteous causes, just human nature. He came to a new understanding of what people were, and it horrified him. He came to a new understanding of what they weren't, and that horrified him even more. He was seeing what people did when there was no one to stop them doing what they wanted to do, when all the checks and balances and restraints were removed, when the illusions and pretences were stripped bare and the reality was revealed. If it had been the work of soldiers acting on orders it would have been bad enough, but the word was that it was paramilitaries operating on their own initiative and acting on instinct. It was men who a few months earlier had been shopkeepers and farmers, builders and bakers and neighbours before they all became butchers. It was ordinary men who wore uniforms but weren't really soldiers.

Cameron's world had been profoundly altered by the realization, and he was no longer able to think of people in quite the same way. Colors didn't seem so bright and sunlight didn't have the same warmth. Friends looked like strangers, and strangers didn't look like people who might become friends. Things he'd previously thought of as permanent suddenly seemed passing. Things he'd once valued above all others suddenly seemed worthless. Things that once held comfort now seemed cold.

Cameron Fraser couldn't believe in God any more.

He found it hard to believe in anything any more.

Laniste, Kacanik, Prizren, Studencarne, Rogovo, Dakovica, Racak, Urosevac, Gorne Obrinje, Likosane, Vucitrn, Mitrovica . . . Somewhere along the line his hands started shaking when he held the camera, and he began finding it difficult to focus the lens. At first he thought it was the Leica's eyepiece that was misting up. He cleaned it with a cotton swab soaked in alcohol but everything still seemed misty when he looked through it, and he realized that it was his eyes he had to wipe.

Even when he managed to focus, it wasn't on what he was looking at, because the images he saw on the groundglass of the camera viewing screen were generated by his mind.

He would close his eyes for a moment but the images filled the darkness inside his head just as they'd filled the viewfinder of his camera, just as they'd filled those hellish holes in the ground. A gallery of ghastly faces with expressions ranging from resignation to helpless rage, bewilderment to awful understanding.

Somewhere along the line he began to be startled by any sudden noise, however innocuous, and even soft sounds set his nerves on edge.

He forgot how to smile and laughter became a foreign language that he no longer knew how to speak and could never hope to learn again. It was accented by cruelty or irony but never by good humor, and while he could understand the subtle accents of the language, he couldn't understand the words.

He started feeling so dirty that even ten minutes under a shower so hot it left him lobster red didn't make him feel clean.

He stopped seeing the victims as purely innocent and began thinking that everyone must be at least a little bit to blame, because that was the only explanation which made any sense for the fate that had befallen them. Then he would see young children who were already old, and others who would never get any older, and the only explanation that had made some sort of sense no longer made any sense at all.

Somewhere along the line Cameron stopped being able to sleep even when he was exhausted, and stopped feeling hungry even when he'd had nothing to eat. He found it difficult talking to people and impossible to concentrate on what they were saying.

He stopped being the person he was and became someone else he didn't know and didn't want to know.

The one thing that allowed him to keep it together was the thought that he wasn't capable of acting anything like those other ordinary men in uniforms had acted, no matter what the circumstances.

But something had happened which meant that soon he didn't even have that consolation. Something shatteringly awful, wholly unforgivable and completely unforgettable.

Even now he couldn't bear to think about it. He'd hoped Jamie's Cottage would provide the distraction he needed to take his mind off what had happened, but instead it was doing the opposite.

Cameron knew he would have to confront the darkness within the ruined shell sooner or later, but decided to put it off another day. He wanted to spend the last light of this day in the sunshine that bathed the glen, not opening a door that led to darkness and the awful ghosts of his past.

Turning away from the cottage's filthy little window, he went over to the camper and took out his two cameras: a Leica M6 rangefinder with a 35mm wideangle lens, and a Nikon FM2 with 105mm telephoto. They lacked any automatic features but he'd never been tempted to trade them in for newer models. He loved using his head rather than a programmed metering pattern to determine exposure, getting so caught up in the challenge of controlling light and composition that for a little while he could forget about everything else in the world, leave his past behind and lose himself in the moment.

With the Leica hanging around his neck and the heavier Nikon slung over his shoulder he started walking back down the track he'd driven up a few minutes earlier. Constantly assessing his surroundings, he appreciated the world around him in a way he seldom did if there wasn't a camera around his neck or in his hands. He continually framed shots with his eyes, experience and instinct giving him a good idea of the coverage he'd get with either the wideangle or telephoto. Whenever he saw something that stopped him in his tracks he asked himself a series of questions without even realizing it: was what had caught his attention unusual or beautiful enough to look good not just as a slide but as a poster-sized print that could be hung on a wall? How could he make the most of the elements that made the shot worth taking? What unwanted details would be included with the wide angle lens? What would he have to compromise and leave out with the telephoto? Was the contrast range between highlight and shadow too great for the film in his cameras to record?

He switched from wideangle to telephoto as the sun started setting and the lochan changed from darkest blue to palest amber. Every so often he pointed the camera directly overhead, determining exposure from that part of the sky as he always did for sunsets, then framing the shots to make the most of the colors of lochan and sky and the dramatic silhouette of the crags in between.

When the sun dipped below the crags he fastened the

studs on the ever-ready camera cases and made his way towards Greystane.

He stopped once, to pick a bunch of wild bluebells . . .

And, watching him from her bedroom window in the tower house high above, as she had been for the last half hour or so, Kate Brodie felt her heart turn over.

CHAPTER 10

CAMERON PUSHED OPEN THE OLD DOOR IN THE WALL AT the top of Castle Crag, having to stoop a little under the low archway. In the twilight he was only vaguely aware of the cobbled courtyard and the crumbling ramparts which enclosed it. Up ahead, the tower house was silhouetted against the darkening sky. As he walked up the flagstoned path towards it, he hid the bunch of wild flowers behind his back to surprise Kate.

The door of the tower house was a bigger version of the one in the outer wall—stout planks hammered together with hand-forged nails and reinforced by enough iron strapping to thwart all but the most determined assaults with a battering ram. There was no sign of a doorbell, so Cameron announced his presence with a giant, hoop-shaped knocker that was in keeping with the scale of the door itself.

There was no answer. He reached for the knocker again, but stopped with his hand halfway there when he heard approaching footsteps echoing inside the tower house. Moments later the door was opened by a dapper old man in tweeds, with a military bearing and neatly-trimmed silver moustache. The man smiled and said, "Mr. Fraser, I take it?"

Cameron nodded, "And you'll be Finlay?"

"Aye, but how did you know that? What's that lass been saying about me?"

"Just that you saw off some bad guy with a camera the other day. She thought it was me."

Finlay smiled, "Let you have both barrels, did she?"

"Point blank."

Finlay's smile turned to a laugh. "Come in, man," he said. "Come in."

Cameron entered the dimly-lit chapel. A door to his left opened and Kate walked through it, wearing a short black dress. "Welcome to Greystane," she said.

Cameron's throat tightened up and for a moment he wasn't able to say anything more than, "Kate!" Then he managed, "You look beautiful."

Kate smiled with delight, and the tightness in Cameron's throat spread to his chest. "I'm sorry I haven't dressed up, but I didn't have anything to dress up in," he told her. "I didn't think I'd need any grown-up clothes, so I didn't bring any with me in the camper."

"I'm sorry: I didn't mean to make you feel awkward. Want me to change?"

"Not in any way," he told her.

Glowing, Kate turned to Finlay and said, "Have I got

time to give Cameron a guided tour, or should I wait until after dinner?"

"Miss Weir'll be a wee while yet," Finlay told her. "In fact, I better see if she needs a hand or I'll be getting called for everything for 'deserting my post', as she puts it when I'm not wherever it is she wants me to be."

Kate and Cameron watched the ghillie leave, then looked at each other. Kate broke the silence that followed, saying, "Have you got something for me?"

Remembering about the flowers, Cameron brought them out from behind his back, and said, "Why do I get the idea that these aren't a surprise?"

"I should make some demure allusion to feminine intuition, I guess, but the truth is that I saw you from my window when you were picking them."

"I wish I had something nicer to give you."

"Cameron, they're lovely," she told him, as delighted with the bunch of wild flowers as if they'd been a hundred-dollar bouquet of roses. "That was so sweet of you."

Looking around at the chapel, Cameron said, "This place is amazing."

"Wait until you see the banquet hall."

Cameron smiled at the way the elegantly dressed woman in front of him was as excited as a child. "Other people have a dining room, you've got a banquet hall," he said.

"Until a week ago all I had was a breakfast bar."

"Where were you a week ago?"

"I had a small craft shop just across the bay from San

Francisco. Well, I still do. I run it with my dad."

"This must be quite a change from California," Cameron said, looking around the chapel.

"The whole thing still seems like a dream," she told him. Her mood changed when she added, "The thought of having to give it up feels like a nightmare. But I don't want to think about that tonight, Cameron. Come on, I'll show you the rest of the tower."

Following her over to the same door she'd entered by, Cameron found himself loving the way the shortness of her hair showed off the elegant, flowing lines of her neck, and the low back of her dress showed off the smoothness of her shoulders. Again he was aware of a tightness in his throat, and of something else—a lightness in his chest, the stirrings of a nameless longing.

When they reached the stairs she said, "Watch the steps, Cameron. It's not very well lit and they're steep—so steep, in fact, that I think modesty dictates you go first."

"I was just about to suggest that myself."

She laughed. "I'm relieved to say you make a most unconvincing liar."

When they got to the top of the stairs she showed him the "big room"—where she picked up a vase for the flowers—and the study. Then she took him up the stairs to the master bedroom, pausing to fill the vase from her en-suite, arrange the bluebells in it, and set them on her dresser. Before she could show him the rest of the tower, Finlay called up from the foot of the staircase: "Lady Kate! Mr.

Fraser!" His voice echoed from the chapel walls. "Dinner's about to be served."

"We're coming, thanks!" Kate shouted down to him.

As the two of them made their way down the staircase, Kate said, "I don't know how Finlay manages all these stairs."

"He looks very fit. Maybe this is one of the reasons why."

"Maybe it would be better for him if he wasn't working here," Kate said, but even as she spoke the words she thought they didn't ring true. Although she'd only known Finlay and Miss Weir for a couple of days, she couldn't imagine them living anywhere else. They were as much a part of Greystane as the portraits in the banquet hall.

As if echoing her thoughts, Cameron said, "I couldn't picture Finlay in an old folks' home."

"I think he'd go from being Finlay to just another old guy in a home," Kate said.

When they reached the foot of the stairs Kate led the way back through the chapel. She didn't know if they'd subconsciously fallen into step with each other, or if it was merely a coincidence, but their footfalls were in such perfect unison that it sounded as though only one person was crossing the stone flagged floor, not two. She wondered if Cameron had also noticed. She glanced at him and saw that he was glancing at her, and somehow she had a strange certainty that in that fleeting moment their thoughts were as in-synch as their footsteps.

And then there was silence in the chapel, because they'd reached the double doors that separated it from the banquet hall. "You're going to love this, Cameron," she told him. After pausing for dramatic effect, Kate flung the doors open and stepped aside to reveal the banquet hall in all its glory.

"Kate, this is incredible!" Cameron told her, looking at the long table with its silver candelabra and, above it, the fully-lit chandelier; and beyond it, a roaring peat fire in the grand fireplace which dominated the far wall. "I'm so embarrassed to be standing here in jeans and a denim shirt," he told her.

"It's just the two of us, Cameron, and even if it wasn't I wouldn't care how you were dressed." Taking his hand, she said, "Come on," and led him inside.

Sensing a hesitation in Cameron's step when they entered the hall, Kate looked at him and saw that his gaze had fallen on the painting that hung the wrong way around. Guiding him over to the picture she said, "Can you give me a hand to turn it?"

"You want it put the right way around?"

She nodded. "I think it's about time, don't you?"

Cameron hesitated, then lifted the picture off the wall hooks, which had been digging into the front of the top section of the ornate gilt frame. As Cameron took a step back to balance the painting on his knee and get a better grip, Kate got her first look at the man it depicted. Her expression changed.

"What is it?" Cameron asked.

"It's your long-lost relative: he looks just like you!"

Cameron appeared taken aback.

Kate laughed and said, "Damn, I wish I had one of your cameras in my hand: that was a 'Kodak Moment' if ever I saw one. Sorry, Cameron, I couldn't resist it."

"You've got me curious about what he really does look like."

"His face is broader than yours, and he's got a beard . . ." Her voice tailed away.

"What is it?"

"The longer I look at it, the more I think there actually *is* something a bit like you, Cameron. It's just across the eyes . . . It looks like he had the same hazel-colored eyes as you."

"Is this you kidding again?"

She shook her head. "If you hang the picture up the right way around, you'll see for yourself."

More than a little curious, Cameron turned the painting around and eased the picture wire onto the wall hooks. At first he was too close to the canvas to get a proper look. He took a few paces back and then stopped in mid-step because he saw what Kate meant. The man in the painting did, indeed, have the same hazel eyes that he saw staring back at him from the mirror when he shaved each morning.

Kate moved back, too, to get a proper look at the picture. All the other portraits were faded to varying degrees by time and dulled by dirt and dust, placing their subjects firmly in the past. However—turned away from the light of day and the smoke of glowing cigar, flickering candle and blazing peat fire for two and a half centuries—Jamie Chisholm's portrait had been spared the ravages of time. Its colors were more vivid than those of any other painting, even that of Colin Chisholm, giving it a presence and immediacy the others lacked. It showed a man in his early twenties with a face framed by dark curls. He wore a baggy white shirt, with a maroon and turquoise tartan plaid over his left shoulder, held in place by a silver brooch in the shape of an owl. "He looks every inch the Highlander," Kate said.

Cameron didn't say anything.

Kate turned from the figure in the painting to the man standing next to her, and got the impression he'd forgotten she was even there. She wondered if he was experiencing a similar legacy of shame to the one she felt when she looked at the portrait of Lady Carolyn. But she guessed there had to be more to it than that, because as she studied him she rocognized the same troubled expression that she'd seen on his face several times earlier that day, when they first met down in the glen. She sensed that as Cameron stood in front of the portrait of Jamie Chisholm he was feeling a connection which went beyond that of distant kinship. It was as if he was being reminded of some sort of shame or disgrace that wasn't simply ancestral, and she wondered what lay behind it.

Whatever it was, she could see it was causing him deep unhappiness. Deciding a change of subject was in order, she moved on down the line of portraits and said, "I think if any picture should be turned to face the wall, it's this one."

Tearing his gaze from Jamie's portrait, he saw that Kate was looking at the painting hanging next to it. He thought the woman it portrayed would have been strikingly beautiful if there had been any hint of warmth and kindness in her eyes. "Who is it?" he asked.

"I take it you don't know anything about the history of the glen?"

"Just what you told me this afternoon about Jamie and his cottage."

"If you've got a skeleton in your closet with Jamie, I've apparently got the Wicked Witch from the North in mine with this woman, Lady Carolyn."

"What did she do?"

"According to Finlay, she kicked most of the clan out of the glen to make way for sheep." Staring at the painting, Kate quietly said, "The way things are looking, I'm going to be the next Lady Carolyn."

"I don't think so, Kate: there's a cold, cruel look in her eyes, where there's warmth and kindness in yours."

"That's sweet of you, Cameron, but I'll feel every bit as cruel as Lady Carolyn if I'm responsible for crofters being forced from the glen."

"It might not come to that."

"It will if nobody comes up with any bright ideas tomorrow night," Kate told him.

"You arranged a meeting, then?"

She nodded. "In here at six o'clock. You're invited, by

the way."

"Thanks. That'll save me pretending I need to borrow a cup of sugar or a jug of milk as an excuse to see you again."

Kate smiled. "At least *you* won't be kicked out of your home if I have to sell, Cameron. That's something. Did you get a chance to look around the cottage this afternoon?"

Cameron didn't want to think about Jamie's Cottage, about the blackness within it and inside himself. So, rather than talk about it even just in passing, he said, "I looked around the glen instead."

"What did you think?"

"It's just about perfect, isn't it?"

Kate nodded. "It'll break my heart if I have to sell it."

"I wish there was something I could do to help."

"Well, if you get any ideas about how to make the estate pay without turning the glen into a ski resort and Greystane into a 'tartan tat visitor center', don't keep them to yourself."

Just then the doors opened and Miss Weir and Finlay came in, each carrying a large silver tray. "If you would like to take your seats," Finlay said grandly.

Two places were set opposite each other at the nearest end of the table, with a neatly folded white linen napkin and half-a-dozen pieces of sparkling silver cutlery at each setting. Kate moved to the nearest seat. Before she could ease it out from under the table, Cameron did it for her.

Miss Weir smiled approvingly and said, "That's what I like to see, manners."

Finlay set his tray down in front of Kate.

Cameron took his seat, and Miss Weir set the other tray down in front of him.

Each tray held a bowl of soup; a main course of roast lamb, boiled potatoes and carrots; and a crystal goblet of cranachan for desert.

"We thought we'd serve the courses all at once so we don't have to keep coming in and out and bothering you," Miss Weir said, all but giving Kate a nudge and a wink.

Kate stole a glance at Cameron, and saw he was trying not to laugh.

It got even harder to keep a straight face when Finlay produced a box of matches from his waistcoat pocket and lit the wicks in the nearest candelabrum.

"Won't you and Finlay join us?" Kate said, not just to be polite but because she had to say something to stop herself from laughing at the none-too-subtle matchmaking.

"That's kind of you to ask, Lady Kate, but not when you have company," Miss Weir said. Looking at Cameron she added, "And such charming company at that."

"Thanks so much," Kate said, looking at the little feast.

"It looks lovely," Cameron added. "I didn't realize how hungry I was until I looked at this."

"You're most welcome, both of you," Miss Weir said. "Finlay'll be back with something to drink. After that we'll not be disturbing you. What can he get you?" she asked Cameron.

"A cold beer would be fine, if you have one."

Kate nodded to show she'd like the same.

When Finlay and Miss Weir had gone, Kate said, "They're so sweet, both of them. They've really tried to make me feel at home—and I do, even after only a couple of days. That must seem a little crazy."

Cameron shook his head. "What seems crazy is that, even though I've only just met you, I feel like you're more than a stranger, more even than just a neighbour."

"If that makes you crazy, then I'm a little crazy, too," Kate told him.

Neither of them knew quite what to say after that, and for a moment it seemed as though a slightly awkward silence might give lie to the words that had gone before.

Then, studying the glittering array of cutlery in front of him, Cameron said, "I'm going to have to apologize for not knowing what spoon to use."

"Damn! I was going to watch you to find out because I don't know either."

They laughed easily and together, the momentary trace of awkwardness gone, before turning their attention to the food.

Kate lifted her bowl of soup and pushed the tray aside.

Cameron did likewise, but paused with the bowl of soup in his hand.

Sensing that something was wrong, Kate looked across the table at him. The happiness of moments earlier had disappeared from his face, along with the color. He was staring at the space on the tray where the soup bowl had been. Kate glanced from his face to the tray in search of an explanation, but all she saw was a folded piece of purple linen, put there to stop the bowl from slipping. From Cameron's expression, the square of cloth might have been drenched in blood. He seemed transfixed by it. She saw his adam's apple move up and down as he swallowed, and watched as he picked up the scrap of linen with the studied calm of someone using every ounce of willpower to conquer a crippling phobia, and slid it under the tray, out of sight.

Before Kate could ask what was wrong, Finlay came in carrying a tray with two bottles of McEwan's lager and a couple of tall glasses. By the time Finlay had poured the drinks and made his exit Cameron had regained his composure. Before Kate could think of a tactful way to ask why he'd been so unsettled by the scrap of purple linen, Cameron said, "I hope I didn't spoil you from opening a bottle of wine by asking for a beer."

Kate shook her head. "Wine reminds me of a time in my life that wasn't too great, when my local tavern was a wine bar and there would be an awkward silence if you asked for a cold beer."

"Back in San Francisco?"

She shook her head. "New York City."

They started on their soup. "Cockaleekie," Cameron said.

"I beg your pardon?" Kate said, bemused by the strange sounding word.

Cameron smiled. "Cockaleekie—it's what this soup

is called."

"What a great name." Kate took another spoonful, and said, "It's marvellous, isn't it?"

Cameron nodded, then said, "I wouldn't have thought of New York as a pretentious kind of city."

"For the most part it's not, but the little part of it I was living in was."

"What part was that?"

"The orbit of the arty circle."

As they pushed aside the soup plates and started on the main course Kate told him how a holiday in New York led to a job as a guide at the Metropolitan Museum, and then a post arranging and promoting exhibitions.

"Sounds good," he said.

"To begin with it was. I was meeting all these people who'd been my heroes when I was at art college—"

"You've got an artistic streak, then?"

She sighed, and said, "I used to think I had."

Cameron thought that was a slightly odd thing to say—you either had some artistic ability or you didn't.

"Anyway," Kate continued, "there I was, making up the guest list for cocktail parties and exhibition previews, so, of course, I invited myself to all of them."

"Doesn't sound too bad to me."

"Like I said, to start with it was great, and I suppose I was hoping some of the brilliance of the people I met might inspire me . . . Hoping that one day I might be arranging the guest list for an exhibition that included some of my own sculptures."

"But . . ."

"Instead of being inspired, the opposite happened. I started feeling I was moving in a cliquey little circle of insufferably pretentious prima donnas with narrow minds and big egos; people who were so in love with themselves they couldn't genuinely like anyone else, let alone love them."

Cameron thought he detected the bitterness of a broken heart in her words. "It's a long way from New York to San Francisco. How come you ended up there?" he asked.

"It's where I was born. Well, just across the bay in a little tourist-trap town called Sausalito. Mom owned a craft shop there; Dad was the sheriff. When Mom died—around about the time I was getting disillusioned at the Met—I quit the Met and went back home. I didn't intend staying there for any length of time; I just wanted to be with Dad for a little while. I told Dad I'd look after the shop as a stop-gap measure, until we could find someone to run it for us and I could work out what I wanted to do with my life.

"And when the telegram from Archibald Cunningham arrived last week—five years down the line—I was still running it."

"And still trying to work out what you wanted to do."

She nodded. "I suppose so. For the first three or four years I was able to do some sculptures and sell them in the shop. But then they started turning out a different way from how I wanted them."

"In what way?"

"Horribly cold." *As cold as Lady Carolyn*, she thought. Something made her glance at the portrait of her reviled ancestor and, as she did so, she realized what was behind the strange familiarity she'd felt the first time she looked at the old oil painting: it wasn't the features that were familiar, rather the expression. The cold look was the same as the loveless look of her later sculptures. At first Kate felt a rush of relief at being able to rationally explain the unsettling feeling of being familiar with a total stranger . . .

Then a horrible notion struck her: the thought that losing her ability to sculpt romantic figures was maybe down to more than a lack of romance in her life . . .

That maybe it was the first manifestation of an ancient cur—

Don't even go there, Kate, she told herself. She tried to laugh at what common sense told her had been a crazy notion, and to put the thought from her mind—but didn't succeed on either count.

"Is everything okay, Kate?"

Cameron's voice broke into her thoughts, and she realized she was sitting with a forkful of lamb poised halfway to her mouth. She forced a smile, and then found she had to force down the food because she'd lost her appetite for a meal that moments earlier she'd been eating with relish.

"Do you never try painting or drawing?" Cameron asked.

"Yeah, but it doesn't give me the same buzz. Sometimes I used to work right through the night on sculptures when I felt like I was doing them well. I've never done that with a painting. It's hard to explain, but there's something wonderfully sensual about shaping with your hands, forming line and curve, feeling texture. I don't want to sound kinky, but it was almost a sexual thrill."

"I can understand—it was almost a sexual thrill just listening to you there."

Kate threw her head back a little, the dark thoughts replaced by delightful ones. For the second time that night Cameron noticed the lovely smoothness of her neck, and then he heard the surprisingly throaty laugh he'd already come to like so much.

After taking a drink, Kate said, "It's such a challenge—making something that's incapable of thought, feeling, or movement look like it can think and feel and move. It's immensely satisfying if you pull it off—and frustrating when you can't. Somehow I don't get the same satisfaction when I'm painting or drawing. But, having said that, the glen's so beautiful it's just a matter of time before I try to capture it on paper or canvas."

Cameron finished his lamb and said, "I can't tell you how much better that was than the food I've been used to."

"Which would be army rations, right?"

He nodded and took a drink.

"So, what made you want to join the army?" Kate asked. "From the way you act with a camera in your hand, I imagine you'd be happier as an out-and-out photographer."

"It was kind of expected of me, joining the army."

Kate remembered Archibald Cunningham's comment about Cameron's ancestors all having a military background.

Cameron's next words bore out the lawyer's: "There's been a career soldier in my family every generation for as long as anyone can remember. You might say it was the family business, and I know my dad would have been disappointed if I hadn't carried it on. The bedtime stories he read to me weren't about Noddy and Tin-Tin, they were about my uncle Calum at The Hook in Korea, where the Chinese attacked in a human wave and The Black Watch dug in and called artillery fire down on their own positions when they were over-run; about my grandfather Sandy being lowered down the cliffs at St Valery on a rope made of rifle slings rather than surrendering; and about my great grandfather storming the Heights of Dargai on the North-West Frontier."

For a few moments Cameron seemed lost in thoughts he'd rather not be having, then he said, "Anyway, you're right: when I left school I did want to be a photographer. The thing was, my parents' marriage had broken up and I stayed with my mum, so I already felt I'd let my dad down in a way by choosing her over him, and didn't want to disappoint him in another way by choosing photography over the army.

"As a compromise I went to college to study photography but also joined the Officer Training Corps. I was hoping the uniform would keep my dad happy, and that when I graduated I could open my own studio and just join the TA—that's like your National Guard."

"But you didn't, you joined the full-time army instead," Kate said.

He nodded. "In my last year at college I met a girl who broke my heart."

"And instead of joining the Foreign Legion to forget, you joined The Black Watch."

Cameron laughed. "Sounds very melodramatic when you put it like that, but that's pretty much how it was. About that time, my dad told me The Black Watch had been picked to oversee the handover of Hong Kong to the Chinese, and were looking for regimental photographers to document what was obviously going to be a historic tour of duty. It seemed like the ideal chance for me to move on, keep Dad happy, and do something I might even enjoy myself, so I took it."

"Any regrets?"

"Not about my time in Hong Kong. It was exciting to be a part of it, capturing a little piece of history on film and seeing an amazing place at the same time. I'll never forget the first time I took the Star Ferry over to Kowloon and then walked up Nathan Road. It was like nowhere I'd ever been, nothing I'd ever seen. There was so much atmosphere I could smell it and see it, touch it and taste it, so much excitement in the air that every single breath I took filled me with excitement."

"I love Chinatown in San Francisco, so I can see why

you'd like Hong Kong," Kate said. "How about after the Far East posting, did you go back to ordinary soldiering?"

He shook his head. "I was a photographer in a uniform. The only shooting I did was with a camera."

Choosing her words carefully, Kate said, "I can't imagine you doing the other kind but, earlier today, you acted like you had."

Cameron looked at her, not understanding.

"When you talked about believing in 'another kind of ghost' this afternoon you had a really haunted look in your eyes."

After a long, reflective look into his drink, Cameron said, "Other people did the shooting, but I saw the bodies."

Kate thought it seemed like there were times when he was still seeing them. "You're not just talking about one or two bodies, are you?" she asked.

"No."

"You must be talking about Yugoslavia, then," she guessed.

"Kosovo. It's a terrible thing to say, but they all seemed the same: Kosovo, Serbia, Bosnia. It wasn't a clash of countries or armies. It wasn't even one village against another, or one soldier against another. It was one neighbour against another, ordinary people doing terrible things to each other for no real reason. It's bad enough when it's just one or two psychos, but at least you can dismiss that as an aberration. When it's whole villages, though, whole countries . . . When you realize it's the behaviour that becomes the norm in situations where people can behave as they please, then you find out much more about other people than you ever wanted to know." He sighed, and added, "You find out much more about yourself than you ever wanted to know."

Kate desperately wanted to learn what it was Cameron had found out about himself. However, she sensed that asking him now might only make him regret telling her as much as he had, not encourage him to tell more. So she just said, "I guess all of that makes you want to get away from people, to a place like this."

He nodded. "Like you, though, I don't know how realistic it is to think I can stay here. I've got vague notions about trying to make a living as a freelancer, specialising in wildlife and scenic shots, but I have an awful feeling that it won't pay."

"I guess the only way to find out is by giving it a try."

Cameron nodded again. "I saved a little when I was in the army, so hopefully I'll be able to renovate the cottage and support myself for long enough to see if the freelance thing is viable."

"And if it isn't?"

"I'll have to try getting a job on the local paper."

"You make that sound like a last resort."

"Take a look at the pictures on its pages: three out of four are check presentations. The others are retirals, wedding anniversaries, school plays. Not the sort of thing you can get too creative or excited about. I'm sure I'd end up just going through the motions, and life should be about more than that, shouldn't it?"

"Most definitely," Kate said, her words heartfelt. She took a drink, then asked, "How about opening a studio and doing portraits and weddings?"

Cameron had considered that, but couldn't see it working out. There was much more to taking portraits than technique. You had to be at ease with people, and able to put people at ease. The best way he could think of explaining things was to say, "It would be like you with your sculptures, Kate."

And she nodded, because she understood.

For a little while they sat without saying anything, just holding their drinks, gazing into them . . .

Then Cameron said, "How about you, Kate. What'll you do if things don't work out here?"

"Go back to Sausalito, I guess."

"It must be a beautiful place if it's a tourist trap, but you don't sound too enthusiastic about going back."

"It is a beautiful place. Nothing like this, but lovely nonetheless. When I said 'back to Sausalito' I suppose what I meant was back to the feeling that life's passing me by."

"At least you'd have whatever money you made from selling the estate," Cameron said.

"I couldn't enjoy spending it, not knowing the price other people had paid to put it in my pocket. I'd feel like I was a second Lady Carolyn . . . And cursed just like she was," she added.

"How do you mean?"

Kate related what Finlay had told her about the deathbed curse on Lady Carolyn and her descendants.

"You don't believe in that sort of stuff, do you?"

"After what Finlay told me about the fate of some of the people in these portraits it's difficult not to," Kate said, looking over Cameron's shoulder at the wall of paintings. "And it's difficult not to get the feeling that history's repeating itself—that I'm destined to be responsible for a second clearance, and punished accordingly." She hesitated, afraid that what she was about to say might seem foolish, but then said it anyway because for some unaccountable reason she was sure that Cameron wouldn't laugh: "Besides, there's the way my sculptures have gone bad . . . It's almost like a curse caused that."

Cameron didn't know quite what to say to that, so he was relieved when Finlay and Miss Weir came in to clear the trays, and the four-way conversation turned to the meal and how much it had been enjoyed.

After a beaming Miss Weir and Finlay had gone, taking the dishes with them, Kate and Cameron were left in silence.

Kate was berating herself for having mentioned the notion of a curse—things had been going so well, then she'd gone and put a downer on the evening and probably made herself seem a little kooky in the process.

Cameron was kicking himself for mentioning the things that weighed him down. He'd been trying to appear bright and funny but, in the end, hadn't been able to keep what was inside from showing.

Kate got up and walked over to the wall of portraits, looking at Lady Carolyn.

Cameron got up and walked over to the picture of Jamie.

Turning to her guest, Kate said, "We make quite a pair, you and me, don't we: a woman with a curse on her family and a guy with a haunted house?"

Suddenly they were laughing at each other and with each other . . .

And then they weren't talking or laughing, they were kissing, neither of them making the first move or thinking about what they were about to do, both of them moving together and acting from feeling rather than thought.

"I didn't think anything like this could happen so quickly," Kate told him after they'd drawn apart, her hands on his shoulders, his clasped around her back.

"I didn't think it could happen at all," Cameron said.

For a few moments they stood like that, suddenly awkward, the way two people are when they've stumbled into the uncharted territory which separates friendship from love.

"Would you understand if I said I didn't want things to happen too fast?" Kate said, finally breaking the silence.

Cameron nodded.

"Would you be disappointed?"

He nodded again.

"I'd have been disappointed if you weren't disappointed," Kate told him.

They laughed easily and together. Some of the awkwardness disappeared, and this time Kate felt able to fill the next silence by asking, "What are you thinking, Cameron Fraser?"

"I'm not thinking, I'm hoping."

"What are you hoping?"

"That you manage to hang on to Greystane, Kate Brodie."

He felt her stiffen in his arms, saw a sadness in her smile.

"That's why I don't want things to move too fast, Cameron—in case I don't manage to hang on to the estate," she said. Then her actions were giving a lie to her words about not wanting things to move too fast, because her hands were running over his shoulders, her fingers clasping behind his neck, her lips pressing against his.

And for Cameron the past suddenly belonged to another time, the faces in the forest belonged to another world.

His heart belonged to Kate Brodie.

And that was when it happened: without any warning, the picture of Jamie Chisholm fell off the wall.

The painting had been hanging directly behind Kate, and she literally jumped with fright as it clattered to the polished wooden floor at her feet. The color drained from her face and, in a shaky voice, she said, "Was that what I think it was?"

"If you think it was a painting falling off the wall then, yes."

Kate broke away from Cameron to turn around and look at the picture lying face-up on the floorboards.

"I wonder if that means Jamie's jealous," Cameron said, trying to make a joke of it.

"I hate to think what it means," Kate said.

Cameron knelt down to examine the painting, and said, "The picture wire snapped." Seeing that Kate was still shaking, he said, "That's all it was, Kate, just an old picture wire that was ready to snap."

"Maybe, but it's really got me spooked."

"I'm not surprised. I got a real fright myself," he admitted.

"Are you going to be okay spending the night in the camper?" Kate asked.

He nodded.

Kate hesitated, then told him, "I meant what I said about not wanting things to move too fast, but you're welcome to the guest room here. In fact, you'd be doing me a favour if you stayed. It'd be nice to know there's someone through the wall."

"I wouldn't like to impose."

"You wouldn't be."

"You're sure? I've got a sleeping bag and fold-down bed in the camper."

"You don't need them. I'll make up the guest bed for you."

"If you're sure . . ."

"Cameron, I'm sure."

"I'll just nip across and get an overnight bag, then. Do you know if there's a quick way to get to the top of Jamie's Crag from here?"

She nodded. "Turn right at the bottom of the steps

outside the wall. You'll come to a bridge, just above the waterfall. It leads to a flight of steps up Jamie's Crag. You'll need a flashlight, though—a torch, I think you call it. I'll see if Finlay has one."

She didn't have to go looking for Finlay because, having heard the clatter of frame on floor, he came rushing in to find out what had happened.

Five minutes later Cameron was heading along the path that led to the bridge.

CHAPTER 11

Cameron was gone for so long that Kate and Finlay were pulling on their coats and getting ready to mount a search party by the time he returned. "Cameron! We were just about to go looking for you," Kate told him. "We thought maybe Jamie's ghost had gotten you."

Cameron didn't even manage a smile, let alone a laugh.

"Is everything okay?" Kate asked.

"The torch died on me," he told her.

Kate and Finlay both looked at the torch in his hand, which was shining brightly, then looked back at him for an explanation.

Cameron didn't know quite what to tell them.

When he set off from Greystane he'd been thanking his long-departed relative Jamie for helping secure him a night under the same roof as Kate Brodie.

However he wasn't thanking Jamie quite so much by the time he reached the end of the path behind the summit of Castle Crag, because the only way down to Waterfall Bridge was by a staircase of wooden sleepers that descended the forested hillside.

Cameron hadn't been able to set foot in a forest since Kosovo, not even by day, let alone night.

He stood there shining the torch down the stairway. The beam of light seemed to heighten the blackness around it. A breeze blew through the branches and they gave a dry rattle that startled him far more than it should have. The trees took on a skeletal quality, their branches like outstretched arms, the twigs like clutching, bony fingers. Staring with horrified fascination into the darkness, Cameron saw things he knew weren't really there, heard things he knew couldn't really be heard. His hand shook as he shone the torch to left and right because he half-expected that, at any moment, the beam would fall on something nightmarish. Something that wouldn't stay dead and buried in a far-off forest clearing.

Eventually he gathered himself enough to twist the front of the torch and tighten the beam so it would travel further, trying to put the forest on either side out of mind by putting it out of sight. He used the torch to probe for the bottom of the steps, but there was no end in sight. Even though he could barely see the trees on either side of the stairway now, he could sense their brooding presence. He felt like they were closing in.

Unable to face what lay ahead, Cameron turned and hurried back along the path and past the staircase that led up to Greystane.

He followed the track that wound its way to the bottom

of Castle Crag and the glen below. After using some stepping-stones to cross the burn, he followed the track up Jamie's Crag until the torchbeam fell on his van.

Once in the camper he put a towel into his rucksack, some underwear on top of the towel, and his toilet bag on top of the underwear. Slinging the rucksack over one shoulder, he left the camper. He had the key in his hand ready to lock up, but something stopped him before he could turn it.

The unmistakable feeling that he was being watched.

His heart started pounding, his pulse racing. Telling himself it was just his imagination working overtime, he took a deep breath in a bid to calm himself, locked the door, and slipped the keys into the hip pocket of his jeans.

But the sensation of being watched grew stronger. So strong that he half-expected a clutching hand to come down on his shoulder at any moment, and was afraid to turn around for fear of what he might see staring back at him.

When at last he turned around it was hesitantly, and the white beam shining out from the torch in his hand was anything but steady.

The circle of light bounced along the bottom of the door of Jamie's Cottage, no more than a dozen yards from where he stood. As it did, so the sensation of being watched vanished.

The lower half of the door was split in the middle, and twisted inwards at one side. Cameron shone the torch upwards, over the rusty iron handle, to the top of the door.

It was buckled outwards at the outer edge. He knew the warping was probably due to the top hinge having rusted away. Yet still he had the thought that it looked almost as if the damage had been caused by someone trying to batter the door down—and it never occurred to him that it might have been someone on the outside trying to kick the door in and break into the cottage, even though that would have been the more logical assumption. *The thought that filled his mind was that the damage had been done by someone inside trying to hammer the door down with their hands in a desperate bid to get out, to escape something dreadful and godforsaken that haunted the darkness within the old stone walls . . .*

Something that moments earlier had been watching *him.*

If there was such a thing as a door to hell it would look like this, Cameron thought. The longer he looked at the door, the more unsettled he became by the prospect of what lay beyond it. Soon he was imagining the sound the door would make if he forced it open, and what he might find if he stepped inside. He didn't have to make a conscious effort to imagine; the thoughts came unbidden to his mind, complete in every detail . . .

The door opening with a jarring shudder, giving way to a drawn-out creaking that went on and on and on.

A darkness revealed that was more complete than the blackest night.

Stepping into it, being enveloped by it, swallowed by it.

Being startled by movement behind him, and turning

around just in time to see the door that had opened so noisily swinging silently, slowly, inexorably shut.

Grabbing frantically for it, but to no avail because it was tantalisingly out of reach.

Watching helplessly as the outside world—the world with his camper van and Greystane and Kate Brodie and Glen Cranoch, with the sun and moon, light and warmth—became a steadily diminishing vertical slash in the darkness before disappearing altogether as the door slammed shut, leaving him standing in the blackness that was deeper than night.

Reaching blindly for the door handle, but finding only splinters that lanced his palm, slit his fingers and wedged under his nails.

The mounting horror of realizing that there was no handle on the inside of the door—realizing there was no way out.

Desperately probing for the crack between door and frame, only to discover it was too narrow to offer his bleeding fingers purchase.

Sinking to hands and knees and searching for the warped section of wood, only to find that it had sprung back into place and was flush with the frame.

Struggling to his feet on shaking legs and reaching for the twisted top of the door only to discover that it, too, was no longer warped.

The feeling of being watched, not from a distance now, but from so close that a bony hand might grab him at any moment.

Looking over his shoulder, seeing only darkness but sensing something more.

Turning back to the door and hammering at it until his hands were black and blue but not managing to break it down, for it would only warp and twist, not splinter and break.

Shouting until he was too hoarse to do more than whisper, and hearing the echoes of voices other than his own getting ever louder . . .

Cameron's dark imaginings were interrupted by the feeling that he was being watched again. The unseen eyes seemed to peer at him not from a crack in the door but from a little to the left. His hand was shaking rather than just trembling as he swung the torch in that direction, over rough old stonework cast in stark relief by the dramatic interplay of light and shadow.

As stone wall gave way to the small, deeply inset window, so the feeling of being watched faded once more. The beam from the torch fell on the bottom right-hand pane. It was cracked and stained and reflected the light, so that all he could see was dirty glass. A weak halo was cast on two of the other sections of the four-paned window, showing they had the same cracked and dirty glass in them. The other quarter of the window—the top left corner—was darker than the deepest shadow, and Cameron remembered from earlier in the day that its glass was missing altogether. Trying to forget his nightmarish imaginings of what might lie within the cottage, he walked towards the window, angling his wrist to shine the torch into the glassless section. Each step he took was smaller and slower than the last because, as the circle of light moved towards the empty quarter of the window, so the beam grew ever dimmer. When he was halfway to the cottage and shone the torch directly at the glassless section, the light died altogether.

"Damn!" he said under his breath. He moved the batteries around, hoping to get some extra charge out of them. Just as he was snapping the cover of the compartment back in place he got the feeling of being watched again. The sensation was so strong that he stopped what he was doing and instinctively looked at the window. The clouds parted and a shaft of moonlight fell on the cottage, which was less than half a dozen yards away now. He looked on in horrified fascination as the pane of glass next to the empty quarter misted up, as if fogged by warm breath.

The misting slowly vanished in front of his eyes until it was gone so completely it was difficult to believe it had ever been there at all.

Just as he was wondering if the misting had been a product of his imagination rather than something within the cottage, the pane clouded over again . . .

Then gradually went from opaque back to clear.

Cameron stood there, transfixed, watching and waiting and somehow knowing that the misting would reappear in a breath's time.

His own breath came out in a rush.

The silence was so intense it was far more disturbing than any noise. Any moment now, he thought . . .

And, sure enough, the window pane misted up again . . .

Then cleared just moments before the silvery light

died as another raft of clouds drifted in front of the moon. The sudden darkness made Cameron remember about the torch in his hand. It lit up when he flicked the switch. He focused its beam on the window pane, waiting for the glass to mist up again.

The moments stretched. The glass remained clear.

Cameron stood like that for a full minute, maybe two, struggling to keep the torch trained on the window pane because his hand was shaking so badly. He didn't know if it was fear or shock or a mix of both, but for that minute or two he was incapable of reasoned thought.

Then adrenalin kicked in, and possible explanations for what he'd witnessed flooded his mind. It could have been the breath of an animal . . .

A squatter . . .

Somebody snooping around from the property firm—the man with the camera Finlay had seen several days earlier, perhaps . . .

Or it could have been a figment of his imagination.

That last thought frightened him more than all the others put together. The idea that madness might lie coiled in the darkness inside him was far more terrifying than anything that could be lurking in Jamie's Cottage, so he pointed the torch at the heather-covered ground to light up the way, and started walking towards the ruin again. His steps were slow and uncertain, and the torchbeam shook with more than just the walk over uneven ground.

After a few paces the circle of light rose in front of

Cameron, no longer falling on bare rock or clumps of heather but instead climbing up the rough stonework of the cottage wall, just a couple of yards ahead of him now. He stopped and slowly raised the torch. Its beam dimmed as it moved over the thick slab of a lintel.

The light got dimmer still as it passed over the cracked and dusty bottom panes of glass, so much feebler now that he knew he hadn't imagined the dimming.

And then, just as what was left of the light fell on the glassless quarter of the window, it died completely. Cameron raised the torch to juggle the batteries around once more. For a moment the torch was pointing up at the sky, and came on full strength. But when Cameron pointed it into the empty quarter of the window it died again, leaving him staring into utter blackness.

Without warning, there was a barely audible sighing from within the cottage. A shadow moved in the darkness, sensed as much as seen, and suddenly a pair of eyes were staring straight into his own. They were unlike any eyes he'd ever seen before: perfectly circular, the irises bright amber, the pupils large and a soul-less black. Cameron took a step back on legs that barely had the strength to support him. The torch fell out of his hand and he stumbled and ended up on the seat of his pants. The clouds cleared the moon, and just then something began to emerge from the empty quarter of the window: tufted, bushy eyebrows followed by those piercing amber eyes . . . A grey face with a cruelly curved beak . . . A white chin and then a dappled chest, dark flecks on light . . . Followed by a pair of talons as vicious as the beak.

An owl.

There was another barely audible sigh as it launched itself from the window, passing so close above Cameron that he could feel the breeze of its passage. He got unsteadily to his feet and watched as the owl disappeared into the night in the direction of the forested hanging valley between the two crags.

Cameron stood there looking into the night for what might have been a little while or a long time, waiting for common-sense to kick in again: for his mind to accept the explanation that the misting on the window had just been the breath of the bird; that the moving shadow within the cottage was nothing more than softly beating wings; that the wistful sighing was simply the sound that went with the motion; that the sensation of being watched was solely due to the amber eyes that had appeared as if from out of nowhere in the empty quarter of the window . . . Waiting for his heart to stop racing, his stomach to sink back down to roughly where it belonged, and the strength to return to his legs.

Then he hurried back towards Greystane as fast as he could. Despite the darkness he wished that the beam from the torch would fade, or at least flicker.

The owl could explain a lot, but not the way the light had died when he tried to shine it into Jamie's Cottage.

By the time Cameron reached Greystane he still

couldn't explain away the dimming of the torch. He could only answer the questioning looks of Kate and Finlay with a lame, "It must have just been a loose wire or something."

Finlay nodded without conviction.

"I maybe shouldn't have told you the cottage is supposed to be haunted," Kate said after Finlay had gone up the stairs to bed. "I don't want to put you off staying in the glen."

"Meeting you has done the opposite of that," Cameron told her.

Kate reached for his hand and clasped it in her own, and Cameron's disquiet disappeared with her touch. By the time they said goodnight to each other with a shy kiss on the landing at the top of the stairs, Cameron wasn't thinking about Jamie's Cottage, the owl or the torch; he was thinking about Kate Brodie.

After breakfast the next morning—which Miss Weir insisted on serving to Kate and Cameron in the banquet hall, albeit without the candles this time—Kate said, "Well, I've shown you mine, how about you showing me yours?"

Finlay came in just at that moment to clear away the dishes. From the way he was trying to hide his smile as he tidied the table, Kate knew he'd heard her. "Houses, Finlay," she explained. "We were talking about houses."

"It's none of my business what you were talking about,

Lady Kate, but I'm sorry if I came in at an inopportune moment."

Kate blushed. "I was just inviting myself up to Jamie's Cottage. Cameron's thinking of renovating it."

Finlay stopped what he was doing, and said, "That reminds me, I have something for Mr. Fraser." Turning to Cameron, he said, "If you'll be so kind as to wait here a few minutes, I think you'll find it worth your while."

"Sounds intriguing," Kate said.

Finlay returned five minutes later with a large cardboard cylinder.

"What is it, Finlay?" Kate asked, unable to contain her curiosity long enough to wait for Cameron to open the tube.

"Plans for doing up Jamie's Cottage, putting in a little kitchen and bathroom, new windows and the like. Not long before Mr. Chisholm died he'd been thinking about renting the cottage out as a holiday home. He was getting desperate to make ends meet. Anyway, he had some plans drawn up for the work that needed done," he gestured to the paper Cameron was unrolling, "and, if I'm not mistaken, he had them approved and got estimates from half a dozen builders. All the paperwork'll still be up in his study somewhere, I'm sure."

Kate said, "This is a pleasant surprise, Finlay."

Cameron didn't say anything; the dark imaginings of the night before were still fresh in his mind.

Kate turned to him and smiled.

Cameron didn't think she noticed that he had to force

the smile he gave her in return, but when Finlay left the room she reached for his hand and gave a reassuring squeeze.

Half an hour later he was standing with her on top of Jamie's Crag. "It is a bit spooky," Kate said, looking at the cottage. "But once it's been done up, once it has curtains on the windows and smoke coming from the chimney, it'll look more like a home than a haunted house."

This time Cameron didn't even manage a forced smile.

Sensing his unease, Kate said, "Just what exactly did happen up here last night, Cameron?"

"I got spooked by an owl flying out the window while I was looking in it."

She searched his eyes, and knew there was more to it than that. "There was something else, though, wasn't there?" she asked.

"Don't you think that would be frightening enough?"

"It would be at the time, but it's the sort of thing you'd laugh about later—yet you're not even smiling about it, let alone laughing."

"Can you laugh about the picture falling off the wall?"

"No, but I'm not trying to pretend there wasn't something spooky about that, the way you're trying to pretend there wasn't something spooky about whatever happened here last night."

Still Cameron didn't say anything.

"Cameron?"

"You're not going to let this drop, are you?"

Kate smiled sweetly and shook her head. "If I've got to

contend with a curse, it'll be some consolation to think that at least my next-door neighbour is having to put up with a haunted house."

Finally Cameron laughed.

"So, come on, out with it. What happened up here last night?"

Cameron took a deep breath, then walked over to the nearest window and said, "When I shone the torch in the window it died on me. I swapped the batteries around and it was working perfectly . . .

"But then, when I shone it in at the window again, the same thing happened. The light died as though the batteries had gone dead. Every time I moved the torch away from the window it came on again, and every time I moved it back it went out."

"That is a bit wooky-spooky," Kate said. "How come you never mentioned anything about it last night?"

"You'd been scared enough as it was by the painting falling off the wall. And besides, I was worried you'd think I was crazy." He paused, then added, "Do you?"

"Not crazy, maybe just suffering from some sort of post-traumatic stress. It's hardly surprising if you are, Cameron. In fact, it'd be more surprising if you weren't. I'm sure you can't see the sort of things you saw in Yugoslavia without being affected by it on some level."

Cameron didn't know what to think about what had happened outside the cottage the night before, let alone what to say.

"You looked haunted before you even saw this place, Cameron. The cottage maybe spooked you because it looks like something you saw in Kosovo. It might have acted as a trigger, a stage for your own ghosts to appear on." She hesitated, then said, "Maybe it wasn't the torch that kept blacking out when you looked through the window, Cameron—maybe it was you."

He didn't say anything, just kept looking at the derelict cottage.

"I don't know what post-traumatic stress syndrome involves," Kate said, "but I'd guess the best cure is to mellow out, lose yourself in other things: your photography, rebuilding this place. I have to admit I'm being selfish—I like having you around—but, even putting that aside, I honestly think it might do you good to rebuild Jamie's Cottage. I guess you've seen too many homes turned into derelict shells; maybe turning a derelict shell into a home might lay some of your ghosts to rest . . ."

Still Cameron didn't speak; his gaze was drawn towards the empty quarter of the window.

"But it might be an idea to stay away from this place by night until you've got it looking like a home rather than a haunted house or the site of an ethnic cleansing," Kate said. "If you want to give the renovation a go, you can crash out at the guest room in Greystane for as long as it takes to turn Jamie's Cottage into your home."

"Thanks," Cameron said, finally turning away from the cottage to look at her. "I appreciate that, but I wouldn't want to get in the way."

"You won't be in the way. And anyway, I've got a battle of my own to face, against Tony Carling. I'd be glad of all the moral support I can get."

Cameron knew exactly what she meant about needing moral support; if it hadn't been for Kate, he would have just got in his camper van and driven away. *Run away*. He could quite happily turn his back on the cottage, but he couldn't turn his back on Kate Brodie. So he took a deep breath and walked over to the door of Jamie's Cottage. His throat was dry and his palm was moist as he reached in his pocket for the ancient key that Archibald Cunningham had given him. He had to use both hands to fit it into the lock, one to keep the other from shaking. After hesitating for the time it took to draw another deep breath, Cameron started turning the key. He hoped the key would jam, the lock would stick and he would have an excuse not to enter Jamie's cottage. Sure enough, the key stuck almost as soon as he tried to turn it. He gave a couple of half-hearted twists of his wrist, but it wouldn't budge. With a sigh of relief he began withdrawing the key—but as he did so it clicked into place, telling him it had just been pushed in too hard for the teeth to engage the tumblers.

His palm was sweating so much now that he had to leave the key in the lock and wipe his hand on his jeans before turning it. This time when he twisted his wrist there was still resistance, but he was able to overcome it.

Something made him hesitate on the threshold. It was

the fear that when he pushed the door it would shudder and scrape and then swing open with a drawn out creak to reveal a blackness darker than night, just as he'd imagined it would when he stood in front of the cottage the night before.

Then he was aware of Kate at his back, and he turned the rusty old handle and pushed.

At first the door stuck fast.

Then it shuddered back a few inches.

It stopped with a scraping jar.

And then shuddered forward another couple of inches.

Caught up in a horrible déjà vu, Cameron couldn't bring himself to push any harder.

He didn't have to. Kate stepped forward and gave a shove, and the door swung open in front of them with a barely discernible creak that slowly died away into utter silence.

To his horror, Cameron saw that the interior of the cottage was impossibly dark, just as it had been in his hellish imaginings of the night before. He froze, unable to move, as if a spell had been cast over him.

"Wow!" Kate said. "Talk about atmospheric. You should have brought your cameras."

Her words broke the spell and Cameron realized that the darkness had a simple explanation; he'd shut his eyes as the door swung open, out of fear of what he was about to see.

Opening them now, he saw sunlight slanting in through the doorframe around him and Kate, casting their shadows onto a stone floor whose only covering was mud and mould and puddles of stagnant rainwater.

A small table sat in the center of a drab room. The table, and the chairs to left and right of it, looked as old as the furniture in Greystane, but that was all they had in common. There was no elaborate carving, no elegantly curved legs and lion's paw feet, and the upholstery of the seats was crudely woven wickerwork rather than plush velvet. A cracked, rainwater-filled bowl sat abandoned on the table, next to a toppled pewter candlestick holder. The only thing that looked as though it must have once been beautiful was the intricately woven lace tablecloth the bowl and candlestick lay on, but now it was so water-stained and filthy that it was almost as dark as the wood it covered.

The far wall beyond the table was bare stone, relieved only by a cracked, badly foxed mirror with a wooden frame whose mitred joints had opened up with years of damp.

The wall to the right held a fireplace with a split wooden bucket, rusty ash pan, and fire-blackened poker in front of it. On one side of the hearth was an ancient rocking chair, lit by a horizontal shaft of light streaming through the window. On the other side of the hearth, illuminated by a sunbeam that shafted through a hole in the roof, was an empty crib lined with more of the filthy but lovingly woven lace, and covered with the gossamer of an equally lovingly woven spider's web.

The light that poured through the window to their left fell on a rusty iron bedframe and a heavy chest of drawers which were all half open and empty but for more cobwebs, glistening with drops of moisture.

Kate and Cameron stood in the doorway, trying to take it all in.

Kate was the first to speak. "Believe it or not, this really could be fantastic," she said.

"I'm going to take some convincing," Cameron told her.

"Don't see it as it is now; look at it in terms of what you can do with it. Just imagine sitting in the rocker with a roaring fire inside and a roaring wind outside." She grabbed his hand and led him into the cottage. Taking him over to the window with the missing pane, she said, "How's that for a view!"

They were looking down on the lochan, and had an unobstructed view of the entire length of the glen.

"There's no getting around it, it'll take a lot of work, but at the end of it you could have something really special here, Cameron." The excitement vanished from her voice when she added, "I just hope I'll still be here for the housewarming."

Now it was his turn to squeeze her hand reassuringly. "How long do you think you can hang on to Greystane?" he asked as they looked down on the glen.

"The estate runs at a loss—what Archibald Cunningham described as a revenue deficit. I think I can make up that deficit from my savings for about two months. After that I'll have to either sell my share in the shop to keep the estate going, or sell the estate."

Cameron thought for a few moments, then said, "I could maybe buy you another few months before it came to that."

"That's really sweet, Cameron, but you're going to need all your money to get on your feet as a freelancer, and to do this place up," she said, looking around.

"There's nothing I'd rather spend my money on than Glen Cranoch and on you, Kate."

She put her hands on his shoulders and kissed him, then said, "I'm finding I want to do that more and more."

"I'm finding I want to do this more and more," Cameron said, and held her in his arms.

CHAPTER 12

CAMERON HELPED KATE ARRANGE THE SEATS IN FOUR rows of four on either side of the table for the crofters' meeting in the banquet hall, while Finlay and Miss Weir set out a light buffet.

As each of the crofting families came in, Kate welcomed them with a smile. She was glad she'd dressed in her nicest clothes—fawn slacks and cream cashmere sweater—because the crofters were obviously wearing their Sunday best. Kate sensed a quiet pride among them, and instinctively liked them for it. She wondered when the banquet hall had last been so full. Not in the days of Colin Chisholm, she guessed. Probably not for sixty years or more, since the "Lost Generation" parties given by Janet and Struan between the wars. However, despite the fact that there were about forty people gathered in the hall, there was nothing like a party atmosphere now. The occasional hushed conversation or two served only to accentuate just how quiet it was. Kate toyed nervously with the "cheat sheet" in her hands and occasionally glanced at it, reading over the notes she'd made for the little speech she was about to give. Public speaking wasn't her thing, and the coming hour would have been an ordeal even if the subject matter hadn't been such a troubling one.

Five minutes before the meeting was due to start all the seats were taken and there were half a dozen people standing, including Miss Weir, Finlay, and Cameron. One of the crofters came over and said, "We're just missing Auld Davie, Lady Kate. He's maybe having a struggle with the stairs. If you don't mind, I'll go out and see if he needs a hand."

Before Kate could answer, the crofter looked past her and said, "Talk of the devil."

The man he referred to was making his way through the chapel with the aid of a walking stick, and made Finlay look in the first flush of youth by comparison.

When the old man reached the door to the banquet hall, Kate said, "I'm sorry, I hope you've not had a struggle with the steps."

"I must be getting old," the man said, as if just realizing it. "I used to take the stairs two at a time when I was coming up here for a ceilidh. Now I have to rest after every single one."

"Well, thanks for coming," Kate told him. "I'll go and look for another chair."

"No need, Lady Kate," the first crofter said.

Kate soon saw what he meant: at least half a dozen crofters got up to offer Auld Davie a seat. Watching them,

Kate got the impression that this gathering was made up of true neighbours rather than just people who happened to live next to each other.

The quiet conversations fell silent row by row when Kate walked towards the grand fireplace at the far end of the hall. She was accompanied by Archibald Cunningham, who'd accepted her invitation to come along and assess whatever ideas were put forward.

There was an expectant hush by the time Kate reached the fireplace and turned to face the people of Glen Cranoch. Looking around the rows of seated crofters Kate saw everything from a young mother with a baby cradled in her arms to the man who was older than Finlay. She was aware that they were all watching her, depending on her, that their fate was in her hands. A wave of panic washed over her, and she froze on the spot.

They could have let her suffer, revelled in seeing the person who lorded over them being humbled. But, instead, the young mother with the baby said in a gentle voice, "I think you've made some notes, Lady Kate."

Kate smiled at her, mouthed a "thank you", and looked at the sheet of paper she'd been holding, forgotten, in her hands. After a deep breath she said, "First of all, I'd like to thank—"

"Lady Kate . . ." It was Miss Weir, calling out from the back of the hall. "You'll have to speak up a bit, or us oldies at the back won't hear."

Kate nodded, glanced down at her notes, and in a

louder voice said, "I'd like to thank you all for coming, and apologize for the short notice. I thought I should call a meeting as soon as possible to let you know where we all stand." She looked up from the notes, and found she didn't have to look back down at them again. "I don't know if Colin Chisholm kept you informed about how the estate was faring, but I think you have a right to know, because The Cranoch is your home as well as mine."

She sighed, then said, "I'm afraid the news isn't good. In latter years Mr. Chisholm only managed to keep the estate going by selling the family silver, so to speak. Now there's nothing left to sell except Greystane and the glen itself. I have a little money, but not enough to keep the estate going much longer. The bottom line is that I'm faced with the choice of coming up with a way to turn The Cranoch's fortunes around, or selling it."

Kate had never heard a silence so loud. She broke it by saying, "Apart from the selfish reason of how much I love it here, and the fact that I dearly want to make Glen Cranoch my home, I feel a responsibility for every one of you. Especially given the fact that some of the people whose pictures hang on that wall," she gestured at the portraits to her right, "seem to have badly let down the people who lived here in the past." It seemed to the people listening that Kate was thinking aloud rather than addressing them when she added, "On top of all the other debts, it seems I face a debt of honor."

The watching crofters could see how heavily that debt

weighed on Kate as she looked at the line of portraits.

Then she turned back to them and said, "I'd hate my picture to be the last one on that wall, and to be looked at in the same way as Lady Carolyn." In a lighter tone she added, "Yes, I saw the looks she got from a few of you earlier!"

There were a few embarrassed little laughs at that.

There was nothing light about Kate's tone when she continued. "What I'm trying to say is that I'd hate to have to sell Glen Cranoch and Greystane, but if things carry on as they are—if the estate isn't paying for itself by the time I run out of money—I won't have any choice." She let out another sigh.

Gathering her thoughts, she carried on: "That's bad enough, but what really worries me is the nature of the only likely buyer." She hesitated, the way a person does when they're trying to work out how to word bad news. "I can hardly bring myself to tell you this . . ."

If anything, the silence now seemed even more complete.

Finally, Kate said, "It's a property company that would change the glen completely, and I don't think any of the changes would be for the better." She looked down at the paper in her hand, not to remind herself of anything she'd written down, but because she couldn't look at the crofters as she said, "They want to turn the lochan into a watersports center and the glen into a ski resort." Kate thought she heard restive stirrings. "They would turn this place—" she held out her hands to indicate the old house around her—"into a visitor center: a 'tartan tat' shop was how their representative put it to me."

There was no doubt now about the stirrings.

"What about the crofts?" Auld Davie shouted out from the back.

"Aye," another voice called out.

Kate looked up from the paper, at all the faces looking back at her. "I wish . . . If there was any other . . ." Archibald Cunningham put his hand on her shoulder in a gesture of support but Kate didn't notice. She literally hung her head in shame as she said, "There wouldn't be any place for the crofts in Glen Cranoch."

The stirrings gave way to a stunned silence, which was broken when the woman with the baby asked, "Could they force us out like that?"

"Once your leases are up, they could," said Archibald Cunningham.

"And they'd be allowed to do all those terrible things to the glen?" another voice asked.

"They must be pretty sure of planning approval, or they wouldn't be prepared to make an offer," the lawyer answered.

"Be honest, Lady Kate," the old crofter asked from the back, "aren't you tempted to just sell up now and have done with it—and with us?"

"No, Davie. It is Davie, isn't it?"

He nodded.

"No, Davie, not even nearly. The money they're offering couldn't buy me another place like Glen Cranoch. I don't think any amount of money could. And it couldn't make up for the guilty conscience I'd have if I thought I'd made that money at the cost of all of you having to leave your homes. To be honest, Davie, I don't feel like I own Glen Cranoch; I feel like I hold it in trust, and that selling it to the sort of people who want to buy it would be an unforgivable betrayal of that trust."

"So what are you going to do?" the young mother asked.

"I really don't know," Kate said. "That's one of the reasons I've called you all here. I wanted to warn you that although I don't want to sell The Cranoch, I might not have any choice—and to let you know what's likely to happen as a result.

"But I also wanted to ask for ideas about how I could turn the place around so that I won't have to sell it. I'm hoping that somebody who knows the glen better than I do might have ideas about how to change its fortunes without changing its nature."

There was another long silence.

"I can assure you that this isn't a token effort to save the place," Kate told them. "It's a plea from the heart for help. If you have any ideas, no matter how outlandish you think they seem, please, please don't keep them to yourself. We're all in this together."

"A distillery!" Auld Davie called out from the back of the banquet hall a few moments later, to some quiet laughter and a few shouts of support.

Kate smiled and turned to Archibald Cunningham.

"It would take a lot of money to set it up, and a lot of

time before there was any return," the lawyer said. "I have a feeling you'd have been just the man to run it, though, Davie."

There was a ripple of laughter, because it was well known throughout The Cranoch that Auld Davie was a master of the illicit still.

"Aye, I suppose I know a good dram when I taste one, right enough," he said.

There was more laughter. "You're too modest, by far," Archibald Cunningham told the old crofter.

The silence that followed was ended by a voice from the back row asking, "How about bottling the glen's water?"

"Mr. Chisholm looked into that, but the soil around here is too peaty," the lawyer said. "Water that's flowed over it doesn't store well in plastic bottles, and glass ones would be too expensive."

The woman sitting next to the young mother—the baby's grandmother, Kate guessed—said, "How about a hotel, Lady Kate?"

Archibald Cunningham answered before Kate could: "Greystane'd look great in a brochure, but it just doesn't have enough rooms to make money."

"What about films, Archie?" a man in his fifties with a bad sweepover and round, pasty-complexioned face shouted from the back of the hall. "What about trying to get movies made here, like *Rob Roy* or *Braveheart*? The Yanks love places like this."

There were more than a few guffaws, and Kate saw the

pasty complexion turn bright red when the man realized why people were laughing.

"Sorry, Lady Kate," the embarrassed crofter said in a voice that was much quieter than the one he'd made his suggestion in.

Kate laughed. "No need to apologize. I appreciate all suggestions. And you're right, Yanks are suckers for places like this. At least, this Yank is."

Somebody applauded her for that. A few others joined in, and soon nearly all of them were clapping and it was Kate who blushed.

When the applause died down, Kate turned to the lawyer next to her and said, "What do you think, Mr. Cunningham—have we got a future in the movies?"

Archie made a note on the pad he held in his hand, but Kate sensed he was doing it just so that he didn't discourage them by shooting all their suggestions down in flames. "The Cranoch is as beautiful as any place I've seen in the movies, so I don't see why we shouldn't look into it," he said. "But we'd be relying on the right film waiting to be made, at the right time. It's a good idea, but not one I'd want to stake my future on."

Half a dozen other proposals followed, most of which Archie Cunningham had to dismiss out of hand as they fell into the same category as the movie idea: long-shots you wouldn't want to stake your future on. The most promising was the idea of a craft collective, using the Internet for marketing. Kate knew it had some potential—she could use Kate's Crafts as a US outlet—but, even without looking at Archie's face as he scribbled the idea in his notebook, she knew it was the sort of thing that could only make a small difference, not transform the fortunes of the estate. Experience told her that the effort needed to produce craft goods was rarely reflected in the price people would pay for them.

When a long silence signalled that nothing more would be forthcoming, Kate said, "I think it's perhaps time to turn to the food which Miss Weir and Finlay have prepared." Trying to hide her disappointment at the fact that nothing promising had emerged from the brainstorming session, she added, "Thanks again for coming along tonight. And remember, any ideas you have in the days ahead will be much appreciated, so I hope you won't hesitate to bring them to my attention. You never know, they might make all the difference."

There was some half-hearted applause, then the hall was quickly filled by the sound of chairs being pulled back and conversations starting up.

Kate turned to Archie and said, "I'm sorry nothing more positive came out of this, Mr. Cunningham. I hope you don't feel I've wasted your time here tonight."

"I hate to say it, but I think *you're* wasting your time, Lady Kate. I sincerely hope you can prove me wrong, but nothing I heard tonight leads me to believe you can."

Just then Cameron came over, and the solicitor said, "So, what do you think of your cottage, Mr. Fraser?"

Before Kate could hear Cameron's reply, her attention was distracted by the approach of a stocky, swarthy man with a thick moustache.

"Lady Kate?" he said in a deep but quiet voice.

Kate smiled and reached out a hand for him to shake.

"I wonder if I might have a word?"

Sensing the crofter wanted a little privacy, Kate said, "Of course," and took a couple of steps to the side.

The man hesitated, then said, "I have a favour to ask."

Absurdly, for some reason Kate felt like Marlon Brando at the start of *The Godfather*, and suddenly pictured a succession of crofters approaching her one after the other, toying nervously with flat tweed caps as they asked her to execute troublesome neighbours, pronounce judgment on blood feuds and the like. So although she said, "Go ahead," the smile that went with her words was a little strained.

"I know you have enough on your mind at the moment, Lady Kate, but . . . it's my daughter, Pamela. She wants to get married."

Kate wondered what that had to do with her. She remembered reading somewhere that back in olden times the lord or lady of the manor had to sanction any marriage among the locals. *Surely that can't still be the case*, she thought.

"I don't know quite how to put this," the crofter said, "but time is of the utmost importance, if you see what I mean."

Kate knew exactly what he meant, but couldn't figure out why he was telling her about it.

"Don't get me wrong, I'm not holding a shotgun to the

laddie's head. Thank goodness I don't have to . . ." His voice trailed away, then he said, "A wedding in Inverness is beyond our means, Lady Kate. It probably still would be even if I had time to save up, because I wouldn't have the money to save up with."

Kate thought she was about to be asked for a loan she could ill afford to give, but instead the man said, "So I was wondering if they could get married in your chapel, here in Greystane."

"Of course," Kate said, relieved. "I'd love that."

Kate's relief was nothing compared to the crofter's. "Lady Kate, I don't know how to thank you," he told her. "I don't know what I would have done. The churches in Inverness charge money to hold a wedding; then there would have been the cost of one of those fancy limousines, or else she'd have been crammed into my car, her dress all creased and crumpled by the time she got out."

"Well, you won't have to worry about any of that. The chapel's at your disposal, Mr. . . ."

"Sandy," he told her, "but I'm also known as Double Ecky."

"I'm trying to work out how 'Sandy' could become 'Double Ecky', but I'm not even coming close," Kate told him, bemused.

"Eck's short for Alec in these parts, and my name is Alexander Alexander.

Kate smiled. "Well, Sandy—Double Ecky—it would be a pleasure."

"Her mother's going to be so relieved," Sandy said. He turned to face a nervous woman who stood beside a tall, gangly youth and a plump teenage girl with a pale face and raven black hair that fell down past her shoulders. The two teenagers made an odd couple because of the difference in their height, but something about the way they held hands made Kate think they were a good fit.

Kate got the feeling Sandy was giving his wife a reassuring smile. His face still had a trace of worry on it when he turned back, however. Kate found out what was bothering him when he said, "The only thing is that they really couldn't wait too long, Lady Kate. Pamela kept things to herself until she could barely hide it any longer, the daft wee thing."

"I understand. Just say when, and the chapel is yours."

He hesitated, then tentatively said, "Would a week on Saturday be too soon?"

Kate shook her head. "It'd be fine."

"I can't thank you enough."

"It's nothing," Kate said.

"No, Lady Kate, it's everything. I'd been trying to think of what else I could do. I'd even thought about seeing if I could persuade a minister to hold the ceremony in the old church at the far end of the lochan, and convince Pamela and young Ross that it would be romantic. I know they'd have smiled to make me feel better, but deep down they'd have felt a chill because it's an unholy place to the people of this glen."

"I can understand why," Kate said, remembering Hamish backing away from the door, the sigh of a Bible page being caught by a breeze that seemed to come from within the old building and not without, and the whispering of old leaves—or something even older—from among the pews. "Anyway," she told the crofter, "there's no need to worry. It won't come to that."

"Aye, thanks to you it won't."

"It's a privilege to be able to help two people get off to a good start, even just in a small way."

"Sorry again that it's such short notice."

"That's all right. It doesn't leave you much time to arrange the reception, though."

"That part of the wedding's no problem. We'll just have it in the croft."

Kate had been in some of the crofters' cottages the day before when she was arranging the meeting, and had seen how small the rooms were. "That'll be a tight squeeze," she said.

"We'll put some tables and chairs out the back."

"What if it rains?"

"Hector next door'll help out and take some of the people in his place."

On the spur of the moment—looking around the banquet hall and remembering what Finlay had said about the windows rattling, the floorboards shaking and the chandelier swinging as a Highland fling was danced—Kate said, "Why not hold the reception here?"

"That's very kind of you, Lady Kate, but I wouldn't dream of imposing on you like that."

"Maybe I won't be able to save the estate in the long run, Sandy, but I won't feel quite so bad if I know I've helped out with some things like this in the short run.

"Besides, from what Finlay's told me, my family owes the people of Glen Cranoch some happy days."

"We couldn't afford—"

"We could use food from the estate, and Miss Weir could do the cooking. I'll help her, and no doubt learn a thing or two in the process." The more Kate considered it, the better she thought it could be. Without realizing it, she was thinking out loud rather than talking to the man in front of her: "Finlay could be the piper, and I'm sure Cameron would agree to take some photos."

For a few moments Sandy said nothing. When he finally spoke, it was to say, "God bless you, Lady Kate."

Kate smiled, thinking it was probably a very long time since anyone from the glen had said that to a lord or lady of Greystane. She put a hand on the crofter's shoulder and said, "It'll be my pleasure, Sandy. I haven't been to a wedding for ages, and I've never had a chance to organise a reception, except in my imagination." She couldn't keep the wistfulness out of her voice when she said that. "I've done it a hundred times in my mind, Sandy. I'd love to find out if it's anything like as much fun as I imagined.

"Besides, it'll be doing me a favour: a distraction from worrying about the estate, and the happiest kind of distraction, at that."

Sandy Alexander reached for Kate's free hand and took it in both his own, before saying, "You can't imagine what this'll mean to Pamela and her mum. You can't imagine what it means to me. I thought I was going to have to disappoint her, and it was breaking my heart. I never dreamed I could delight her."

"You're most welcome Sandy. Just let me know how many people will be coming."

"This is the guest list, Lady Kate," Sandy told her, half turning to take in the assembled people with a sweep of his arm. After taking a deep breath, as if unable to believe it all, he said, "You are sure about this?"

"Completely certain. There's just one condition."

"Just name it, Lady Kate. In fact, you don't even have to; I agree to whatever it is. I'd do anything to make Pamela happy."

"It's actually something I want Pamela to do: when she throws the bouquet over her shoulder, could you tell her to throw it in my direction?"

Sandy smiled and said, "I'll do that, Lady Kate." Barely able to conceal his excitement, he looked at his wife, daughter, and Ross, and said, "Can I tell them the good news?"

Kate nodded. "Tell the world, Sandy. I'd want everyone to know if *I* was getting married. In fact . . ." she stopped him as he was about to turn away ". . . why not make an announcement now, and invite everyone to the reception while you're at it."

"I wouldn't like to invite people into a house that's not my own."

"Ask Finlay to make the announcement, then—if you can prise him away from the sandwiches for long enough. He'll be glad to do it, especially with the thought of a wedding feast as a prospect."

"If you're sure . . ."

"Yes, Sandy, I'm sure."

Sandy reached for her hand and kissed it in a spontaneous gesture.

Cameron turned away from Archibald Cunningham a moment too late to see that. All he saw was Sandy hurrying away, and Kate beaming.

"You look like you've just had some good news. Has someone come up with a bright idea?"

"Yes," she told him, "me!"

"Something that might turn the estate around?"

"No, just something that'll make a few of the people who live in it very happy. I hope you don't mind, but I've kind of roped you into it, too." Seeing the puzzlement on Cameron's face she said, "Don't worry, I'm sure you'll enjoy it. All you have to do is take some photos."

Before Cameron could ask any more questions the chime of silver teaspoon on crystal glass rang out three times. All eyes turned to the head of the table, where Finlay stood with Mr. and Mrs. Alexander and the little-and-large couple.

By the time the echoes of the third ring died out,

Finlay had complete silence. "Ladies and gentlemen, your attention please," he said. "It is my happy duty to inform you of a forthcoming wedding in the glen." Gesturing to the small, raven-haired girl and the gangly young man, he said, "Miss Pamela Alexander, and Mr. Ross Anderson."

There were a few wolf-whistles, some cheers and a round of applause. Then someone shouted out, "We're going to have Pamela Anderson living in Glen Cranoch, then!"

When the laughter died down, Finlay continued. "Furthermore, I've been asked to invite one and all to the wedding ceremony, in Greystane's chapel, a week on Saturday—and to a reception afterwards, here in the banquet hall."

There was more applause.

Miss Weir appeared at Finlay's side, holding a bottle of whisky in each hand.

Finlay said, "Now, if you'll bear with us while we charge the glasses, I think a toast is in order." That got even louder applause.

Miss Weir worked her way down the crowd on the left of the table with one of the bottles, while Finlay used the other one to fill the glasses on the right. He poured a couple extra, and brought them over to Kate and Cameron. "You've done a fine thing, Kate Brodie," he said. "A fine thing, indeed."

Finlay turned and walked back to Sandy Alexander, whispered something in his ear, then rang teaspoon on glass for silence again.

Sandy looked down at the floor for a few moments.

Then, in a voice that was close to breaking, he turned to his daughter and son-in-law to be, raised his glass to them, and said, "To Pamela and Ross."

"Pamela and Ross!" echoed around the room.

Sandy next raised his glass to Kate in a quiet salute.

Kate raised hers in return. Turning to Cameron she said, "You don't mind taking the wedding photos, do you."

"No," Cameron said, smiling at her and looking like he was trying not to laugh.

"What is it?" she asked.

"You're glowing."

"It's just great to think about doing something that'll make people happy, rather than worrying about having to do something that'll make them sad. And besides, I'll get to arrange a wedding. Even if it isn't my own."

"Now it's my turn to say I hear the sound of distant violins."

"A whole string orchestra," Kate said, laughing at herself as she said it.

"Are you sure you can afford to do all this?" Cameron asked.

"It won't cost much. The more I thought about it, the more I realized we already have pretty much everything we need. We can put on a pretty fantastic meal with food from the estate—salmon and venison and the like. Finlay plays the pipes, so we'll have music; and we've got a great venue right here in the banquet hall. It's exactly the sort of thing it was built for, after all." Thinking about the wild flowers Cameron had given her, she said, "We've even got flowers for the bouquets."

"Sounds like you've got it all thought out."

"Not the details, but I'm excited at the thought of working them out, too."

"You seem to be a bit of a natural at this," Cameron told her.

"What?"

"Planning weddings."

"It's not that, it's just that everything we'll need is right here in the glen . . ." Kate's voice trailed away after she said that, and her expression changed from one of excitement to a much more thoughtful look.

"Just thought of a snag?" Cameron asked.

She shook her head.

Cameron couldn't work out what she was thinking of, so finally he had to ask. "What is it, Kate?"

The excitement returned to her face, and there was even more of it than there had been before. "I think it could be the bright idea I was looking for. The one that just might save Greystane and Glen Cranoch and the people in this banquet hall."

"I don't follow."

"Weddings, Cameron! Think about everything you need for a wedding, and we've got it in Greystane and The Cranoch. We've got a chapel for the service; a banquet hall you can hold a dance in; flowers; food; a dozen fantastic places for taking the most romantic of photos . . ." She was so excited that the words weren't coming out in any particular order. "It's all here, Cameron, right here."

Cameron thought about it, then said, "I don't want to put a damper on things like Archie Cunningham was doing all night, but unfortunately 'here' is the middle of nowhere. It's an ideal, convenient location for people who live in the glen, but beyond that—"

"You've obviously never read a wedding magazine."

"You've got me there."

"People get married in Mauritius, the Seychelles, the Maldives—they want somewhere remote and romantic. And let's face it, where are you going to find anywhere more romantic than a Highland glen with a castle on a crag?" She was on a roll. "It's like that crofter shouted out from the back of the hall: us Yanks love places like this. Everybody laughed at him, but he's right. We are suckers for this sort of thing. In the States our idea of history starts about 200 years ago, and an old building is one that dates to 1900. Millions of us can trace our roots to this part of the world, and we're curious about what it's like, about where we come from. We long to see it for ourselves, get in touch with the romance of it, the wild beauty, the pride and passion—to feel that those things are part of where we came from, and so a part of who we are. All those things are here, Cameron, in spades and for real, not in some made-up, theme park version.

"And besides, it really is the best of both worlds. It looks remote, like it belongs to another time, but there's an airport not even an hour's drive away."

"Sorry to play the part of Archie Cunningham again, but what he said about the problems that stop it being any good as a hotel still follow for what you have in mind. You're right about the banquet hall being designed for things like weddings and dances, but back then the guests were locals who could walk back to their cottages at the end of the night. You couldn't offer to put dozens of wedding guests up in Greystane, because there's nowhere for them to go."

Kate thought about that for a few moments, and a smile crossed her face. "The answer's in what you just said about how the guests would go back to their cottages after parties in the old days. I'm guessing the crofters of The Cranoch are always looking for ways of making money—they'd be glad to offer bed and breakfast. And can you imagine how American wedding guests would feel at the thought of being able to say they'd stayed in a Highland croft rather than in some bland, chain hotel? Maybe we could even renovate some of the old township crofts around the lochan, Cameron."

Archibald Cunningham chose that moment to came over and say goodnight. Before he could open his mouth, Kate said, "Ah, Archie, just the man."

He looked taken aback—he'd seen Kate crying and dejected; he'd never seen her looking anything like this.

"I think I might have an idea for saving The Cranoch," she told him.

The lawyer raised his eyebrows, and before he could

ask what the idea was, Kate was telling him. The words were the same as the ones she'd used to explain things to Cameron, but again they came out in a jumble rather than in any particular order. Archibald Cunningham didn't interrupt her, sensing that he wouldn't have had a chance of getting a word in edgeways no matter how hard he tried.

Once Kate finished, the lawyer thought over what she'd said.

"What do you think?" Kate asked him. When he didn't answer right away she said, "Come on, Archie, what do you think?"

"I think it might work . . ."

Kate was almost jumping up and down.

"But—"

"Don't dare make this a big 'but,' Archibald Cunningham."

"It's not a small one, but it's not insurmountable. It'll just take some thought to get around it, that's all."

"What is it, Archie?"

"Your product is a winner, I'm sure of that. It's just that it's a niche product, and to sell enough of it you'd really have to get your act together when it comes to putting it out there in the marketplace."

Kate took some deep breaths, trying to get her head together. "There are ways to do it. There have to be."

"Aye, well, remember that people plan weddings a fair while in advance."

"But they also pay deposits well in advance," she

pointed out.

"You're determined to make this work, aren't you?" Archibald Cunningham said.

"Yes, I am."

"I hope I made it clear that the estate can't keep going much longer. You don't have much time, Lady Kate."

"I'll buy as much time as I can. I'd sell my share in Kate's Crafts without a second thought if I believed there was a realistic chance to make The Cranoch a going concern, rather than just keep it staggering along on its last legs for another few months."

"If you feel that strongly, it might just be worth giving it a go."

"It is worth it, Archie. More worth it than anything else I've ever tried to do."

"Well, let me know how I can help," he told her. "And let them know, too." He pointed at the crofters, who were enjoying the food that had earlier lain untouched. "They're resourceful and they have skills and talents you might not expect."

Kate smiled, shook his hand, and then gave him a parting peck on the cheek.

When Archie had gone she turned to Cameron and said, "You could be a big part of this, too. You said you thought being a freelancer might not pay. Well, how about doing the wedding photos—not just for this marriage, but for all the others that, with a bit of luck, will follow. It might help you to stay in the glen, rather than have to look for a dull job and a flat in Inverness."

Cameron didn't say anything.

"Somehow I get the impression you're not completely sold on the idea," Kate said, unable to keep the disappointment from her voice.

"I think your idea's great, and there's a chance it could work. It's just my part in it that I'm not so sure about."

"Why?"

"It's like you were saying last night, about not being able to do sculptures any more; that's what I'm like with taking photographs of people."

"You'll mellow out once you have a few of these inside you," Kate said, holding up her glass.

"And besides," she smiled demurely, "maybe if you fall in love yourself you'll have a greater empathy with your subjects. I'll have to see what I can do about that."

Sandy Alexander and his family came over before Cameron could respond to that. Gesturing to Pamela and Ross, Sandy said, "They've got something they want to say to you, Lady Kate."

"We want to thank you, Lady Kate," Ross said.

"You're most welcome," Kate told him. Looking at Pamela as well, she added, "Don't ask me how I know this, but something tells me you're going to be very happy together."

The young couple blushed and turned to leave. Sandy hung back to say, "Once again, Lady Kate, my heartfelt thanks."

"Actually, Sandy, it's me who should be thanking you," Kate told him.

CHAPTER 13

KATE AND CAMERON STARTED BECOMING MORE THAN simply friends in the days that followed, and Glen Cranoch became their home. There were times when they forgot about the world outside the glen, and there were moments when they forgot about everyone else in the world except each other.

Cameron phoned the various contractors who'd given estimates for renovating Jamie's Cottage, picked one who could start doing the work immediately, and helped out as an extra laborer.

Meanwhile Kate set about her new role as a wedding planner with enthusiasm and excitement, using the forthcoming marriage of Pamela and Ross to gain experience of putting together the kind of package that would be her product. With help from Miss Weir—whose inspired suggestions revealed unfulfilled dreams of love and marriage and a hitherto well-concealed romantic side—Kate set about compiling a list of all the ingredients for a fairytale wedding. The next stage involved Finlay as well as Miss

Weir—the three of them went through the list, working out what the estate and its people could provide, and what would have to be sourced from further afield.

Their lives soon fell into a pattern. They got up early and breakfasted together in the kitchen. Finlay found an extra couple of stools, and Miss Weir took it upon herself to feed Cameron up as he was obviously "another sufferer of that dyslexia nervosa".

After that Cameron walked to Waterfall Bridge with Kate at his side and Hamish scampering along just ahead of them, setting the pace. It was a slow pace but they didn't mind because there was so much to enjoy in the surroundings and each other that they didn't want to hurry.

Kate and Hamish turned back at the foot of the steps cut into Jamie's Crag. Cameron climbed them and got things ready for the workmen, or just sat outside the cottage and looked out over the lochan and the dramatic sweep of the hills on either side. His favourite mornings were the ones when there was a mist over the water and the hillsides were hidden, with only the rocky summits visible. At such times he could imagine he was looking at little islands in the sky and he'd feel a swelling in his chest at the beauty of it, a peace in the present that was so different from what he saw when he looked into the past.

By the time the workmen arrived at the cottage Kate was back in the study at Greystane, scribbling down a list of things to do for the day and then working her way through it. Before long she'd head down to the kitchen to seek the advice of Miss Weir about something or other. As often as not she'd stay there for the rest of the morning, discussing solutions to little difficulties, embellishing ideas—and sharing a pot of tea and plate of scones. She found an empty cardboard folder in Colin Chisholm's old bureau and neatly printed WEDDING PLANS on the front, but before long it was bulging at the seams and she had to appropriate one of his black family tree ringbinders to accommodate her wedding planner's file.

Just before noon Finlay would appear by magic at the kitchen door, as often as not with a fish for the pan or a rabbit for the pot. He'd announce his presence with a not too subtle cough, or a peeved, "I'll just see to my own lunch," and Kate and Miss Weir would look up from a table covered in files and folders, empty mugs, and crumb-filled plates.

After hastily clearing the table they'd prepare a sandwich for Finlay and lunch hamper for Cameron and the builders.

Hamish would be waiting for Kate outside the kitchen or at the door in Greystane's walls and they'd take the path to the right, down through the forested hillside to Waterfall Bridge. Kate would set the wicker basket down at the foot of Jamie's Crag and lift Hamish up on top. Then, with the hamper cradled in both arms, and Hamish perched on top of it, she'd climb the rough-hewn stairs.

If Cameron was outside the cottage Kate would just stand there for a little while watching him work with pick or shovel, mason's hammer or bricklayer's trowel—enjoying the sight of him stripped to the waist, loving the play of the lean muscles in his arms and across his back—and usually it was a bark from Hamish that alerted him to her presence.

If Cameron was working inside, he'd hear Kate calling "Lunchtime!" through the doorway. She'd hand a flask of tea and bag of sandwiches to the workmen, and keep another flask and some sandwiches for herself and Cameron. Then, with Hamish in her arms, she'd lead the way down Jamie's Crag while Cameron followed with the hamper.

Sitting on the parapet of Waterfall Bridge, with the crags on either side and the lochan shimmering below in the mid-day sun, they'd recount the morning's little problems and how they'd been resolved, and discuss the challenges that lay ahead and how they might be overcome. Sometimes they'd talk about the beautiful things around them; sometimes they'd just look at those things and listen to the water running beneath their feet and cascading into the glen below, not feeling the need to speak because the timeless sound of river and waterfall said it all.

Then, with the food eaten and the tea drunk and no more excuses for not doing the things that still had to be done, Kate and Hamish would head back up Castle Crag to Greystane, while Cameron climbed the steps back up to Jamie's Cottage.

The next time they saw each other was in the hour before sunset, just after the builders left. Cameron was usually tidying up for the day when he heard Hamish's welcoming bark. Looking out of window or doorway he'd see the little white terrier scampering towards the cottage.

Then he'd look beyond Hamish, to the edge of Jamie's Crag, and his chest would tighten while he waited for Kate Brodie to appear. In those moments he'd wonder what she'd be wearing—the blue-and-white striped T-shirt, maybe; the cream roll-neck sweater, or the pale blue cardigan with the sleeves pulled a little way up her slender forearms; the faded jeans that showed off the length of her legs, or the peasant skirt that gave even more grace to her movements—and his breath would catch in his throat at the first flash of her hair, not white gold as it was in the morning but a darker gold in the light of the setting sun.

She'd tell him how her day had gone, sometimes in a slightly subdued voice if there was a problem yet to be resolved; more often with the words tumbling out the way they do when you can't wait to say them to someone, and the someone you most want to say them to is standing right there in front of you.

Cameron would tell her about his own day by showing her around the cottage. At first—when the work was all about weatherproofing—it was the outside they walked around, and he'd proudly point to new roof slates or windows or repairs to the gables. But, as the days passed and the work progressed, he was able to show her things they were doing inside to turn the house into a home: one day pointing out the new partition walls of a bathroom, the next day a kitchen sink, and the day after that laughing along with her when he realized how proudly he'd been showing off the soil pipe for a toilet.

When Hamish started barking to let them know he was feeling left out or just plain hungry they'd head back to Greystane. The first few days they walked back hand-in-hand a little self-consciously. But, as the days passed, they began walking with arms linked, and one afternoon Cameron found Kate's arm around his waist, and she found his arm around her shoulders. Neither of them could say who'd reached out first, or when; each had acted without conscious thought, just feeling.

Dinner was eaten in the banquet hall. Although Miss Weir was now happy to serve breakfast for four in the kitchen, she made it clear she expected them to be seated in a more appropriate setting for the evening meals she took such a pride in preparing. The meal usually lasted the best part of an hour—not just because of all the food, but because of the conversation that followed it.

After thanking Finlay and Miss Weir and offering to do the washing up—an offer that was never accepted but always appreciated—Kate and Cameron would grab a couple of beers from the fridge and head up to the "lounge" to talk some more about the day just past or the one to come.

They never stayed up too late because the days were so demanding. Arranging the forthcoming wedding and putting together packages to offer in future left Kate exhausted mentally. Cameron was worn out physically from the effort of turning Jamie's Cottage into a home; stiff and aching from head to foot, he'd be ready to crash out by ten o'clock. For all the demands of the days, though, they never complained at night. Kate never said she had headaches, just welcomed the fact that she was no longer completely powerless to prevent the loss of Greystane and the spoiling of the glen. Cameron never mentioned his aches and pains, because they were a small price to pay for having the chance to rebuild his life, and live it next to Kate. Much as they enjoyed the challenge of the days, it was those nights they looked forward to most—the sharing of a sense of satisfaction, the easy conversation and comfortable silences, the simple pleasures of a cold beer and a warm fire.

At around ten o'clock they'd put the guard over the fire and climb the stairs to the next floor, then say goodnight with a kiss in the landing.

At first Cameron welcomed the moment when he turned out his bedside lamp and his head touched the pillow, so exhausted that he'd be deep in a dreamless sleep within minutes.

By the end of the first week, however, the heaviest work was done and his body was more accustomed to manual labor. That made the days easier but the nights hard, because sleep was more elusive. He still had thoughts he didn't want to be having, and that was the time it was hardest not to think about them: in the early hours of the morning when there was no sight or sound or distraction, no one to talk to about other things. Even when sleep finally came it was far from restful because it was filled by a harrowing mix of guilty conscience and nightmarish memories.

Kate noticed little differences in him as the days went

by: his smile wasn't so carefree or frequent; his laughter wasn't so loud or long-lasting; and, when he stared into the fire, his silences were more brooding than companionable. She wanted to ask what was wrong, what he was seeing when he looked into the flames, but realized he would only tell her when the time was right.

Although the time wasn't right for that, Kate soon felt it was right for something else. One night just before the wedding, when they got up from the fireside in the big room at the usual time, she lit a candle and said, "Cameron, there's something I want to show you." She led him up the flight of stairs to the bedrooms, and then up the next flight of stairs, too. It was different from all the others as it formed a tight spiral rather than a series of straight switchbacks, and opened in the center of a landing. The landing had four doors, one in the middle of each wall. Kate opened the one straight ahead, revealing a small room with an attic roof.

Cameron couldn't work out what it was she wanted to show him: there was a dark wooden chest of drawers and matching wardrobe on the left; and an ancient bed on the right, with what looked like a cupboard angled into the corner at its foot. He turned to look at Kate for an explanation after he'd looked around the room.

In a quiet voice, because she didn't want to wake Finlay in the room on one side or Miss Weir in the room on the other side, Kate gestured to the cupboard and said, "Open the door, Cameron."

When he did, he was surprised to see the stone steps of an even narrower, more steeply-pitched spiral staircase.

"Take this," Kate said, handing him the saucer with the candle in it.

The flame flickered in a cold draught as Cameron climbed the stairs. After a few steps the draught became a breeze. Four steps later he saw why: he was looking at the inside of a stone cylinder with a narrow slit in the curving wall—the interior of one of the little turrets that jutted from each corner of the square tower.

As he climbed the last two steps, Cameron heard the quiet roar of falling water from far below. A gust of wind blew out the candle when he stepped into the turret, but he barely noticed because by then he was looking through the slit in the thick stone wall. Then glen was sketched in quicksilver below and the sky high above was brightened by stars without number.

A suggestion of perfume on the crisp, clean air told him Kate was at his side. "I couldn't sleep last night," she told him. "It must have been the excitement of the wedding, the worry that maybe I've forgotten something. Anyway, I realized I'd never been up here, and got curious. I came up at midnight, and was blown away by what I saw."

Cameron could understand why. Looking up at the stars he was lost in the wonder at the dizzying thought that there were as many below the slowly spinning world he stood on as above, as many behind as ahead. Kate put her arm around his waist and he felt her hip brush his thigh as she moved closer to him, and in that moment he forgot all about the stars; all he could think of was Kate Brodie. She took the candle from him with her free hand and set it down on the floor. When she straightened up she put that hand around his waist along with the other one, moving them up his back until they were clasped behind his neck, drawing his lips down towards her own.

And then they were kissing, touching at hip and thigh as well as mouth.

They moved apart only to draw breath, and when they moved back together they were somehow even closer than before. Kate broke off to whisper in his ear, "Sleep with me tonight and every night, Cameron." Moving away, she said, "Five minutes, just give me five minutes. I'll leave my door open, and you don't have to knock."

Then she was gone and Cameron was alone in the tiny turret at the top of the tower, listening to the falling water and measuring time not by the sweeping hand of the watch on his wrist but by counting stars in the sky above, one for each second.

When he'd counted 300 stars he went down the stairs. Kate's door was ajar. He paused in front of it, feeling things he hadn't felt for longer than he could remember and had thought he might never feel again, and things he'd never felt before. Then he gently pushed the door.

For a moment he just stood there, his heart not able to beat.

Kate, too shy to have undressed in front of him, had

switched off the light and was standing barefoot on a sheepskin rug in front of the fire. Her back was to him and she was wearing only a white cotton shirt that reached half-way down her thighs. The tails of the shirt hung out at each side, so that even though she was facing away from him he knew that the shirt must be unbuttoned. The thin, pale material was translucent in the flickering glow of the fire, and her body was a silhouette half-seen in front of him, half-imagined in his mind.

"Kate," he said, not managing to say more than her name, and even that as little more than a whisper.

She turned and smiled shyly, hands clasped in front of her and hiding what the open shirt would have revealed. *It must have been as long a time for her as it has for me*, Cameron thought. He took a step towards her ...

And as he did so Kate forgot her inhibitions and opened her arms to him, the shirt spreading like gossamer wings, the flames of the fire backlighting her so that as much was left to Cameron's imagination as was revealed.

Kate put her hands up to his face and did something she'd longed to do since the first time she saw him—traced the hard line of his cheekbones with her fingertips. She let her fingers slide down his neck and inside his collar, undoing the buttons of his plaid shirt one by one before running her hands up over his lean stomach and well-muscled chest and then out over his shoulders, peeling his shirt away as they went.

Then her hands were moving down his back and

around his waist until her fingers were at his belt buckle. While she undid that, Cameron worked one boot off with the edge of the other and kicked off his socks.

Kate wrapped her arms and the folds of her shirt around him, hands clasped in the small of his back, drawing his hips into hers so that when they kissed all of their bodies were touching, not just the parts they kissed with.

The four-poster bed was only a couple of steps away but it might as well have been on the other side of an ocean; Kate didn't feel able to take one step, let alone two. Barely able to stand, she sank to her knees, drawing Cameron down with her. She said his name once in a voice she barely recognized as her own, and then couldn't say it any more because they were kissing. It was a kiss like no other she'd ever known, but instead of satisfying her it made her hungry for more.

Now she couldn't even kneel, let alone stand, had to take one of the hands that had been cupped behind his neck and place it palm down on the rug at her side for support . . .

And soon one hand was running through the sheepskin and the other was running through Cameron's hair because she was rolling over onto her hip and then on her back, and he was moving with her.

One moment the flickering amber glow from the fire was on her back, the next on his as they rolled and touched and moved until they were moved without moving, couldn't move any more, could barely even breathe.

And in those entwined moments there was no yesterday or tomorrow. There were no words except his name and hers, and all the other ones were forgotten in the learning of a new, unspoken, unforgettable language of feeling rather than thought, a language that had a thousand words for joy and laughter and none at all for what comes after, none at all for anything beyond the sheepskin rug and the dancing shadows of the fire.

In those entwined moments there were only two people in the world, and they moved and breathed and lived as one.

CHAPTER 14

WHAT HAPPENED IN THE WEEK THAT FOLLOWED LEFT Kate hurt and confused. Although she shared a bed with Cameron each night, there were moments when she knew he was having thoughts he couldn't talk about—and every passing day seemed to bring more of them.

At first she asked Cameron what it was he couldn't put behind him, what stopped him from opening up and moving on. She asked what he was looking at when she woke beside him early one morning and he was staring into the darkness with his eyes focused on something she couldn't see.

She asked what he was listening to when she came across him sitting on the cottage doorstep one afternoon and spoke his name and he didn't seem to hear.

She asked what he was thinking about one night when the gentle touch of her hand on his shoulder as they sat in the lounge startled him so much that it startled her.

And she asked why he'd been so unsettled by the purple napkin on the night of their first meal together; and why one evening in the cottage, when they were about to clear up after the builders, all the color left his face when she took out a purple scarf to wrap over her head and keep the dust out of her hair.

But each time she asked he just said, "I'm sorry, Kate," and finally she stopped asking what he was seeing or hearing or thinking about at times like that. Just as the good moments of love and laughter drew them together, so those other moments kept them further apart than they should have been.

Cameron understood Kate's hurt but was powerless to do anything about it. He couldn't tell her that the more he came to love her, the less he could contemplate sharing the future with her: she deserved a man who didn't carry around memories he was too ashamed to reveal to the woman he loved, a man who didn't have to avoid looking into his own eyes in the mirror when he shaved each morning, a man who wasn't un-nerved by the color purple.

He knew that Kate must wonder if his worries about their relationship had something to do with her, and being unable to tell her that the person he doubted was himself broke his heart. He couldn't tell her because his doubts weren't the kind you could share with another person—not if you wanted that person to respect you and feel safe with you, let alone live with you and love you.

Cameron was sure the things he'd have to tell Kate in order to close the distance between them were things that would drive them apart.

Any hopes he had that Kate didn't perceive the gulf between them as being as wide as he did were dashed one night just before the wedding. He was staring into the fire when Kate, who'd been putting together a seating plan for the reception, suddenly broke into his reverie by saying, "Cameron, would you sit for me?"

At first he didn't understand what she meant. But when she tore the seating plan from her clipboard to leave a blank sheet of paper, he realized she wanted to draw him. The troubled look slipped from his face and he smiled the quiet, boyish smile she loved so much.

Kate got out of the armchair, sat cross-legged opposite him, and began to draw. At first her hand moved quickly, and Cameron guessed she was roughing out general proportions and outlines.

But gradually her movements slowed, and as many involved a rubber as a pencil.

Finally she ripped the paper from the clipboard, her eyes filling with tears.

"Can I see it?" he asked.

She shook her head, screwing the paper up.

"What's wrong?" he asked.

"It's your face, Cameron. I couldn't draw your face. It came out like my statues, like a stranger."

He thought about telling Kate the things she needed to know to capture his true likeness. Then he thought about what the drawing would look like if she knew those things. He didn't like what he saw, and didn't think she would either, so he didn't say anything.

The silence between them sounded very loud, and seemed to last forever.

Finally Kate said, "I feel like you're rebuilding the cottage but not your life, Cameron. I thought I could help you, but you won't let me in. It's as though your life has rooms that you're scared to go into and rooms you sometimes can't get out of, and I can't help you do either because you won't give me the keys."

Unable to meet her searching gaze, Cameron looked into the fire instead.

"As long as there are doors that are locked we can maybe share a house, Cameron, but we can't make a home—and it's a home that I long for, and to share it with you. Why won't you let me in?"

"I can't," he said, still looking into the flames.

"Don't you trust me?"

"I'd trust you with my life, you must know that."

"That doesn't add up," she said, exasperated. "If you really trust someone you don't have secrets from them, things you're frightened to tell them."

"What I'm most frightened of is losing you."

"You're saying you want us to be together, but by shutting me out you're doing the one thing that's certain to keep us apart. Have you any idea how much it hurts when the person you most want to be close to holds you tight for a few moments each night, and then the rest of the time keeps you at arm's length? I want to share my life with you, Cameron, but I can't share my life with someone who's shutting me out of half of theirs."

"I'd give you the keys to the locked doors if I could, you have to believe that."

"What I believe is that if two people love each other then they're much stronger together than apart. I believe that together there's nothing they can't face."

"That's how it would be in an ideal world, Kate, but I've spent the last year learning that the world is a lot less than perfect, and that I'm one of the far from perfect parts of it. I can't forget that, and it gets harder to face you every time I remember it."

"God, Cameron!" she said, infuriated. "Part of me is mad at you, and part of me is crazy about you, and I don't know what to do."

He didn't know what to tell her.

For a few moments it seemed like Kate didn't know what to say, either. Finally she told him, "I'm going to Edinburgh tomorrow to pick up some stuff for the wedding. I think I'll stay overnight and hope that things make more sense when I get back, because they don't make any sense at all right now."

Cameron knew he was supposed to say something at this point, but didn't know what it was.

Kate sighed, then said, "I feel like part of you is a part of me, Cameron, but there's another part of you that's a complete stranger. Maybe when I get back you can introduce me to him."

Wanting hard work to occupy his mind while Kate was away, Cameron spent most of the next day on his hands and knees putting a new finish on the stone floor of the cottage. It was back-breaking work, and after it was done he collapsed into the rocking chair for a rest before the walk back to Greystane. Within moments he was asleep, and within minutes he was dreaming . . .

Hearing warlike whoops and taunts and ranting bagpipes all around, and the steady, disciplined beating of military snare drums in the distance.

Blackness gave way to misty grey, as if his eyes were adjusting to the lighting of the dream. Gradually the fog cleared to reveal rank upon rank of scarlet-clad troops barely a quarter of a mile away across a sleet-swept moor. Battle standards of crimson and mustard and green emblazoned with regimental badges fluttered above the lines of men, vivid against the leaden sky.

Without warning a thunderous series of booms from close by shook the ground beneath his feet and a sulphurous cloud engulfed him, stinging his eyes and burning his throat, leaving him blinking and blind, coughing and choking and deafened by a high-pitched ringing in his head.

A gust of wind blew the smoke away in time for him to see a salvo of round-shot arching towards the immaculately ordered scarlet ranks up ahead. Most of the cannonballs fell short but a few bounced and rolled far enough to topple some of the men like toy soldiers on a wargame board or pins in a bowling alley.

As if by magic the gaps were filled almost as soon as they appeared. Again as if by magic, grey puffs blossomed between the scarlet formations, followed by distant claps of thunder, as the Redcoat artillery opened up.

For a few moments nothing happened, and he thought their aim was badly off.

Then the sky was peppered with black dots that grew steadily larger and nearer, moving with deceptive slowness until they were overhead and then whistling past with an ear-splitting rush to land behind him. Each impact was marked by a dull thud that shook the earth beneath his feet, and followed by piercing screams of such agony that they sapped the strength from his legs and whatever courage had been in his heart.

A voice from near at hand shouted, "Stand fast!"

Another hoarsely commanded, "Fire!"

The guns around him roared out again, but there were fewer of them now. Even as the last one fired, the air to left and right was ripped asunder by another salvo of enemy roundshot.

A piper stopped in mid skirl, and there was another unconducted symphony of visceral screams.

There was no answer from the artillery around him now, just another barrage from the guns ahead. This time instead of the air being split above him it was shredded all around, as if by a swarm of angry bees. From the corner of his eye he saw men being knocked backwards, staggering forwards or sinking to their knees as if in slow motion, and as he turned to look he got a face full of someone else's blood.

He blinked warm blood from his eyes and spat it from his mouth just as a man to his right broke ranks to walk with reckless defiance and awesome courage towards the Redcoat lines. He wore dark plaid and a blue bonnet with white cockade. In his left hand was a small round shield of wood and leather, in his right hand he held a yard-long basket-hilted broadsword. Raising the sword behind his head, he shouted, "Wait no more, men of Clan Chattan!" Slashing the broadsword forward with a cry of "Life or death! Claymore! Claymore!" he charged without waiting to see whether the men behind him followed, as if sure they would storm the very gates of Hell if he asked them to.

Cameron hesitated but those around him did not, surging around him with shouts of "Life or death!" and "Claymore! Claymore!" so that while Cameron had lined up in the front row, he was in the second or third row of the charge.

The charge seemed to go on forever. On either side he could hear wordless cries of pain and hate and fury; from up ahead the earth-shaking thunder of cannon; and, all around, the high-pitched whistling of lead balls and jagged pieces of iron that shredded the smoke and indiscriminately splintered the wood of targe and musket stock, pinged off the steel of sword blade and pistol barrel, ripped into flesh and shattered bone.

The mix of mist and smoke shrouding the moor was so thick that he could no longer see how far he was from the Redcoat lines, but he knew they must be close because the thunder from up ahead was almost deafening now and even the bagpipes were drowned out and only heard in memory, in the music of the blood that bound the charging men like brothers.

With each stumbling, staggering step the shrieking swarm of lead seemed to grow more intense, the screams around him louder, the battle cries fewer and hoarser.

When another gust of wind cleared the smoke away he saw three ranks of mitred Redcoats barely twenty paces ahead of him. The first rank dropped in unison to one knee. Butts of bayoneted muskets slammed into their shoulders with a meaty slap audible even above the sounds of battle. The commander of "Fire!" was followed by a ripple of innocuous little puffs blossomed along the line, stabbed through here and there with brilliant orange flashes. A heartbeat later came the noise that went with smoke and flame—a succession of pops that was ragged at the start and end but almost a solid sound in the middle.

The next thing he knew he was tripping over a body and the air above him was singing with the deadly song of another swarm of vengeful bees. Looking up from where he'd fallen on the cold, wet heather he saw that most of the charging men charged no more.

Up ahead came the command, "Second rank, present arms!"

The next line of Redcoats shouldered their muskets.
"Fire!"

More puffs of smoke and spikes of flame...

Another Pop! Pop! BOOOOOOOOM!!! Pop! Pop!

More Highlanders falling as if they'd stumbled just like him, only never getting up again. There were so few clansmen left on their feet now that he had a clear view of the ranks of scarlet-clad soldiers they charged towards. He saw every detail vividly...

A Redcoat ramming a rod into the barrel of his musket, tall mitred hat on his head, white leather neck stock rising above his collar, broad belt and bandolier of buff leather over knee-length coat of scarlet with wide collar and cuffs of mustard yellow, mud-spattered grey gaiters cinched at the knee with black garters...

Another trooper next to him biting a cartridge open and spitting darkly to one side, his lips ringed with black powder...

A drummer beating time, chevrons sloping up his sleeve from wrist to shoulder, drum banded in red at top and bottom and criss-crossed with rope...

An officer with a black tricorn and silver wig, sabre in hand, looking down the line of his men and calling out, "Third rank, make ready... Present... Fire!"

More kilted men tumbling: one, barely more than a boy, hit by so much shot that he was lifted several feet of the ground and flung half a dozen yards backwards...

A young man caught in the shoulder by a musket ball

and spun around, like a rag doll doing a grotesque parody of a pirouette, with an accompanying shower of crimson blood . . .

Another hit square in the forehead and stopped literally dead in his tracks.

The few remaining clansmen were almost at the first rank of kneeling soldiers now, flailing and hacking with boundless fury but falling victim to Redcoat bayonets before their unblooded claymores could land a telling blow.

A cry of "Dunmaghlas!" from close behind announced another charge, and moments later more kilted warriors were rushing past him. Unable to make himself get up off the heather to join them after witnessing the full horror of what had happened to the first wave, he just watched as the charging men stumbled over the bodies of fallen friends and kinsmen before being stopped in their tracks by another rolling volley. At least half of the Highlanders went down, and those who remained on their feet just stood there for a moment that for many was a lifetime, too proud to go back but unable to force themselves forward into such a ferocious weight of shot. Some shook their swords in desperate frustration or reached down to pick up stones to throw in helpless rage. Others raised their plaids over their heads and tried to shelter behind the tartan.

One held high the gold and scarlet colors of the clan, but the next volley turned him this way and that before driving him from his feet and dumping him halfway between Cameron and the Redcoat ranks. Cameron thought the clansman was dead, but then the standard shivered as the man tried to lift it. His body heaved and fell back with a shudder. Seeing Cameron out of glassy eyes, the standard-bearer said, "Jamie, the colors . . . Save the colors."

Cameron just lay there, looking at him.

"The day's lost," the fallen Highlander croaked, "but at least save the col—"

The voice was drowned out by another volley.

Cameron jumped in the chair. He came half awake before falling back into the dream.

He was up and running now, but away from the gunfire, screams, and moaning rather than towards them. His right shoulder throbbed as if he'd been struck with a red-hot sledgehammer. Pain spread out from it in pounding waves that almost sickened him, each one blacking his vision with a pulsing darkness that he struggled to blink away.

The dream kaleidoscoped into a nightmare of pursuit and concealment:

Running through trees with the branches whipping his face; tripping over roots; hiding behind trunks.

Splashing through fast-flowing icy water, teeth chattering, shivering uncontrollably.

Struggling to get over waist-high dykes and then sheltering behind the drystane walls with heart in mouth as he listened to the hoofbeats of mounted men, the creaking wheels of gun carriage and baggage wagon, the regimented footfalls of marching men . . . Holding his breath or burying his head in his plaid and biting the folds of wet wool to stifle cries of pain until the only sounds were the light patter of raindrops, the heavy pounding of his heart and a moaning that he thought was the wind until he tried to move and the moan turned into a howl of agony that issued forth from his own wind-chapped lips.

Then there was blackness and silence, finally broken by a gentle but insistent sound: *Tap* . . .

Tap-tap . . .

Tap-tap-tap—

Cameron woke up and for a few moments could almost feel his eyes smarting and taste acrid smoke in his throat, feel his chest heaving and a strange numbness in his shoulder. There was a ringing in his ears, and another sound, too . . .

Tap . . .

Tap-tap . . .

Tap-tap-tap.

It came from the window. He turned to face it with dread, unsure of what he was about to see.

An owl was perched on the outside sill, pecking at the glass with its beak. As Cameron watched, the bird turned and spread its wings and was gone, leaving him to wonder if it had ever really been there at all.

By the time he got back to Greystane his eyes were no longer stinging and his throat was clear. The echoes had gone from his head, and the feeling had come back to his arm.

But the whole thing was still so vivid that it seemed much more like a memory than a dream.

CHAPTER 15

KATE WAS ONLY GONE FOR ONE DAY, BUT CAMERON MISSED her more than he would have believed possible.

When she appeared in the doorway of the cottage the next afternoon he felt the same thing as the very first time he saw her, but even more strongly. Earlier that day he'd picked her some flowers and put them in a vase of lochan water, and after the hug he broke away to hand them to her.

She kissed him and said, "They're lovely, Cameron."

"They're from the stranger you wanted to get to know."

"Are you ready to tell me something about him?"

"I can tell you that he loves you very much."

"I need to know more than that, Cameron. He's tall, dark and handsome—but there are times when I feel like that's all I know about him, and that's just enough for a crush, not for lasting love."

Cameron took a deep breath, hesitated, and said, "Have you ever heard of Srebrenica?"

The name was vaguely familiar to Kate from TV news programs. However they were the kind of reports she tended to quickly switch over because they were so grim. "I've heard of it," she said, "but I've no idea what happened there."

"Something terrible," he told her. "Not unlike what happened here in Glen Cranoch all those years ago, I suppose—except that there were people in Srebrenica who could have tried to stop the terrible thing happening, who should have tried to help the people who couldn't help themselves."

"And they didn't?"

"No. They didn't fight the battle that needed to be fought because they were outnumbered and thought it was a battle they couldn't win."

"Was the stranger one of them?"

Cameron shook his head.

"Then I don't understand."

"The stranger had his own private Srebrenica, Kate."

"I'm afraid you've lost me."

"I'm afraid I'll lose you for good if I try to explain."

"The one thing that's certain is that you'll lose me for good if you don't at least try."

Still he hesitated, and Kate felt her heart breaking at the depth of his anguish and at the knowledge that she might be losing him forever.

Then he seemed to come to a decision. "Take a seat, Kate," he told her.

"Because it's a long story or because it's one that's going to shock me?"

"Both."

Filled with dread, Kate sat in the old rocking chair

beside the fireside.

Unable to look her in the eye, Cameron stared into the blackened hearth, hands resting on the slate mantelpiece. When he finally started speaking, Kate thought it was as though he was thinking aloud rather than talking to her. "I'd always been afraid of finding myself in a situation where I'd have to act like a soldier as well as just dress like one," he said. "The uniform might have fitted me perfectly, but I wasn't at all sure *I* measured up to *it*. My own little Srebrenica was the day I found out that I didn't."

He was quiet for such a long time that Kate finally said, "What happened?"

"I'd been sent out in a Land Rover with a squaddie driver to a village called Vorce to take some photos."

He fell silent, as if lost somewhere closer to there than here and then than now. Again Kate had to prompt him. "Photos of what?" she asked.

Her voice brought him back to the present. "There were rumours that a whole lot of people had disappeared from the village, so I was looking for evidence of an 'ethnic cleansing'. It's amazing how two words can describe an infinity of cruelty and suffering, isn't it?" he said.

"Anyway, the Land Rover broke down about a mile short of the village: close enough to see the cluster of whitewashed walls and red tile roofs, but not quite close enough to make out individual houses. It appeared to be a tranquil scene until I studied it through a pair of binoculars while the squaddie looked at the engine of the Land Rover. Most houses were undamaged, but others had blackened patches on the walls and ragged shell-holes in the tile roofs. A few were almost gutted.

"The pristine homes would be the ones Serb families had been living in, I guessed.

"The damaged dwellings would be the homes of ethnic Albanians who'd been driven out.

"The gutted ruins would have belonged to Albanians who'd refused to leave; old people who were too frail or weary or proud to flee the fury that had been unleashed in the valley. These were the houses I'd been sent to photograph, because the word was that the people who'd once lived in them had died in them. The chances were that the people who actually pulled the triggers would never be brought to justice, but my photographs would provide evidence for an indictment against the Serb commander who'd either ordered the killings or done nothing to stop them."

Cameron was still looking at the hearth, but Kate got the feeling he was seeing the blackened stones of Vorce.

"The late afternoon sun streaming over my shoulder had a modelling effect, casting dramatic shadows, making straights lines stand out with razor sharpness and throwing even small things into stark relief," Cameron said, obviously remembering the scene in every detail. "It was perfect light to capture the horror of what had happened there: the gutted shells would have a depth that made it clear people once lived in them; the last remaining traces of their everyday lives would be recorded—the little things that showed these ruined houses had once been homes.

"I knew there was only about an hour of that light left. When I asked the squaddie how long the Land Rover would take to fix, he said 'about an hour.'

"I looked at the road leading to the village, trying to work out how long it would take to walk along it. Twenty minutes at the most, I thought. I could get there and take my shots before the light faded."

"Wasn't it a bit risky going into a place like that alone?"

"It was against standing orders to go *anywhere* alone, but the alternative was to wait for the Land Rover to be fixed, and by then the light would be gone. I'd have wasted the afternoon and would have to spend the next morning making the same journey again. It would be about noon when I got there, and the sun would be high in the sky or obscured by clouds. Either way the light wouldn't have been as good as it was that afternoon. It seemed crazy to be so close and just turn back, so I told the squaddie I'd walk to the village and grab the shots I needed while he fixed the Land Rover."

"That took guts, Cameron."

"No, it didn't. I knew there weren't any Serb paramilitaries or regulars within 20 miles of the village. According to all the intelligence it had been 'freed' by the Kosovo Liberation Army. Any men with guns would be ethnic Albanians, and I thought they'd be glad to see someone taking pictures that showed what had happened to their friends and families, photos that would help bring those responsible to justice."

"Seems like sound logic, so what went wrong?"

"The fact that logic had long since ceased to apply in Vorce and a thousand other places like it . . . The fact that even after all the things I'd seen I was still so naïve it never occurred to me that the survivors would be hell-bent on taking matters into their own hands, evening up the score without counting the cost or distinguishing between right and wrong, good and evil."

He fell silent, then turned from Kate back to the hearth and said, "I'd counted five burnt-out houses when I first looked through the binoculars. Photographing the first four was perfectly straightforward. The light was as dramatic as I'd hoped, and I hardly even had to think about how to make the most of it.

"I was looking around the ruins of the fifth house when I heard a vehicle approaching. Thinking it was the Land Rover, I walked over to the door, ready to flag the squaddie down. But, as I approached the doorway, I realized the sound was coming from the wrong direction. I began to get a bad feeling, and crouched down in the shadows to one side of a broken window.

"The engine-beat grew steadily louder, then changed pitch, and I could tell that the vehicle was coming to a halt just outside the house I was hiding in.

"Moments later came the squeal of badly-worn brakes. It's a sound I still hear in my sleep. If I'm lucky I wake up in a cold sweat at that point."

"And if you're not lucky?"

"The nightmare continues, and I relive the rest of what happened in Vorce," he said.

Kate thought his voice sounded almost like that of a stranger, an automaton. She had to wait so long to hear it again that she thought she was going to have to ask him what did happen next, but he started to answer her question just before it was asked. "An old truck passed by the window," he said. "It was moving so slowly I had time to make out a mud-streaked, maroon-colored cab. There were two men in it, both wearing the black berets and tiger-striped battledress of the KLA."

Now Kate sensed that although he was looking into the hearth of Jamie's cottage, he was seeing out of the broken window of a ruined house.

"Moments later the back of the truck came into view." He swallowed several times, as if fighting back a wave of nausea.

Kate's dread mounted. This time she didn't prompt him to continue.

But eventually he did. "There was a wooden-slatted cargo section of the sort that might have held cattle or sheep on their way to the abattoir in the days before the madness began," he said.

Kate had an idea what he was about to say, so that she was fighting back a wave of nausea herself even before she heard his next words.

"It wasn't the bewildered eyes of farmyard animals on

the way to the slaughterhouse that peered out from between the slats, though," he said. "It was the eyes of bewildered people. That's all I could see of them—just their eyes—but it was enough to know that some of the people in the cattle truck were old and some were young and some were men and some women, some resigned to their fate, others frantic with fear—"

"Oh, Cameron!"

Either he didn't hear her words or was far beyond the consolation they expressed. Whatever, he carried on in the same un-nervingly matter-of-fact tone of voice. "They weren't looking at me, but in my nightmares they are. In my nightmares they look straight at me without blinking, and when I wake from the nightmares I have the feeling that they're still staring at me, plaintively, accusingly, desperately." He swallowed, as if it was getting harder to force the words out. "Sometimes even long after I'm awake I can still feel them staring at me. I can't see them but they can see me. I know that they're watching me, judging me, damning me."

Kate got up from the rocker and put an arm around him. The touch of her arm startled him back from past to present and he looked at her with eyes almost as haunted as the ones he'd just been talking about.

"I'm sorry, Cameron, I didn't mean to bring all this back," she said.

"It's never gone away. I don't think it ever will," he told her, and Kate was glad when he looked away again because it was frightening and heartbreaking to see such a look in anyone's eyes, let alone in the eyes of someone you loved.

"Maybe if it hadn't been for the purple . . . The purple . . ."

"The purple what, Cameron?"

"The purple headscarf," he said finally. There was something so unsettling about his voice and expression that Kate let her arm drop and took a step away from him. She felt the same thing that she did when a movie became too scary for her and she had to switch channels. Only this time the fear wasn't contained in a little box that could be turned off and on at will.

"What headscarf?" she asked, filled with a mix of horrified curiosity and dread.

But Cameron was staring into the hearth and once more seeing the past rather than the present, and when he spoke it was to pick up from where he'd left off, rather than to answer her question. "The engine died just as the lorry disappeared from sight, and I knew it had pulled up outside the house next door."

He lapsed into silence.

"What did you do?" Kate asked.

He didn't answer right away. When he finally spoke it was in his own time, and Kate suspected that he hadn't even heard her question. "I crawled across to the side window," he said. "From there I could see the back of the truck. Sitting on the tailgate was a third uniformed man, machine gun at the ready, his back to me, guarding the human cattle.

"The doors on either side of the cab opened and the other two KLA men got out.

"They started walking towards the house next door. The driver unholstered a pistol. It was a Luger, and I remember thinking how appropriate that was. The other man unslung a shotgun. The driver banged on the front door of the house but there was no answer. He banged again, while the man with the shotgun made his way around the gable end, passing just a few yards from me.

"Just then, the back door of the house opened. An old woman in a black shawl and a purple... A purple..."

"A purple headscarf," Kate said.

Cameron nodded. "Yes, an old woman in a purple headscarf hurried out just as the man with the shotgun turned the corner.

"The man shouted something, but the woman—she must have been the last remaining Serb in the village—ignored him and started to hurry away.

"The man shouted again. I couldn't understand the words, but the tone of voice left me in no doubt that he'd shoot if the old woman didn't obey his command. She must have sensed the same thing, because she stopped and turned slowly to face the man with the shotgun—and me.

"The man gestured towards her with his gun, indicating the direction he wanted her to go in. When she didn't move he walked towards her, jabbing the muzzle into her side. I was close enough to see her wince and hear her groan.

"I knew that a good soldier would have drawn his gun at that point, and a good photographer would have raised his camera.

"A good man would have done something.

"But I also knew that even if I dropped the soldier with the shotgun there was a better-than-even chance I'd be shot by one of the others. So I didn't draw my pistol.

"And I knew that if I took a photo there was a chance the man with the shotgun would hear the shutter being tripped, and that he'd let me have both barrels if he did. So I didn't raise the camera.

"I just crawled on my hands and knees around to the front window, kneeling in the shadows and watching as the back of the truck was unhinged and the woman was herded towards it.

"There were a couple of moments when a brave man had a chance of taking out all three KLA fighters: the driver had holstered his Luger and was on his way back to the cab; the front-seat passenger had slung his shotgun and had both hands wedged into the old woman's behind, shoving her into the lorry; and the soldier on the tailgate was reaching out to grab the woman's shawl and pull her inside.

"Those were the moments when I found out that I wasn't a brave man, because all I did was watch."

"It was three against one, Cameron. You can't beat yourself up for not taking on those odds," Kate said. "You wouldn't have saved her life, just got yourself killed."

Cameron didn't turn to look at her, and she didn't

know if it was because he was too ashamed or if it was because he was so caught up in his memories of those awful moments that, again, he hadn't heard.

"I didn't even take a photo, even though there was little danger of being heard by then," he said. "If I'd had a photographic record of those moments I would have had to explain to others what I was ashamed to admit to myself. So I just listened to the bolt of the tailgate sliding home and watched the woman disappear into the shadows of a truck that I knew might well be making the same sort of journey as the ones that take animals to an abattoir."

Finally Cameron turned from the hearth at his feet to the woman at his side and said, "I didn't tell anyone what had happened, Kate, so there was no court martial or disciplinary hearing, no blemish on my service record.

"There was plenty on my conscience, though. At best I was guilty of dereliction of duty or conduct unbecoming. At worst I was guilty of outright cowardice.

"The one plea in mitigation I could offer in the court of my own conscience was the notion that maybe the old woman and the others in the truck were being taken to a prison camp rather than a place of execution. I wanted to believe that so badly that, in time, maybe I would have . . . If I hadn't seen the old woman's purple scarf again a couple of weeks later." Again he had to turn away from Kate.

"Where did you see it?" she asked.

He sighed heavily, then said, "At the bottom of an unmarked grave."

"Oh, Cameron!"

"I didn't feel fit to wear an officer's uniform after that so I resigned my commission, and wasn't pressed too hard to explain the 'personal reasons' I'd cited for doing so because my term of enlistment was almost up.

"I had vague notions of trying to make a living as a nature photographer in wild and lonely places, as far away from people as I could get. Then the telegram from Archie Cunningham arrived out of the blue."

"And you came to Glen Cranoch to see if Jamie's Cottage was the sort of place where a fresh start could begin."

He nodded. "Life's not that simple, though, is it?"

"Cameron, the evil men are the ones who drove former friends and neighbours from their homes, not the ones who didn't sacrifice their lives in vain for strangers they couldn't even have saved."

"Who was it who said that all it takes for evil to prevail is for good men to stand by and do nothing?"

"Probably somebody who'd never been in a position where stepping forward would cost him his life," Kate said. She tugged Cameron's arm so that he faced her, and said, "You have to move on, Cameron. Dwelling on the past just screws up your future, and you deserve better than that—and so do I."

"It's not that simple."

"I understand that it can't be easy, but not why you think it's impossible."

"I can tell you why, Kate: it's the knowledge that if

I found myself in the same situation again I probably wouldn't handle it any better than I did the last time."

"You don't know that."

"Deep down I do. Maybe it does run in the family."

"What?"

"A yellow streak."

"It took courage to tell me what you just told me."

"That's a different kind of courage."

"But a kind of courage all the same."

He didn't say anything.

"Cameron, in that village you probably acted just how anybody else would have acted in the face of odds like that—one pistol against a shotgun, a machine gun, and a handgun."

For a few moments he didn't respond. Then he said, "Kate, I wanted so badly to be the man of your dreams, because you're the woman of mine."

"Oh, Cameron," she said, hugging him.

When they moved apart, she saw that the unhappiness was still there in his eyes. "Cameron," she said, "Miss Weir told me something a few days ago, when she saw how worried I was about what would happen if I had to sell the estate. She said, 'You can't take the weight of the world on your shoulders or it'll crush you'."

"I should have tried to carry that old woman's share, though," Cameron said.

"If you want to carry more than your share, how about helping me carry the weight of a little part of the world, a beautiful part that won't stay that way if I have to hand it over to the people who want to take it from me."

"You know I will, Kate."

Again he was quiet, and she could tell how deeply troubled he still was. "I'm sorry for the old woman, Cameron," she told him, "but I'm not sorry that you didn't do something that would have got you killed, because then I wouldn't be able to do this . . ." she ran a hand through his hair, brushing it back from his brow.

"Or this . . ." she hugged him even harder.

"Or this . . ." she kissed him.

CHAPTER 16

"So, Kate, do you think you could do this on a regular basis?" Cameron asked.

The wedding reception was in full swing. Miss Weir's meal had been thoroughly enjoyed; everybody from the happy couple to Kate Brodie and, somewhat bizarrely, Bonnie Prince Charlie, had been toasted; the table top had been cleared and propped against the wall beneath the portraits, and now the old hall was echoing to a joyful bagpipe tune played by Finlay McRae and the carefree "heuchs!" of a Highland reel.

Kate nodded in answer to the question, thrilled by what she was seeing.

Cameron smiled and for some reason they both laughed, enjoying the feeling of getting closer to each other rather than slowly drifting apart.

Kate turned to look back at the wedding party: at the dancing men with their kilts constantly threatening to reveal all but somehow stopping just short of stopping short, their Braveheart shirts with lace-up fronts instead of buttons, their hands held high above the head when their arms weren't swinging partners away from them with wild abandon or drawing them close enough to kiss.

And the women beautiful in their baggy-sleeved white linen arisaids, black velvet waistcoats, and long tartan skirts, dancing the way people do when their forefathers have written the music and their fathers are playing it and they understand what every note of it really means.

Kate looked at the flush of youth on even the oldest faces, thought that too often people forget how to have fun as they grow older, and that the dances were a way of remembering. Even those who simply stood and watched weren't just wallflowers because they stamped their feet and clapped their hands in time to the music.

She looked at Pamela and Ross, seeing the happiness of two young people who believe everything is possible except disappointment, who were just starting to realize that it was all ahead of them and that there was no reason why much more of it shouldn't be good than bad if you had someone to share it with.

And she looked at Sandy Alexander, "tired and emotional" already, as happy as his son-in-law and daughter put together although far more of life was behind him than ahead.

She heard the windows rattling, felt the floor shake beneath her feet, saw the chandelier swinging from side to side above her head, and said to Cameron, "There's nothing I'd rather do than this, nowhere in the world I'd rather be."

Finlay stopped for a break and another whiskey, the dancers stopped to get their breath back, and Kate turned to Cameron again, saying, "I hope you can capture even a little of this in your photographs. It's just amazing."

"You've done a great job," he told her.

She shook her head. "I simply told people when and where to turn up. It's Miss Weir in the kitchen and Finlay on the bagpipes; it's the flowers from the glen, the chandelier on the ceiling, the portraits on the wall; it's the wild romance of the dances, and the fact that they're being danced in a banquet hall that has half a thousand years of history."

Finlay filled his bag and fingered the drones again, signalling the start of another dance. Watching the floor fill up, Kate said, "There isn't a girl from my part of the world who wouldn't want to get married in this little part of the world, Cameron." There was a sparkle in her eyes and real belief in her voice when she said, "This wedding thing really could work; maybe not well enough to make me rich in terms of money, but well enough to save the glen and safeguard the way of life of the people who want to live in it—and that would make me richer than any amount of money.

"The more I think about it, the more possibilities I see," she told him. "The crofters could make souvenirs—every guest's going to want them—and clothes for hiring: kilts and Braveheart shirts for the men, arisaids for the women—"

"I've got more than a few photos of you in yours," Cameron said. "You look every inch the Highland lady, Kate Brodie. You'd sell the outfit so well that people won't just hire it, they'll want to buy it."

Kate smiled with a different kind of happiness on hearing his words and seeing the look in his eyes when he spoke them. Suddenly she didn't just want to be organising the whole affair, looking on from the sidelines; she wanted to be one of the people doing the wild abandoned dance. She made her way down the hall—which almost involved a jig in itself to avoid the spinning, advancing, and retreating dancers—until she reached Finlay in the far corner. His ruddy cheeks puffed in and out, and his foot tapped to keep time as he played a happy Highland tune. Kate let him finish before whispering something in his ear.

The old Highlander smiled and nodded. He waited until the floor had cleared and Kate Brodic had returned to Cameron's side, then gathered his breath and filled first his lungs and then the bag.

As Kate led a surprised Cameron on to the dance floor, Finlay played the opening notes of her request. One of the loudest cheers of the day went up from the people of The Cranoch, not just because it was such a fine tune, but because of who was dancing to it. They all saw that Kate had taken the trouble to learn the steps, and they clapped and cheered her on. Finlay McRae, wearing a dark green beret with the Commando dagger badge on it, and a short kilt jacket bearing the ribbon of the medal he'd won with his bagpipes on a very different occasion, played like a young man again; Mabel Weir looked on, as full of pride as Finlay, because she was the one who'd taught the willowy American the steps of the dance that was making her life come alive; and the banquet hall of Greystane echoed to clapping hands and stamping feet, to breathless "heuchs!" and a tune called *The Waterfall Glen*.

When the music stopped there was applause for Kate and Cameron as well as Finlay, but the two dancers barely heard it because Kate had her head pressed tight against Cameron's chest and all she could hear was the beating of his heart; and Cameron was caught up in trying to think of how to ask her the question he suddenly wanted answered because he felt like he was holding all he'd ever wanted from life right there in his arms, and it was more than he'd ever thought he could have.

Before he could say anything, there was a loud shout of "FIRE!"

Instinctively Cameron looked over Kate's shoulder in the direction of the shout.

Kate turned and saw what he was seeing: one of the guests pointing out of the nearest window at a pall of black smoke rising into the cloudless late afternoon sky.

Already people were heading for the doors, not stampeding in panic because the smoke wasn't coming from Greystane, but hurrying in alarm because it came from down in the glen.

By the time Kate and Cameron reached the arched doorway in Greystane's outer wall the first guests had reached the bottom of the steps and were running to the edge of the crag. "It's Double Ecky's croft!" one of them shouted. "It's going up in smoke!"

Sandy Alexander hurried down the steps, Ross and Pamela standing dumbstruck for a moment before rushing after him, still holding hands.

When Sandy reached his croft it was already past saving, and the fight was all about stopping the fire from spreading to the cottages on either side.

By the time Kate and Cameron got there a chain had formed from the lochan to the cluster of white crofts at the foot of Castle Crag. Water was being scooped up in pails and iron cooking pots at one end of the line and thrown onto the flames at the other. Even the youngest children were helping out, running with the empty vessels from the cottages back to the lochan so they could be refilled and passed from hand to hand back up the line again.

The blaze was almost out by the time a fire engine arrived in the glen. Sandy Alexander, his wife, daughter, and new son-in-law were looking as gutted as the cottage, and their clothes and faces were almost as smoke-blackened as the stone walls.

Two of the firefighters unreeled the hose, and another two came up to the still smoking croft, ushering people back. The older of the firefighters asked, "Are there any gas cylinders inside?"

"Oh, Christ, aye!" Sandy said.

The fireman turned from Sandy to the crowd and said,

"Get right back, everybody! Right back!" Looking back at Sandy, he said, "Whereabouts is it?"

The father of the bride looked at him from glazed eyes.

"Whereabouts is the cylinder, man, and what's in it?" the fireman asked.

Responding to the urgent tone, Sandy said, "It's calor. Come on, I'll show you—"

The fireman stopped him with an outstretched arm and the words, "Your family could lose more than their house if you do that. Just tell me where it is."

Sandy pointed to the right of the ruined cottage, saying, "There, round the back."

"Inside or outside?"

"Outside."

"That's probably all that's stopped it going up already. Now go to your family and keep them back—and everybody else, too."

Sandy hesitated.

"You can help us or hinder us . . ." the fire chief said.

Sandy nodded and helped the other firefighter usher the crowd back. There was some reluctance until the firefighter told everyone exactly why it was better for them to get as far back as possible.

The fire crew trained the hose on the cylinder for a good ten minutes before moving it out of harm's way and venturing into the blackened shell of the cottage itself.

When the chief firefighter came out a few minutes later Sandy was the first to approach him. Before Sandy could say anything, the fireman said, "It was the chip pan. It's always either the chip pan or a cigarette butt."

Sandy looked at him, not understanding.

"Your wife must have left the cooker on and forgotten about it."

"We weren't making chips," Sandy told him. "We were at a wedding, my daughter's wedding."

"Maybe you weren't making chips, but the cooker must have been left on."

Sandy's wife, who'd been comforting Pamela, walked over and said, "The cooker was never on today—we were all too nervous to eat a bite."

"I've seen enough chip-pan fires before to know I've just seen another one now," the fireman told her. "With all the excitement of the wedding it would be easy to lose track of what you were doing," he added.

The racing engine of a vehicle approaching at high speed made them all look around. They watched as a dark green Range Rover tore along the track that ran by the lochan. It drew up with a screech of brakes beside the fire engine. They expected to see a couple of policemen get out, but instead it was a man in jeans and a sweatshirt. He grabbed a camera from the front seat and, not even bothering to close the door, hurried towards the crowd.

He stopped a dozen paces from the gathering, eyes darting from side to side until he saw the young girl with the tear-stained face and dress more black than white and the tall young man with his arm around her. He grabbed a couple of shots before the wrathful figure of Double Ecky started running towards him, followed by the taller figure of Cameron Fraser and half a dozen crofters.

The man scampered back to his Range Rover and drove off with wheels spinning and the door still open.

"What in God's name was that all about?" Sandy said, as they watched the Range Rover disappear towards the far end of the glen.

"An ambulance-chaser from Inverness who must have seen the smoke, by the looks of things," Cameron said.

Sandy sighed. "That's all we need—and Lady Kate, too."

"Right now it's the least of our problems," Cameron said. "Come on, we better see what we can do." He led Sandy back to the crowd. Kate was trying to comfort Mrs. Alexander, but looked as though she needed comforting herself.

Sandy took over from Kate, who stared helplessly at Cameron. He put his arm around her and she buried her face in his shoulder. He could tell from the shuddering of her chest that she was sobbing, and rocked her gently from side to side.

"Oh, Cameron, if only I'd let them have the reception in their house like they wanted to," she said. "Maybe there really is a curse, Cameron."

"There's no such thing as curses," he told her, trying to convince himself as much as her when he said it.

Then another Range Rover was drawing up at the head of the glen, not dark green but white with a bright orange stripe along the side and flashing blue lights on the roof. This time it *was* a couple of police officers who got out. They took statements from the firefighters about the cause of the blaze, then moved on to Sandy Alexander and his wife.

Kate looked at Cameron when she heard the police ask the couple if anyone had a grudge against them, "Should I tell them about Yeoman wanting to buy the estate?" she said to Cameron.

He nodded, and Kate approached the two policemen as they headed back to their Range Rover. "Excuse me," she said, "it might be nothing, but . . ."

She told them about Tony Carling and Yeoman Holdings.

"And did this Tony Carling make any threat against you?" the older officer asked.

Kate shook her head.

"Did he imply he'd harm anyone or anything in the glen if you wouldn't sell?"

"No, but he just acted like a bully," Kate said, aware of how lame it sounded.

"I'm sorry," the policeman told her, "but there's not a lot we can do unless he made some specific threats. To be honest, the chances are that Mrs. Alexander or her husband left the hob turned on and have either forgotten they did or are too ashamed to admit it. I don't think there's anything more sinister to it than that."

"Yes," Cameron said, "there is." He told the policeman about the other Range Rover that had entered the glen, and the man who got out of it.

"Did you get the licence number?"

Cameron shook his head.

"It was likely just a passing opportunist with a camera who saw the smoke and sniffed a picture in it."

"Bit of a coincidence, is it not?" Cameron said.

"Aye, but coincidences do happen. That's why there's a word for them."

"This jerk in the Range Rover just pulled up and took photos of the bride in tears and the house going up in smoke, then rushed off again," Kate told him.

"Not very tasteful," the policeman said, "but there's no law against it."

"It was almost like he knew there was going to be a fire," Kate said.

"Maybe he just knew there was going to be a wedding, and thought that would be a good story because it's been so long since the last one in Greystane."

Looking at the smoking cottage and the crowd of shocked crofters, the other policeman said, "He's got more of a story than he bargained for. The bride's house gutted on her wedding day—the poor lassie."

"Can we stop those photos being used if he takes them to a newspaper?" Cameron asked, thinking not just about the further distress their publication would cause to the Alexanders but about the harm it would do to the business Kate was trying to get off the ground.

"If you could find out who took them and what paper

he works for or sold them to, then you could ask nicely," the older policeman said. "But, quite frankly, I'd be surprised if you got anywhere; it's too good a story to pass up on, I'm thinking."

Cameron nodded, and put his arm around Kate again. They went over to see what they could do for Sandy Alexander, his wife, and the devastated newly-weds. However, neighbouring crofters were doing all that could be done, providing everything from words of comfort to more practical help such as beds for the night.

All their excitement of earlier in the day completely gone, Kate, Cameron, Finlay, and Miss Weir made their way slowly back up Castle Crag to Greystane, which seemed strangely quiet now.

Together the four of them set about clearing the banquet hall. There was no conversation, just the chink of china and crystal echoing from the old walls.

Kate and Cameron offered to help with washing the dishes, but Miss Weir shooed them away.

As Kate turned to leave, Miss Weir stopped her, saying, "Don't let what happened today put you off, lass. I think your idea is going to work."

Kate summoned a strained smile in thanks, but couldn't manage any words. With Cameron at her side, she headed through to the chapel.

"Miss Weir's right," Cameron told Kate as they walked behind the pews, towards the staircase. "I really think this whole thing could work, and I'm not just saying that because I know how much it means to you and the glen."

Kate didn't say anything.

"It's not just wishful thinking, Kate, or an attempt to cheer you up. Everyone was having a great time, and they're used to this sort of thing—they're not the kind of people who'd be blown away by the novelty and charm of it all," he said. "I'm so sure you're on a winner that I'll put up whatever money I have left to help you get it off the ground."

Kate smiled her thanks, then sighed and said, "I just feel so awful about what happened." She stopped in the aisle, which Pamela had walked down just a few hours earlier, and said, "Cameron, do you think it was an accident, or something more sinister?"

"It would be easier to believe it was just an accident if it hadn't been the bride's croft that went up in smoke, and if it hadn't been for that guy showing up with the camera, wouldn't it?"

"A whole lot easier."

"Of course, that could all just have been coincidence, like the policeman said."

Kate didn't answer. She didn't say anything at all until a few minutes later when she was sitting in the lounge with a stiff drink inside her and another in her hand. "There really could be a curse, Cameron," she said. "Maybe my family's fated not to be able to hold on to the glen. It would be a fitting punishment, given what they did to the people who once lived here."

"Kate, if the fire wasn't an accident then it was a dirty

trick by Yeoman, not the result of a curse from beyond the grave."

"It could almost be the same thing. Curses work through ciphers, don't they? Maybe Yeoman is a cipher for this curse."

Cameron put his arm around her. "I won't let anything happen to you, or the glen," he promised her.

"Maybe there's nothing you or anyone else can do—look what happened this afternoon. That's why a curse is so frightening, I suppose: you can't fight it. Or at least you can't fight it and win. You're powerless to stop it running its course."

Cameron wasn't sure what to say to that, and was glad to be saved by the ringing of the ancient Bakelite telephone.

Kate got up from the chaise longue and answered with a weary, "Kate Brodie."

She listened for a moment, then angrily said, "I'd rather not talk to you," and slammed the receiver down so hard the cradle almost broke.

"Who was that?" Cameron asked, never having heard her be so curt with anyone before.

"Some guy from *The Inverness Morning Herald*."

"What did he say?"

"'I believe you had a bit of a drama at a wedding in The Cranoch today'," Kate told him, before adding, "Vulture!"

"I don't want to interfere, but I think you should talk to him. Or, at least, let me talk to him."

"Why? Like I said, he's being a vulture."

"He would say he's just doing his job."

"Well, it's a pretty nasty job."

"That's beside the point."

"What is the point?"

"That he's going to write a story anyway, so it'd be better to have some influence on how it reads. I know from the PR stuff I did in the army that it pays to have good relations with the Press—they can either help you or they can crucify you."

"Well, in this case they're not going to help us. We needed good publicity, Cameron, not the sort we're going to get from this."

"Yes, but at least we can do some damage control. We can maybe also find out if the guy with the camera was a staffer or freelancer they regularly deal with, in which case the fire probably was just an accident and the photographer showing up probably was a coincidence. But if it was some mysterious third party who took the pictures, then the odds on accident and coincidence are a whole lot longer."

Kate thought about it for a few moments, then said, "Could you talk to him, Cameron? My head's spinning after everything that's happened today. I really can't think straight."

Cameron nodded and picked up the phone. He used 1471 for the callback service to get the newspaper's number, then asked Kate, "Do you remember the name of the man who phoned?"

"McLaren. Harry McLaren, I think."

Cameron dialled the number. When he got through to the newspaper switchboard he said, "I'd like to talk to Harry McLaren, please."

"One moment."

There was a click, then a twenty-Marlboro-a-day voice said, "Harry McLaren speaking."

"Hello, this is Cameron Fraser calling on behalf of Lady Kate Brodie. I believe you rang a few moments ago."

"I believe Lady Kate Brodie didn't want to talk to me a few moments ago."

"You called at a bad time."

"Can I ask exactly who you are?"

"My name's Cameron Fraser. I'm a friend and neighbour."

"Aye, well, thanks for calling back, Mr. Fraser. Somebody looked into the office here a short while ago, said they'd been driving past The Cranoch and saw smoke. Out of curiosity they went to see what was happening, and got some photos of a wedding party with the bride in a smoke-blackened dress. There are some quite dramatic shots. We just wanted to ask a few questions, fill out the story we're putting together to go with the photos."

"First of all, can *I* ask *you* a question: who handed the spool in?"

"He didn't leave a name or address."

"Not even for payment?"

"He told us to give any fee to charity, said he just liked taking photos for the fun of it."

Cameron didn't say anything.

"You're not suggesting there was any foul play, are you?" the reporter asked.

"I was just curious," Cameron said.

"Aye, well, we've been on to the police and fire brigade, and they've said no one was hurt in the fire and there are no suspicious circumstances. They've also said it happened during the wedding ceremony, and that the cottage of the bride's family was gutted."

"Yes, it was, so I'm sure you can understand how upset everyone is. Any chance you'd pull the photos?"

"None at all. As I'm sure *you* can understand, it's way too good a story. Especially given the other circumstances."

"What other circumstances?"

"You know, the curse that's supposed to be on the Chisholm family."

"The bride wasn't a member of the Chisholm family."

"No, but the wedding was held in Greystane, wasn't it, and we believe it was a trial run for a wedding business the Chisholm heiress is trying to start up."

"Where did you hear that?"

"Come on—no journalist worth their salt reveals a source. Anyway, I was just wondering if Lady Kate would like to make any comment."

"I'll have to ask her about that. Can I get back to you?"

"Of course. Ask for extension 3212."

Almost before Cameron hung up, Kate was asking, "What was that all about?"

"Better take another drink," Cameron told her.

"Why?"

"They're going to run the story and picture."

"It sounded like there's more to it than that."

He nodded.

"Well?"

"He knows you're trying to start a wedding business . . . And he knows about the supposed curse."

"How did he find all that stuff out?" Kate asked.

"I suppose the curse thing will be common knowledge, and the local journos will drag it out and dust it down at every opportunity—it's exactly the sort of thing that sells papers. As for the plans for a wedding package business, I'm guessing he was tipped off by the same person who 'just happened' to be driving past the glen after the fire."

"It wasn't a staff photographer, then?"

Cameron shook his head. "It really is starting to look like a dirty tricks campaign by Yeoman, trying to kill your wedding business plan stillborn with some bad publicity."

"Couldn't we tell that to this Harry McLaren? That'd be a good story in itself. Maybe the bad publicity for Yeoman would scare them off."

"We've nothing solid to back it up, Kate. A newspaper—especially a small one that doesn't have the resources to fight legal battles—wouldn't print an allegation like that without hard facts to substantiate it, and we simply don't have them. Besides, the curse aspect is probably a far better one as far as they're concerned."

"Like I said, Cameron, maybe they're one and the same story, anyway."

"If you honestly believe that, then you might as well just hand The Cranoch to Tony Carling on a plate."

"You know I'd never do that. What I'm frightened of is that I won't be able to stop him taking it."

"Kate, all the great ideas you've been telling me about for putting together a wedding package—using the resources of the glen, including the crofters—they all work. They create a chemistry that's really special. What happened before the fire today proved that, so the day's not been a total disaster."

"Tell that to Pamela and Ross. I tried helping them and look what happened because they got involved with me: the misfortune, bad luck, curse, whatever you want to call it, rubbed off on them."

"Sabotage is what I'd call it."

"Well that's not what the papers are going to call it."

"It's one paper, Kate, and a local one at that."

"If it is Yeoman behind this, I don't think they'll have stopped with a local newspaper. I wouldn't be surprised if they've fed the story to the national papers as well."

"Even if they have, it's not the end of the world. You said yourself that the main market is going to be overseas. I think the best thing we can do is phone Harry McLaren back and tell him the important thing is that nobody was hurt.

"Then we just have to move on: take the positives from today—the way your package worked so well—and think about how to sell your idea in the States, Canada, Australia, New Zealand; everywhere with ex-pat links to Scotland. I'll get our photos developed, and with a bit of luck there'll be some we can use for adverts in wedding magazines, Scottish interest magazines, clan society newsletters, that sort of thing."

Kate didn't say anything.

"It really can work," he told her. "It's a great product. It's just up to you to sell it—and I'll help in every way I can."

Kate managed a hint of a smile and squeezed his hand in thanks.

The phone rang once more, and she picked it up.

Cameron watched the smile die on Kate's face as she listened to the caller. There was no trace of happiness left by the time she said, "The only comment I'd like to make is that no one was hurt, and that's the most important thing."

There was a short silence while Kate listened to the person on the other end of the phone.

Then she said, "No, I don't believe there's a curse on my family," and hung up.

"Another paper?" Cameron asked.

She nodded, "And not just a local one this time."

CHAPTER 17

"So much for the old saying that any publicity's good publicity," Kate said disconsolately.

It was the morning after the fire. Cameron had driven her into Inverness for a paper and they were standing outside the newsagents, looking at the billboards.

The Northern Star billboard read:

BLAZE BLACKENS
BRIDE'S BIG DAY

The Inverness Morning Herald billboard was even more damning:

BRIDE HIT BY CURSE
OF THE CRANOCH

Kate sighed heavily. "I can't think of much worse publicity."

"Neither could Yeoman Holdings, apparently," said Cameron.

"I hate to think they can get away with something like this."

"They won't if you can make a go of the business and

hold on to the glen."

"It's going to be harder now than ever. I'll tell you something, though, it's made me more determined than ever."

Cameron saw the steel in her now, as well as the sweetness, and when he put an arm around her shoulder he was feeling admiration as well as love.

She put her arm around his waist and said, "Doing any work on the cottage today?"

"There's nothing that can't wait, though I'm longing for the day when I can say to you, 'Your place or mine'?"

"When you do, I'll say 'your place and mine'."

They laughed for the first time since the fire.

"If you've nothing planned today, how about helping me make up an advertisement to put in magazines in the States and Canada?" Kate asked. "It's like Archie Cunningham said: people organize weddings a long time in advance, so there's no time to waste."

Cameron nodded. He looked at his watch. "I've brought the spools from the wedding. The chemist should be open by now, so I could drop them off, we can grab a bite to eat, then pick them up and see if the photos have come out okay."

"I'm sure they'll be fine," she told him. "Better than fine."

"I really hope so. I'd love to be able to give Ross and Pamela something for an album, and you something for an advert. I just hope there's even one really nice shot."

"I'm sure there'll be a lot more than just one. I was watching you at work. When we first met I remember you told me you were scared of doing wedding photos because you didn't feel you could put people at their ease, or believe in what you were doing. Well, yesterday you looked like you were having as much fun as the guests."

"I have to admit I was getting quite into it."

"Think you'd like to do it on a regular basis?"

"Better wait until you see how these come out before you offer me the job," Cameron said, taking half a dozen plastic film canisters from his pocket.

He needn't have worried. A little over an hour later, after bacon rolls and coffee in The Piper's Arms, they went back to the chemist and picked up the cardboard folders of 9 by 6 prints. He'd ordered two sets, one to give Kate for promotional use, and one for the Alexanders. Cameron handed the first bundle to Kate, and started looking through the other one himself.

"Cameron, these are fantastic," Kate said as she flipped through the glossy photos.

He smiled with quiet pride, and said, "They're okay."

"They're a whole lot better than okay. This'll cheer the Alexanders up." She kissed him and whispered in his ear, "You're hired!"

When they got back to the glen they stopped off at the cottage Sandy was staying in, and handed in his set of photos. He looked through the first half-dozen pictures, then, without saying a word, shook Cameron's hand.

"How are Pamela and Ross?" Kate asked.

"Still sleeping."

"Sandy, I'm so sorry about what happened."

"Lady Kate, you've nothing to apologize for."

"The paper's are talking about the cur—"

"I'll make sure Ross and Pamela don't see them."

Kate was about to leave but, before she did, she couldn't help asking, "Sandy, do you think there really is a curse on my family?"

The little crofter couldn't meet her eye. Instead he looked down the length of the glen, at the deserted townships around the lochan and the abandoned church in the distance.

Kate put a hand on his shoulder and said, "Sorry, I shouldn't have put you in an awkward position like that."

Still not able to meet her gaze, he reached up and clasped her hand in his own.

When he finally looked at her, it was to say, "Does this mean you're going to sell up and go back to the States?"

Kate shook her head. "It means I'll have to work even harder to save the glen, though. Mr. Fraser and I are about to make up an advertisement to put in magazines around the world. Do you think Pamela and Ross would mind if we used one of their photos in it?"

Sandy Alexander's face brightened, and he said, "They'd be thrilled if you did."

"Meantime, is there anything we can do to help them or you?" Kate asked.

"It's okay, Lady Kate. Everybody's been so kind. They haven't let us want for anything. I don't think I could ever repay them."

"If the business works out like I'm hoping it will, you'll have repaid them a dozen times over," she told him.

When they got to Greystane, Finlay greeted them with an anxious look and a question: "You didn't see Hamish when you were coming up the crag, did you?"

Kate shook her head.

"The rascal's disappeared. He sometimes wanders off through a hole in the wall and scrambles down the crag, but it's not like him to miss his lunch."

"Want us to have a look for him?" Kate asked.

"It's okay. I'll give him a wee while yet."

"Let us know if he doesn't turn up, and we'll mount a little search party."

Finlay nodded.

Kate and Cameron carried on up to the sitting room. Kate settled on the chaise longue with a pad and paper to note down ideas for an advert. Similarly equipped, Cameron sank into what had become "his" armchair.

"Okay, where do we start?" Kate asked.

"How about with a name for the firm."

She nodded. "Any suggestions?"

"I'm trying to come up with something inspiring involving the names Greystane or Glen Cranoch, but nothing's springing to mind."

Kate thought for a few moments, then said, "What about The Highland Fling Wedding Company?"

"I like it," Cameron said. "How about some sort of

slogan to go with it—you know, the way Pepsi has *The Real Thing*."

Kate thought about that, then said, "Finlay told me a Highland Fling is a dance people do until the music stops or until they drop, not caring where the steps take them or whether all that it makes them is tired in the end. He told me it was a dance people did to the beat of their heart. How would that sound: *The Highland Fling Wedding Company—Dance to the Beat of Your Heart*."

Cameron nodded, and said, "Works for me."

Kate wrote the name and slogan at the top of the page, then said, "Okay, how do we go about describing everything that Greystane and Glen Cranoch can offer a couple who want to get married?"

Cameron thought about that. "Difficult knowing where to begin, isn't it?" he said.

Kate nodded.

"It might help if we break it down into the different parts that make up a wedding, then try to come up with some evocative words for each one," Cameron suggested.

"Okay," Kate said. "There's the ceremony itself, of course, and the meal . . ." she wrote the words down and underlined them as she spoke.

"And the photos," Cameron added.

Kate looked up from her pad and smiled, loving the way he was getting as caught up in the idea as she was.

"And the dancing," he added.

But by now Kate wasn't listening to him any more, or

writing anything down. She'd turned over a new page and was sketching Cameron as he noted ideas under each of the little headings, so caught up in what he was doing that he didn't realize he was the subject of her attention.

She finished before he did, and by the time he said, "Kate, I think I've got it," and looked up from his page, Kate was holding up a sheet of paper with an almost perfect likeness of him drawn on it.

"Kate!" he said, taken aback by what he saw.

She just smiled.

Cameron took the paper from her and studied the drawing, then looked at Kate, seeing her in a new light. "I knew you could draw, but I didn't realize you could do anything like this," he said.

"Neither did I," she told him. The portrait was as lifelike as a photo, but her pencil had also recorded things no camera lens could capture; a hint of hidden depths, a suggestion of what made the man.

Modestly changing the subject, she said, "I hope at least one of us was doing what we were supposed to be doing: what did you manage to come up with?"

Cameron tore his gaze away from the portrait, looked at his own sheet of paper, and read out what he'd written: *"For vows exchanged in a hilltop castle, and photos taken beside a cascading waterfall; for a feast in a banquet hall, and all the enchantment of a Highland ball; for the history, mystery, and romance of Scotland's most beautiful glen; for the love of your life, and for memories that will last a lifetime: Highland Fling*

Weddings—dance to the beat of your heart."

Kate clapped her hands with delight, and said, "This calls for a drink."

"Want me to go downstairs for a couple of cold ones?" Cameron asked.

Kate nodded.

Cameron opened the sitting room door just as Finlay was about to knock on it. There was a worried look on his face, and Cameron guessed what had put it there. "Still no sign of Hamish?" he asked.

Finlay shook his head.

"Want a hand to look for him?" Kate said.

"I wouldn't mind, but I don't want you and Mr. Fraser having to change any plans because of Hamish and me."

"I wanted to get some more pictures of the glen to go with the adverts, anyway," Cameron said to make Finlay feel better.

"Hamish has never been gone this long before," Finlay said. "I hate to think he's got himself lost or cragfast somewhere."

"Crag what?" Kate asked.

"Cragfast—you know, climbed up somewhere he couldn't get back down from."

The thought of the lovable little dog whimpering away on a cliff ledge made Kate drop everything.

Five minutes later they were heading through the door in the outer wall and down the summit steps. When they got to the path at the bottom, where the Land Rover was parked, Kate said, "Should we split up?"

"It might be best, if you don't mind," Finlay told her. "How about if you look down by the lochan and Mr. Fraser and I go this way," he said, pointing down the path that led to Waterfall Bridge.

Kate nodded.

"Do you want to take the Land Rover?" Finlay asked, reaching in his pocket for the keys.

Kate shook her head. "It's too nice a day. I'd rather walk." She kissed Cameron, waved to Finlay and headed down the track that wound around Castle Crag and led to the lochan below.

Cameron and Finlay started along the path to the right, towards the hanging valley between the two crags. At the end of it Finlay said, "If I take this bank, could you take the opposite one, Mr. Fraser?"

Cameron nodded. He hurried down the steps, looking at the wooden sleepers below his feet rather than the wooded slope on either side, and crossed the bridge.

Jamie's Crag was too steep for Hamish to climb, and so was the staircase cut into it, so if the little Westie had crossed the bridge the only way he could have gone was to the left, along the forested lower slope of the hanging valley. Cameron hesitated on the edge of the woods, trying not to think about the last time he'd searched in a forest, then took a deep breath and headed into the trees.

He was startled by every twig that snapped underfoot, unsettled by the movement of each branch in the breeze.

He didn't notice that the trees weren't bare-branched but had leaves that were a dozen beautiful shades of green...

He didn't notice the little specks suspended in slanting shafts of late afternoon sunlight...

The resilient give of the forest floor beneath his feet...

Or the sweetness of singing birds from high above.

All he noticed was the silence between the birdsongs, the menace in the shadows between the shafts of sunlight, the tree roots like half-buried bones, the dryness in his throat and the moisture on his brow.

After he'd been walking for about ten minutes he noticed something else, too, something so un-nerving that it stopped him in his tracks. The feeling that he was being watched: not from the left, where the embankment sloped down to the river a dozen yards below; but from the right, where the rising slope steepened and forest gave way to crag and heather.

The first time he looked he saw nothing. Telling himself his mind was playing tricks, he started walking again.

However the sensation of being watched was so strong that he stopped a few yards further on and looked up to his right again. This time he noticed a black slash in a rocky outcrop about thirty yards up the slope. It was like a large, irregular letterbox, and he guessed it was the mouth of a cave that had been almost covered with boulders, either by hand in an attempt at concealment, or by chance in a rockfall. The opening was just big enough for a small dog like Hamish to climb into.

Glad of the excuse to get out of the forest, Cameron scrambled up the slope. Once, as he looked up at the black slash in the rocks above, he thought he saw the flash of a pair of eyes staring at him out of the darkness. "Hamish?" he called out. But there was no answering bark, and the small eyes disappeared before he could even be sure he'd seen them.

The shadows cast by the setting sun advanced rapidly up the rocky slope, drawing closer to the small opening. Cameron quickened his pace, racing to get to the cleft before it was swallowed in blackness because he didn't have a torch with him.

He reached the small opening just before the sunset shadows merged with the blackness of the cave. For the first few seconds his eyes weren't sufficiently dark-adapted to see anything other than a thin band of warm orange sunlight slanting across the rock floor.

However, as his eyes adjusted and he was able to distinguish shape and shade, he saw what looked like a rusty strip of metal lying at an angle across the band of light. It was like part of a sword, he thought, but the band of sunlight narrowed even as he watched. Before he could get a closer look, the inside of the cave was swallowed up by the darkness that marks the end of the day.

"My kingdom for a torch," Cameron said. He'd heard that the surviving Jacobite clansmen hid their weapons after Culloden, and guessed he'd stumbled across a little horde of them now. Peering into the depths of the cave, he wondered what else might lie hidden in the darkness. An old flintlock musket, maybe, some rusty dirks and a pistol or two—

And then from the blackness in front of Cameron came a sighing that would have frightened the life out of him if he hadn't heard it once before and known what to expect next. He moved his head out of the way and, sure enough, an owl flew out of the opening, passing so close that his face was caressed by the draught from its soft-feathered, slowly beating wings.

Cameron turned to follow the bird's flight. As he did, he noticed a movement from the corner of his eye: a small white dog trotting along the edge of the treeline, about to head into the forest below. "Hamish!" he called out.

The terrier stopped and looked around, as if not sure where the voice had come from.

"Hamish, over here!" Cameron called out, scrambling down the scree towards the terrier. Cameron got the feeling Hamish was relieved to see him: the little dog barked a couple of times and started hurrying up the slope.

When Cameron got to the Westie he lifted him up in his arms, gave him a comforting little hug and got a lick on the cheek in return. Cameron was more of a cat person than a dog-lover, and normally wouldn't have taken too kindly to a canine lick on the cheek. But now he just smiled, won over by the display of affection and delighted to have found the little pal who meant so much to Finlay and Kate.

And besides, he was glad to have a little buddy himself for the twilight walk back through the woods.

Cameron and Hamish arrived back at Castle Crag just as Finlay was about to get into the Land Rover. After a joyous reunion with his beloved little terrier, Finlay said to Cameron, "Kate's not back yet—I was just about to see if I could give her a lift up from the glen. Want to come along?"

Cameron nodded. He strapped himself into the passenger seat, Hamish sitting in his lap, as Finlay gunned the Land Rover into life.

Cameron wished he had a Nikon or Leica in his hands rather than a West Highland Terrier as they made their way down the dirt track, because the setting sun was turning the sky to a great flat canvas streaked by a thousand fiery shades of red and orange.

"Does this place ever stop seeming beautiful to you?" Cameron asked Finlay.

There was no answer.

Even before he turned to look at Finlay, Cameron knew something was wrong because they were approaching the first bend far too fast.

"The brakes have gone!" Finlay said. He repeatedly pressed the brake pedal, but to no avail.

They took the sharp bend much faster than was

comfortable, using every inch of the dirt road. "Sweet Jesus!" Finlay said, fighting with the wheel to get the Land Rover back into the middle of the track.

A cold trickle of sweat ran down Cameron's back. The Westie in his lap started yelping, alarmed by the tone of his master's voice and the increasing speed with which the crag was flashing by.

The second bend—the turn that would bring them from the side of the crag to the long, steep stretch of track that led down the sheer front face of the outcrop—was approaching at an alarming rate. Finlay was working the brake pedal so frantically now that even above the roaring engine, crunch of gravel, and Hamish's panicked barking Cameron clearly heard the *clack-clack-clack* as the little rectangle of metal slapped uselessly against the floor.

The clacking suddenly stopped, and Cameron tore his horrified gaze away from the rapidly approaching bend and looked at Finlay, half-expecting to see that he'd had a heart attack with the shock and fear of what was happening. Instead, the old Highlander seemed completely calm. There was a steely look in his eyes, and a calmness in his voice when he said to Cameron, "Keep a tight hold on Hamish, Mr. Fraser. This is going to be a little dicey."

Then the bend was upon them, and they were taking it so fast that Cameron thought they must surely hurtle over the edge and plummet into the glen below. His mouth was bone dry and he could feel the dog in his arms trembling, hear it barking above the roar of the engine. Too afraid to keep looking ahead, Cameron turned again to look at Finlay McRae.

There was no sign of fear on the Highlander's face, just total concentration and grim determination. As Finlay turned the wheel he seemed to be wrestling the vehicle rather than steering it, controlling it with force of will as well as the strength of his hands, arms, and shoulders.

For a terrible moment it appeared as though gravity and momentum had defeated him. The back of the Land Rover swung so far out that the rear offside wheel left the track, and the rest of the vehicle seemed doomed to follow.

Finlay threw his whole body into the turn and for a moment of dog-barking, engine-roaring madness their lives literally hung in the balance.

Then the sideways momentum of the skid slowed just enough for the front wheels to bite and drive forward. The rear offside wheel bumped back onto the dirt trail with a sickening jolt, and then they were hurtling down the track rather than over the side of the crag.

Cameron breathed again and gave Hamish a reassuring hug, saying to the little Westie, "Finlay's just saved our lives."

"Maybe not for long," Finlay said grimly.

Looking up from Hamish, out of the windscreen, Cameron immediately saw the cause of Finlay's concern: Kate was coming up the track, and there was barely room for them to pass her. She waved to them, but froze with her hand in mid-air when she realized something was very wrong.

Finlay only had a split second to decide whether to pass her on the right and flirt once more with the precipice, or take the safe option and steer left, towards the inner edge of the track, and leave Kate to take her chances with the drop. Without hesitation he steered the Land Rover as close as he dared to the right.

Kate flattened herself against the rock face and the Land Rover hurtled past her so fast that Cameron just got a fleeting glimpse of her horrified expression.

There was another sickening jolt as both offside wheels went over the precipice, and the dreadful scraping of metal against rock as the underside of the Land Rover ground against the edge of the track. Again their lives were in the balance, and once more it seemed to be only Finlay's force of will that saved them, with first one bone-jarring jolt, then another, signalling that all four wheels were back on the dirt road.

The gradient flattened out as they approached the bottom of the glen, but they were travelling so fast that Finlay couldn't take the last bend in the track. Fortunately there was no drop to plunge over, and when they were finally brought to a shuddering halt it was by the burn up ahead. Without the seatbelts they would have been catapulted through the windscreen. As it was they were flung forward with rib-bruising, whiplashing violence. One of Hamish's legs was caught between Cameron and the dashboard, and as soon as Cameron heard the dog's pained yelping and saw the awkward angle of its leg he knew a bone was broken.

Then he was aware of Finlay slumped over the steering wheel. For a few awful moments he feared the worst. Trying not to hurt Hamish, Cameron reached out a hand to Finlay's shoulder. Even the slight movement was enough to make Hamish let out a little yelp and whimper. Finlay stirred at the sound of the dog rather than the touch of Cameron's hand, and slowly straightened up with a groan. He shook his head as if trying to clear it, grimacing as he did so.

"Finlay, are you okay?" Cameron asked.

Clutching his chest with one hand and reaching up with the other to gingerly massage his neck, Finlay said, "Aye. I think so."

Hamish let out another little whimper.

Finlay slowly turned his head to look at the little terrier. He saw the limp forepaw dangling at an unnatural angle. His own aches and pains immediately forgotten, he said, "Hamish! My wee pal!"

Kate appeared at the window, having run down the track, and said, "Cameron, Finlay! Are you okay?"

Cameron nodded. Finlay didn't say anything—he was too busy reaching out to take Hamish from Cameron's arms.

Kate saw the dangling leg and winced. "Broken?" she mouthed to Cameron.

He nodded.

"What happened?" she asked.

Finlay looked up from Hamish and said, "The brakes went on me, Lady Kate. I don't understand it—they were fine the last time I used the Land Rover."

Kate went very quiet. Cameron guessed what she was thinking, and knew he was right moments later when she quietly said, "I'm not superstitious, but I'm starting to believe there maybe really is a curse."

"That's exactly what Tony Carling wants you—and anyone who might be considering getting married in the glen—to think," Cameron told her.

"You think this wasn't just an accident?" Finlay asked, gently cradling Hamish in his arms.

"I think it was about as much of an accident as the fire," Cameron said.

Finlay winced as he straightened up. Seeing his pain, Kate said, "Finlay, do you want me to call an ambulance?"

"No," Finlay said, "but I'd like you to call a vet."

Kate nodded. "I will. And the police."

While Kate hurried away, Finlay turned to Cameron and said, "If I find out Mr. Tony Carling was behind this, I'll teach him what it really means to be cursed."

CHAPTER 18

"I KNEW WHAT TO EXPECT, BUT IT LOOKS EVEN WORSE in black and white," Kate said. She was sitting beside Cameron in the accident and emergency area at Raigmore Hospital in Inverness, looking at the latest edition of the local newspaper while they waited for Finlay to come out of a curtained consulting area.

He'd refused to go to hospital the day before, showing more concern for Hamish than himself, but Miss Weir "insisted" after a night of listening to his groans through the wall. Kate and Cameron had driven him into town in the courtesy car left by the garage when the Land Rover was towed away.

There was a copy of the local newspaper among the pile of *National Geographic* and *Scottish Field* magazines on the coffee tables in the waiting area, and the headline leaped up at them in bold black capitals: **NEW DRAMA IN "CURSED" GLEN**. Below it was a photo of Greystane and Castle Crag.

With an air of resignation, Kate picked up the newspaper and started reading the story aloud. "It says: 'Two men narrowly cheated death yesterday in a dramatic accident on the troubled Glen Cranoch estate.

" 'Estate worker Finlay McRae and Cameron Fraser, close friend of American heiress Kate Brodie, were driving down Castle Crag when the brakes of Mr. McRae's Land Rover mysteriously failed, leaving them to negotiate the sharp bends in the steep, winding road at dangerously high speeds.

" 'Skid marks on the roads and damage to the verge at each of the bends pay testament to how close the Land Rover came to a deadly plunge down the sheer face of the crag.

" 'The vehicle finally came to rest in . . .'" Kate turned over to an inside page, which showed a photo of the Land Rover pitched forward in the burn, and picked up where she'd left off. " '. . . the burn at the foot of the glen's waterfall.

" 'Both men were said to be shaken and bruised. Mr. McRae's West Highland terrier was not so fortunate, however, suffering a broken leg in the accident.

" 'Coming only a day after fire destroyed the croft of a bride's family on her wedding day, the crash is the latest misfortune to befall Glen Cranoch, whose very name is a corruption of the Gaelic for Glen of Tears.

" 'No one from the estate was available to comment on whether they believe this latest accident lends weight to the notion of a curse dating from the days of the infamous Highland clearance . . .'" Kate's voice tailed away into a despairing sigh. "They go on to recount the story of Lady Carolyn and the old woman's deathbed curse." Looking up from the paper, she said, "It's difficult to imagine any worse publicity, Cameron. Doubtless the nationals'll pick it up tomorrow. It might even make the TV news." She gave another sigh, then said, "If only the police could have proved foul play."

The local constabulary had sent an accident investigator to examine the Land Rover, but the severe scraping to the underside of the vehicle prevented him from saying whether the brake lines had been deliberately cut.

Kate stared at the photo, then said, "I just hope Finlay's okay. If there's anything wrong with him I really will start believing there's a curse. In fact, I'm still not sure there isn't."

"We have to think of a way to prove there isn't."

"How?"

"By showing that Tony Carling is behind the run of 'bad luck'."

"Just how are we going to do that?"

Cameron, who'd been giving the matter some serious thought since the crash, said, "I think you might be holding the answer in your hands."

"I don't understand."

"He's been using the newspapers against us—we can use them against him."

"I still don't follow."

"If we announce another plan to save the estate I'm sure Carling will try to sabotage it. When he does, we have to catch him in the act."

"That all sounds easier said than done, Cameron. What sort of plan did you have in mind to act as bait?"

Before Cameron could confess that he hadn't thought out the specifics, the green pull-around curtains of the consulting bay parted and Finlay walked slowly out, clutching a bottle of painkillers. Seeing the concern on the faces of Kate and Cameron, he said, "There's no need to worry. Nothing's broken; it's just some bruising.

"Now, if you don't mind, I'd like to get back and see how poor wee Hamish is doing."

Cameron spent most of the drive back to Glen Cranoch thinking of how to make his plan work, but without success.

As they drove past the lochan, Finlay looked at it longingly and said, "It'll be a while before I'm able to cast a rod again."

"That just means there'll be all the more fish to catch," Kate said to cheer him up.

"That's it!" Cameron said.

Kate and Finlay both looked at him, and then at each other . . .

And then they smiled as Cameron explained what he had in mind.

"Pity it's not on the front page," Kate said as she looked at *The Inverness Morning Herald* the next day. The paper had been delivered by one of the crofters who'd gone into town on an errand.

"It doesn't matter, I'm sure Carling will still notice it," Cameron said.

They were standing with Finlay and Miss Weir in the kitchen, looking at a story halfway down Page 3. It was headlined *Fish farm plan for troubled glen*.

"What exactly do you expect him to do when he sees it?" Miss Weir asked.

"I'm not sure, but I'm certain he'll try to do *something*, and I want to be there to catch him on camera when he does. I'll set up a night-time OP—sorry, an observation post—at the far end of the glen. If Carling tries to dump poison in the lochan, or something like that, he'll do it as far away from the crofters' cottages as possible, and probably under cover of darkness."

Thinking about the far end of Glen Cranoch, Cameron realized he had a choice between setting up camp in the ruined cottages or the old church. He couldn't bring himself to go inside the blackened cottages by day, let alone night, so he said, "I'll use the church as a base."

Finlay and Miss Weir exchanged uneasy glances, and Kate looked down at the stone flagged floor. Cameron looked from one to another for an explanation, but nobody would meet his questioning gaze.

"There's an old shooting blind on the hillside above the road into the glen," Finlay said at last.

"It'd be too far away from the water to take a good

enough photo of any dirty tricks in the lochan," Cameron told him. "What's wrong with the church?"

There was another awkward silence.

"Don't tell me it's supposed to be haunted, too," Cameron said. "I would have thought a church was the ideal place to go when you want to get away from ghosts."

Again the silence was deafening.

Finally Miss Weir said, "I suppose you'd say it's a haunting place rather than a haunted one, Mr. Fraser."

"Something tells me that's going to seem like a meaningless distinction once darkness falls."

"It's just that the last minister who preached there played an ungodly part in the clearing of the glen," Finlay told him. "You could say he sold his soul to the devil, so it's hard for the people who remain in Glen Cranoch to think of his church as a house of God."

Cameron knew that Tony Carling would need time to work out a plan of his own in response to the newspaper article, and so was unlikely to try anything that night. However, he didn't want to take the slightest chance of missing a clandestine visit by the businessman, so he spent the afternoon setting up his observation post in readiness for the fall of night. He packed his camera gear and flash units into a rucksack, while Kate carried a blanket to keep him warm through the chill of the night, a bottle of water, and some sandwiches.

Although it was a warm summer's afternoon Cameron shivered when he entered the old church. Looking at the mould-speckled walls, empty pews, and deserted pulpit, he said, "The word 'godforsaken' somehow springs to mind, but I don't know why. I've been in other disused churches and they don't have an unsettling atmosphere like this one."

Kate didn't say anything.

Looking around, Cameron said, "I'm glad I don't believe in God, because if I did I'd have the feeling this place had been abandoned by Him as well as by His worshippers."

"Do you want me to spend the night here with you?" Kate asked in the sort of voice that made it clear she was hoping he'd politely decline the offer.

Her reluctance was so obvious that he couldn't resist asking, "What would you do if I said 'yes'?"

"Hope you changed your mind. There's no one else I'd rather spend the night with, Cameron, but there are plenty of other places I'd rather spend it in."

He smiled. "It's okay, it's probably better if I'm on my own, otherwise I'd end up talking to you instead of listening for Tony Carling."

Kate couldn't hide her relief, and Cameron couldn't hide his amusement at it.

Later, though—once Kate had left and the bright shafts of sunlight had turned to gold and then disappeared into thin air, gone as completely as vanished youth and lost innocence—Cameron didn't feel like smiling any more. As he looked around the empty church he tried telling himself that the coming of darkness would be a blessing, because it would hide the haunting signs of neglect and abandonment.

But he changed his mind when night began to fall because it seemed to bring the opposite of a blessing. He sat there mesmerized as shadows appeared all around like black magic spells made visible. He watched them slowly lengthen as if they were animated by some dark, relentless force, swallowing pulpit, pillar, and pew and leaving in their wake a darkness so complete it was hard to believe he would ever see daylight again.

When he turned his back on the interior of the church and looked out of the broken window he felt the darkness like a threatening presence at his back, one that might reach out and claim him at any moment.

The hours before the moon broke through the clouds were an eternity of long, empty silences punctuated by moments of heart-stopping alarm. Unable to see anything but the impenetrable depths of night when he looked out of the broken window, he became totally reliant on his sense of hearing, and even the slightest sounds were accentuated as a result. Every so often, just as he was on the point of dozing off, a sudden noise would startle him frightfully and for several awful moments he'd use imagination rather than common sense when considering its cause: the squeak of warped door swinging on rusty hinges and rattle of ill-fitting window panes against wooden frame in a gust of wind; the scratching and scurrying of small animals in the foundations beneath his feet; the creak of roof timbers contracting overhead in the chill of night. Always the sounds came from within the old building, so that gradually the desolate church became his whole world and he almost forgot about the glen outside.

He soon began to feel as if his weren't the only pair of watchful eyes in the creaking old building and that, while he was looking out into the blackness of night, all the other eyes were looking at him, judging him, condemning him to some unspeakably awful fate. He felt as if the pews were filled by a silent congregation of the damned—and that he was destined to join their ranks in a never-ending night. He half expected to feel a clutching hand fall on his shoulder at any moment, and spent almost as much time looking into the darkness of the church behind him as he did out of the broken window into the pitch black of the glen.

When the moon finally broke through the clouds even the glistening lochan, plunging quicksilver waterfall and magically limned outline of Greystane and Castle Crag appearing like something from a fairytale in the distance couldn't hold his attention completely, for the interior of the church around him was, in its way, even more striking. Milky white moonbeams slanted through the arched windows, creating pools of ghostly light and monstrous shadows that bore no apparent relation to the things they were cast from. Cameron found himself in one of the shafts of silvery light and, even though he knew he would be silhouetted against it to anyone looking into the church from outside, still it took him the best part of a minute and all his strength of will to step into the shadows.

He was glad when clouds obscured the moon once more because, although he wouldn't have believed it was possible, the spectral glow and slowly moving shadows within the church had been even more menacing than the total darkness.

Unsettling as the atmosphere in the church was, it only accounted for part of his disquiet. The rest was down to the thought of what a sound from outside the church might signal. Even with high-speed film and a fast lens he'd need a photographic flash to capture evidence of any wrongdoing—and from what he'd heard of Tony Carling, the big Englishman wouldn't exactly behave like a deer caught in the headlights when the bulb went off.

There was no way around it: if he wanted to help Kate Brodie, he was going to have to take his chances with Tony Carling—and he knew the odds of coming out of such an encounter unscathed weren't good.

Just when Cameron thought the night was never going to end, the sky showed the first signs of changing from black to blue. He thought at first he might be imagining it, but then palest amber appeared on the horizon, as though a dark canvas was being delicately colored by some great, invisible hand.

Slowly but surely the hills rose up out of the darkness on either side of the church, their dark, brooding bulk lightening as first the grey of rocky summit ridges appeared, then the mauve of heather and green of forest.

Soon the distinctive outline of the twin crags and Greystane emerged in the distance at the far end of the glen.

When Cameron rushed out of the church to greet the day, he felt like he'd escaped from a hellish halfway house between the living and the dead.

The walk back to Greystane eased the stiffness out of his bones but didn't take the kinks out of his mind, for the disappointment he felt at a fruitless night was tempered by guilty relief at the fact that he hadn't been forced to confront Tony Carling.

The smell of sizzling bacon as he approached the lean-to at the back of the banquet hall stimulated an appetite that had been suppressed by fear; the sandwiches lay behind in the church, and he hadn't eaten all night.

Finlay and Miss Weir were just finishing breakfast when he walked into the kitchen. He tried to give them a "good morning" smile, but knew from the concerned look on their faces that he hadn't come close to pulling it off. "It must have seemed like a long night, Mr. Fraser," Finlay said.

Cameron nodded. He wanted to forget about the night behind him, and the one that lay ahead, so he quickly changed the subject by asking, "How about you, Finlay—did the tablets help?"

"Maybe they did, but I'm more inclined to think it was the wee dram I washed them down with that did the trick. Whatever, I slept like a baby and woke up feeling more like my old self." His chirpiness deserted him when he added, "I'll be able to take a turn in the church tonight, Mr. Fraser."

Miss Weir gave a phoney little cough, and said, "Excuse me, I was just choking on the smell of burning martyr."

Cameron laughed and felt better, thinking how good it was to be back in the land of the living. He sat down on a stool next to Finlay just as the kitchen door opened and Kate walked in. She wrapped her arms around him from behind. Resting her head on his shoulder, she whispered, "I missed you," in his ear, and suddenly the darkness of the church seemed like part of another world.

By halfway through his second night in the old church Cameron recognized the sounds of the building for what they were, and so they no longer startled him. Without the prick of terror that unfamiliar noises had brought the night before, boredom rather than fear became his biggest enemy. As the night wore on, so he increasingly woke up with his chin hitting his chest after dozing off to sleep.

He came to with a start after one such sleepy interlude and was in mid-yawn when a sound from outside the church stopped him. At first he thought he'd imagined it.

But it grew louder the longer he listened, until he was sure of what it was: the crunch of tyres rolling very slowly over gravel. He had a clear view of the lochan, but the sound came from the track behind the church, to the left, near the pass that led into the glen. For a few moments all he saw was the dim glow of the water in the light of the waxing moon . . .

Then, to the accompaniment of a lightly revving engine, a dark shape came into view. The angular bulk of a Range Rover.

The crunch of gravel died away as the vehicle left the track and trundled down towards the lochan.

Cameron reached for his Nikon, palms sweating despite the chill of the night. As his hands closed on the camera sling he clearly heard the ratcheting of a handbrake being engaged, then a car door squeaking open.

A heavy footfall on shingle was followed by another as the driver got out onto the small pebble beach at the water's edge.

Moments later a burly silhouette appeared against the quicksilver of the loch. The figure moved to the back of the vehicle, raised an arm and opened the top half of the hatchback trunk, then lowered the bottom half. There was a scraping, as if something heavy was being dragged from the trunk. The figure stooped, and for several seconds the silhouette was lost in the shadowy bulk of the car before reappearing against the lochan as the man carried a big crate down towards the water's edge.

Cameron knew he was too far away for his flash to reach the Range Rover, let alone cast any light on what the man was doing down by the water, but he was too afraid to move closer. He just stood there, watching the silhouette disappear as the man squatted to set down the heavy crate.

After several seconds of noisy splashing the silhouette reappeared as the man stood up, lifting the crate easily now that it had been emptied.

Watching the man walk back to the rear of the Range Rover, Cameron's legs were shaking, his whole body damp with the fear sweat that had been confined to his palms moments earlier. He was almost physically sick at the thought that he'd blown the chance to capture the man on film, and at the knowledge that he'd never be able to look Kate Brodie or Finlay McRae in the eye again as a result.

Filled with self-loathing, he waited for the man to close the boot, knowing the sound would have a finality that marked the end of his own hopes of ever finding happiness.

But instead of the soft thud of a closing door there was more scraping.

The man was taking another crate from the boot.

Feeling nothing that could happen to him in the moments to come could be as bad as the prospect of the future he'd been faced with moments earlier, Cameron slung the Nikon around his neck and padded quickly but silently out of the church and down towards the Range Rover.

He got to the edge of the narrow shingle beach just as the silhouetted man set the crate down at the water's edge, no more than half a dozen yards away. Taking a deep breath, his hands shaking, Cameron tried to raise the camera.

Nothing happened. He felt powerless to move, capable

only of listening.

The scrape of a crate being opened was followed by the frenzied splashing of living things entering the water.

The sounds somehow brought Cameron to life and, before he knew what he was doing, he raised the camera and pressed the shutter. Suddenly the night was ablaze with a cone of light as the flash fired, illuminating a stocky figure crouched at the edge of the lochan and a crate of big-clawed, lobster-like creatures that thrashed furiously when they entered the water. The man turned in surprise to face the blinding light. Cameron kept his finger on the shutter and fired off the whole roll of film. The man in front of him was captured in an action sequence of postures that went from crouching to standing, and a range of expressions from shock to snarling anger and then a mocking, challenging look that was even more intimidating than the snarl.

By the time the camera's motor drive had fired off the last frame of film the man was advancing towards Cameron, into a slanting shaft of moonlight. Despite never having seen Tony Carling before, Cameron knew from Kate's description that he was facing the Yeoman boss now.

"What do you think you're doing?" Cameron said, trying in vain to keep the fear from his voice.

"A little fish farming of my own," the man said in a London accent. He took another step towards Cameron, saying, "Now hand over the film, and I'll let you keep the camera."

Cameron stood rooted to the spot. He wasn't giving away anything in terms of height or age, but knew by Carling's bull neck, heavy shoulders, and barrel chest that he was giving away a lot in weight—and could tell by the look in the man's eyes that he was giving away even more in terms of aggression. He tried to summon up the courage to fight a battle that he knew was well worth fighting . . .

But wasn't able to, because he knew it was a battle he couldn't hope to win.

Reading Cameron's expression and what lay behind it, Carling sneered and reached for the Nikon.

There was something about the look on Carling's face in that moment that reminded Cameron of the expression on the face of the bully who'd herded the woman with the purple headscarf onto the cattle truck—and suddenly, without thinking what he was doing, Cameron clenched his right hand into a fist and threw a haymaker that came out of the past and all the way up from his hip, connecting solidly with the other man's jaw.

Carling staggered back but didn't go down. Cameron knew he hadn't knocked the fight out of him, but somehow he wasn't scared any more. Instead of thinking about how he might get hurt in the coming fight, he was thinking about a crofter's gutted cottage and a bride's ruined wedding . . .

About Finlay McRae standing on a Normandy beach at the age of nineteen and playing *Highland Laddie* . . .

About Glen Cranoch and Kate Brodie, and how they were so well worth fighting for.

In place of fear, Cameron Fraser felt a wild abandon, and as the big Londoner took a step forward the Scotsman stepped in to meet him, hands raised in a high guard.

Just as they were about to close to striking distance a face appeared in the slanting shaft of moonlight Carling had just walked through.

Carling saw Cameron's apparent distraction, and thought it was a crude ploy to divert his attention. "You'll have to do better than that, Jock," he said.

His smile froze when he felt a tap on the shoulder. He turned around in time to receive a heavy blow to his cheek with the butt of a shotgun, knocking him flat on his back and out cold.

Standing over the fallen Englishman, Finlay McRae said, "That was for wee Hamish and Double Ecky." Then he winced with pain and clutched at his chest.

"Finlay, are you okay?" Cameron said, fearing the old man was having a seizure.

Finlay managed to smile through the pain. "Aye, it's just my ribs," he said. "But it was worth it."

"Where did you appear from?"

"I couldn't sleep, so I went for a wee walk up to the shooting blind, just in case the chance presented itself to settle my account with Mr. Tony Carling. My compliments on the way you settled your account and Miss Brodie's, by the way. Oh, to be young again," he added wistfully. Gesturing to the Nikon around Cameron's neck, he said, "I take it from the flash of your camera that you got some photos?"

Cameron nodded. "I'm not sure what he was up to, though."

Finlay walked over to the wicker crate by the edge of the lochan. There was one thrashing creature left in it. Shining a torch on it, he said, "American crayfish!" in disgust.

"I don't understand," Cameron said.

"They're vicious predators that eat everything else around them. They would have been the kiss of death if we had been planning to start up a fish farm."

"Has he broken any laws by releasing them into the loch?"

"Aye, he has, indeed. It's just a pity he won't be convicted for the fire in Double Ecky's croft and causing the Land Rover crash as well. Still, when your photographs appear in the paper, I don't think anyone will have the slightest doubt about what's been going on in The Cranoch over the last couple of weeks."

A groan told them Tony Carling was coming to. Finlay shone his torch on the fallen man, who blinked and rolled over onto his side before struggling groggily to his knees. Finlay handed Cameron the torch and, shotgun in his right hand, used his left hand to grab Carling by the hair. "If you ever, ever set foot in The Cranoch again, I swear I'll use the other end of the gun on you," Finlay said before swinging Carling's head down so forcefully that the Londoner ended up on all fours.

Turning to Cameron, Finlay said, "Now, Mr. Fraser, I think it's time to go home."

And they did. Finlay McRae whistled *Highland Laddie* as they walked alongside the lochan in the moonlight, and Cameron Fraser thought about his Highland lady.

It was almost dawn by the time they got back to Greystane. Cameron went up to the lounge to phone the police, while Finlay headed for the kitchen to fix up some breakfast. There was a light in the window, and when he opened the door Kate was sitting at the table, hands wrapped around a mug of cocoa.

"What are you doing up at this hour, lass?" Finlay asked when he entered the lean-to.

"I couldn't sleep for worrying about Cameron. What are *you* doing, Finlay? You look like you've been up and about for ages."

"I took a little walk to the far end of the glen to keep Mr. Fraser company."

"Is everything okay?"

"Everything is fine, lass. Everything is just fine." He poured himself a mug of tea, and said, "There was a wee spot of bother, but it's all taken care of."

"What sort of bother?"

"Nothing to trouble yourself about."

"Finlay! Where's Cameron?"

"He's just giving the police a little phone call."

"Finlay, what happened?"

And then Finlay was recounting the events at the far end of the glen, glad to have someone to tell them to because he was proud of Cameron Fraser and wanted to share his pride.

When Cameron came back, Kate waited for him to say something. When he didn't, she said, "Is everything okay?" She waited for him to tell her what had happened in his own words, talk about the part he'd played.

But he didn't even hint at it. He just nodded, and all he said in his quiet voice was, "Yes, Kate, everything's okay."

She threw her arms around him, loving him not just for the courage he'd found, but for the modesty he hadn't lost, and believing him when he whispered, "Everything's going to be all right, Kate."

EPILOGUE

"You have to hand it to him, the American crayfish was a nice touch," Harry McLaren said.

The *Inverness Morning Herald* reporter was standing with Cameron and Kate outside the town's sheriff court. "With Lady Kate being from the States, a species from America scuppering plans for a fish farm has the sort of irony that would have added weight to the notion of a curse if it hadn't been for these." He looked at Cameron's grainy black and white photos of Tony Carling poised beside a crate at the edge of the lochan. "Talk about being caught in the act," the reporter said, chuckling away to himself. "It'll be tomorrow's front-page lead. We can't explicitly blame Carling outright for things he hasn't been found guilty of, you understand, but you won't have to read too far between the lines to realise what's been going on in the glen."

"I can't tell you what a relief this is," Kate said.

"I can let you hear what I've got so far, if you'd like..."

Kate nodded.

The reporter took a spiral-bound notebook from the

inside pocket of his tweed jacket and started reading the shorthand he'd scribbled in its pages: " 'A London businessman has been fined £1400 at Inverness Sheriff Court after the latest in a series of incidents apparently intended to add weight to the notion of the so-called Curse of The Cranoch.

" 'Tony Carling (36), of Westminster Way, admitted willfully releasing a non-native species, namely American crayfish, into the lochan at Glen Cranoch in the early hours of Tuesday in contravention of the Wildlife and Countryside Act (1981).

" 'Carling is chairman and managing director of Yeoman Holdings, the property firm which has been trying to buy The Cranoch Estate in the hope of turning it into a leisure resort.

" 'The dramatic photo above'—I'm not sure which one we'll use, but they're all pretty dramatic—'led to a change of plea when produced as evidence in court. The picture was taken by Mr. Cameron Fraser, a close friend of Lady Kate Brodie, the American heiress who recently inherited the estate.

" 'Apparently suspecting foul play was afoot after recent incidents in the glen—including a fire which destroyed a bride's cottage on her wedding day, and a car crash caused by brake failure—Mr. Fraser and ghillie Finlay McRae set about trying to prove their suspicions. This photo was the result.

" 'Asked outside the court whether he had been

attempting to add substance to the notion of a Curse of The Cranoch, and intimidate Lady Kate into selling the wildly beautiful estate, Carling refused to comment.

" 'He also declined to comment on how he sustained the severe swelling which marked one side of his face.

" 'One person who was prepared to comment was Mr. McRae. The sprightly 76-year-old-former commando, a decorated D-Day veteran, said that Carling had been 'sent homeward tae think again'." The reporter chuckled to himself at that and said, "I think I'll use that quote in the heading: how does 'London businessman sent homeward tae think again' sound to you?"

"Better than you'd believe," Kate told him.

"If you don't mind, I'd just like to add a few paragraphs about your plans for the glen, and how they might have been affected by all this."

Before Kate could answer, her attention was distracted by a commotion when a van marked "NorthScot T" pulled up only yards from where they stood. She looked over the journalist's shoulder to see a film crew piling out of the back and setting up a camera. An attractive young auburn-haired woman stepped out of the front of the van, sized up the scene at a glance, and said to Harry McLaren, "Excuse me, do you mind if we butt in—we'd like to do a live feed in time for the *North Today* lunchtime news."

The newspaperman responded with a gallant bow and said, "They're all yours."

"Do you mind doing a quick interview?" the TV reporter

asked Kate and Cameron.

Before Kate could answer, a man with a large pair of headphones said, "Paula, we're on in ten!" and handed her a microphone.

The woman turned from Kate and Cameron, watching the hands of the man in the headphones as he counted down from ten with his fingers. When his last finger folded into his palm, she looked into the camera and said, "I'm standing outside Inverness Sheriff Court where London businessman Tony Carling has just been found guilty of an offence apparently aimed at perpetuating the notion of an ancient curse. With me is the American heiress at the heart of the story, Lady Kate Brodie."

The TV reporter turned to the side, and the cameraman pulled back to include Kate in the shot. "Lady Kate, thanks for joining us. First of all, can I ask if you ever at any stage believed that the unfortunate incidents which plagued your arrival in Glen Cranoch might have had a supernatural explanation?"

"I wasn't sure quite what to think," Kate said into the proffered microphone.

"And what do you think now?"

"I think it's quite obvious what's been going on."

"Do you still plan to try and start up a fish farm?"

"The fish farm was what you might call a red herring, if you'll pardon the pun."

"So you're sticking to the plan to save The Cranoch by using it as a venue for weddings?"

Kate nodded.

"Aren't you afraid some people might still be put off by the notion of a curse, given the glen's unhappy history?"

"If there is such a thing as a curse, I think it would only work against those who try to harm the glen and its people—the Tony Carlings of this world."

"But surely you must recognise that people might think twice about getting married in a place with such a checkered history. I mean, would you be happy to get married there?"

Kate's surprise at that question was as nothing compared to the shock she felt moments later at the next one, for it wasn't asked by the TV reporter, but by Cameron Fraser: "Well, Kate," he said, "Would you?"

Kate turned to Cameron, oblivious of the frantic gesturing of the director, who'd guessed what was about to happen and was signalling to his cameraman to pull back for a group shot.

"Kate, would you marry me in the chapel at Greystane?" Cameron asked.

Flash bulbs started going off all around, people began clapping, the TV reporter clasped her hands in delight—and Kate Brodie didn't notice any of it. The only thing she could see was the face of the man she loved with all her heart; the only thing she could hear was his voice, saying, "Marry me, Kate Brodie . . ."

And then, safe and secure and completely sure in his arms, she said just one word.

"Yes."

INVERNESS MORNING HERALD
Wednesday, August 26, 1996

Skeleton found in Glen Cranoch

POLICE FORENSIC investigators and archaeologists from Historic Scotland spent most of yesterday in a cave in Glen Cranoch following the discovery of human remains thought to date from the 1745 Jacobite rebellion.

The discovery was made by Mr. Cameron Fraser, owner of a nearby cottage and fiancé of estate owner Lady Kate Brodie, while looking for a missing dog last week. Initially he thought he had simply stumbled on a cache of clansmen's weapons hidden in the bloody aftermath of the '45. With light fading and lacking a torch he was unable to investigate further at that time.

He intended going back the next day, but was sidetracked by a series of dramatic events including a car crash, a violent confrontation with London businessman Tony Carling, and a sensational marriage proposal made on live TV following the conclusion of the Carling court case.

Little wonder, then, that it was several days before he remembered about the cache of weapons and went to investigate further.

Entering the cave he found not only the basket-hilted broadsword which had originally caught his attention, but also the skeleton of the clansman who once carried it.

Experts say it is still too early to positively date the remains, but indications suggest they are those of a clansmen who may well have fought alongside Bonnie Prince Charlie.

INVERNESS MORNING HERALD
Thursday, August 27, 1996

Startling twist in case of Cranoch clansman

IN A startling twist it appears that the body found in Glen Cranoch earlier this week may be that of a distant relative of Mr. Cameron Fraser, the man who discovered it.

A distinctive owl-shaped silver brooch found on the remains of the clansman's plaid matches that in a portrait of disgraced Jamie Chisholm which hangs in nearby Greystane Castle. Chisholm was known to have been present at Culloden in 1746, but was branded a coward after being seen fleeing from the field of battle. His eventual fate had hitherto been unknown.

However, in a dramatic turn of events, it appears that a discovery made with the body may not only clear Jamie Chisholm's name but in fact make him something of a hero. A silk battle standard was found folded inside the plaid which clothed the skeleton, leading experts to believe that the clansman had been trying to save the colours and return them to Greystane, the seat of his clan. The standard is covered in blood from the chest wound which it appears the gallant clansman succumbed to while being hunted by the Redcoats of "Butcher" Cumberland in the brutal aftermath of the battle.

Mr. Fraser said, "It seems he must have run into the full force of musket fire and grape shot to save the colours and salvage some honour for the clan.

"Had he been caught with these colours as he tried to make his way home he could have expected no quarter.

"For two and a half centuries Jamie Chisholm has been reviled as a coward. Now I hope he'll be remembered as a hero, and that not only his body but his soul can rest in peace."

INVERNESS MORNING HERALD
Monday, September 21, 1996

A Highland fling

LADY KATE BRODIE was married at the weekend to Mr. Cameron Fraser, descendant of Jamie of the Colours—the Highland clansman whose name he helped to clear.

Lady Kate was born in America and lived in Sausalito, near San Francisco, until inheriting the Cranoch Estate on the death of Mr. Colin Chisholm earlier this year. She has resisted renewed overtures by London-based developers Yeoman Holdings to buy the estate for one-million pounds, saying she fears it would lead to the despoiling of the glen, a "second clearance" of the crofters, and the end of a "gentler, more decent way of life that's in danger of being lost forever".

She hopes to turn around the fortunes of the estate by using Greystane Castle for wedding packages, with particular emphasis on the US market.

It was therefore fitting that Greystane was the venue for her own wedding, which was attended by her father Mr. Keith Brodie and godfather Mr. John Hammond, both retired law-enforcement officials from Sausalito.

There had been considerable media interest in the wedding, given recent events in the glen and the troubled history of the Chisholm family. However, despite tabloid speculations relating to suggestions of a curse, the wedding went without a hitch, and a happy day was had by all.

INVERNESS MORNING HERALD
Monday, December 16, 1996

Fairytale romance

EVERY WEDDING is special to the friends and family of those involved, but some strike a chord even with strangers because they have a fairytale quality that shows romance is not dead.

That was certainly the case with a wedding held at Greystane House in The Cranoch Estate at the weekend.

Cranoch owners Kate and Cameron Fraser—who hope to turn around the fortunes of the ailing estate by using it for wedding packages—said few weddings will mean as much to them as the one they arranged on Saturday.

The marriage was between estate worker Miss Mabel Weir and Mrs Fraser's godfather Mr. John Hammond. The happy couple met at the recent wedding of Lady Kate and Cameron Fraser, hit it off, and kindled the flames of their romance by means of email!

Estate ghillie Finlay McRae said that no one should be too surprised by the wedding—after all, to the amusement of all concerned, Miss Weir had caught the bridal bouquet at Lady Kate's wedding!

INVERNESS MORNING HERALD
Tuesday, September 22, 1997

Generous gesture

LADY KATE FRASER has given the crofters on the former Cranoch estate—now renamed Waterfall Glen—title to their land for a nominal sum of £1 each.

She said that *Highland Fling Weddings*, the business which she and husband Cameron formed in a bid to save the once ailing estate, had succeeded beyond their wildest dreams and the gesture was a way of sharing that success and celebrating the happiness of their own marriage with the people around them—people they did not want to look on as tenants, but rather as friends.

Asked if she thought this would lay to rest the "Curse of The Cranoch" which was said to have dogged the family since Lady Carolyn Chisholm cleared the glen to make way for sheep two and a half centuries earlier, Lady Kate said, "I guess only time will tell."

INVERNESS MORNING HERALD
Monday, June 21, 1997

INTIMATIONS
(HATCHES, MATCHES & DISPATCHES)

FRASER: Cameron and Lady Kate of Waterfall Glen are delighted to announce the birth of a bouncing baby boy in Raigmore Hospital on Sunday—and proud to call him JAMIE.

If you enjoyed reading Waterfall Glen,
you may also enjoy this special presentation of
By Honor Bound *available from Medallion Press:*

By Honor Bound

Helen A. Rosburg

A PERFECT TEN!

"In my opinion, BY HONOR BOUND is a must-read for any romance fiction fan, and assuredly deserves the distinction of a Perfect 10. It's just that good!" —*Romance Reviews Today*

Prologue

October 16, 1793

The final few steps were difficult. Though the injury to her leg had been a long time healing, and the pain had lessened greatly, it was still not gone completely. The last stairs to the ground floor had to be taken carefully, and Honneure leaned heavily on her cane. Finally at the bottom, she rested against the wall for a moment to catch her breath and wipe the moisture from her brow. As she did so, the hood of her cape fell back and she immediately stiffened with fear.

A quick glance up and down the narrow street assured Honneure that no one had noticed her. She pulled her hood back up, tucking in stray wisps of pale, wavy hair. The sidewalks usually teemed this time of day. No doubt the crowds had all gone to the square to witness the execution.

A wave of nausea coursed through Honneure's frail form, so strongly it rocked her. She fought to keep down the meager breakfast of bread and tea Dr. Droulet had pressed upon her.

She could not be sick now. She could not. She had to be at the square also. She had to be there, at the end. She could not allow her friend to die alone. No matter how great her own personal danger, the bonds of love could not, would not, be denied.

Honneure squeezed her eyes tightly shut. It was ironic, she thought. So ironic. All of her adult life she had lived for and served her queen. Again and again she had sacrificed her own wants and needs for her sovereign's. She had believed it to be her duty and had been bound by honor to fulfill it. Honor bound. All her life, honor bound. And now?

Honneure shook her head, a humorless smile on the curve of her mouth.

Once again she risked all for her queen. Once again she was about to take the chance that she would never again see her beloved Philippe. This time, however, it was not from a sense of duty, but out of love. It was a lesson she should have learned long ago. If she had she might, even now, be in the arms of . . .

No. She mustn't think that way. There was no going back, only forward. The choices she had made in the past had led her to this moment in the present. She had to take what she had learned and keep moving. For as long, at least, as she was able.

Another swift glance up the street assured Honneure she was virtually alone. Leaning on her cane, she started on her journey. She only prayed she would arrive in time.

The closer she came to the square, the more crowded the streets became. A few people glanced at her curiously. But perhaps it was only because of her limp. Or, because of the dark cloak and hood she held close at her throat on such a warm, fall day. She recognized no one, and no one recognized her. No one had the slightest clue that she was a fugitive from the revolution. No one could possibly guess that she, too, had been slated to be fodder for the hungry blade of the guillotine.

Nausea churned again in Honneure's stomach. She could almost feel the blood drain from her face. But she did not hesitate. With one leg in rhythm with her sturdy cane, she hobbled onward.

Urgency quickened her lopsided gait, however, when she heard a cry from just ahead.

"She comes! The Widow Capet comes!"

"The Austrian whore!" came another shout. "The whore meets Lady Guillotine!"

Urgency turned to rising panic. Honneure stumbled as someone jostled her shoulder. "Sorry," she mumbled under her breath, although it was not her fault. "Sorry."

An overweight man with grizzled hair scowled at her. "Watch where yer goin'," he growled. Several others around him turned in her direction, all with thunderous frowns riding their brows.

Honneure lowered her gaze and tried to push her way through the mob in the opposite direction. She was going to have to be very, very careful. The mood of the crowd was murderous, indeed.

"There!" a woman's voice screamed. "There she is!"

Honneure felt her bladder weaken. But the woman was

not talking about her. Taking a deep breath, she dared to glance up from the littered ground.

All heads were turned to the left. Fathers hoisted little children up on their shoulders so they could see better. Women stood on tiptoes.

Honneure could see nothing. She was only able to hear the creak and groan of the tumbril's wooden wheels as it rolled through the crowded, cobbled square. Emboldened by her growing horror, Honneure elbowed her way through the massed and stinking bodies.

Irritated grunts and rude curses filled her ears. She ignored them. She had but one thought, one purpose. She had to get there in time. Her friend must know she did not die alone.

There was so much pushing and shoving by all that hardly anyone paid any attention to Honneure. Ducking, squeezing sideways, and pushing by turn, she managed to make her way to the front of the crowd. Only a few heads bobbed in front of her. She was able, at last, to see her Queen. Tears immediately rushed to Honneure's eyes.

She sat facing backwards, hands tied behind her back. Her posture was rigid, chin held high. The cart rumbled to a halt.

The former Queen had to be helped from the tumbrel. Honneure noticed her pretty plum shoes as she slowly climbed the ladder to the scaffold. Her white pique dress and bonnet were immaculate.

How like her. How very like her. A sob caught in

Honneure's throat.

Though she remained erect, Antoinette began to tremble at last. The executioner seized her roughly and forced her to her knees. He tied her to the plank. The guillotine towered above her, blade glimmering in the sun.

"You're not alone," Honneure whispered. "Antoinette, dearest friend, you're not alone," she said a little louder. Heads turned in her direction, but she paid them no heed. Pressing closer still to the scaffold, she slipped the hood from her head.

For one brief moment, Antoinette raised her eyes.

"My Queen!" The tortured cry rasped from Honneure's throat. She stretched out her hand, cane clattering to the ground.

The blade fell.

Pandemonium erupted. A thunderous roar, as if from a single, giant throat, burst from the crowd. General cheering followed. A few screams punctuated the tumult as the mob surged forward, crushing a few of its own under its terrible weight. Honneure feared she would be carried along with them, but the few who surrounded her were not moving. They had noticed her when she cried out. Now they stared at her.

Though choking on her tears, Honneure quickly pulled her hood up. It was too late.

"It's the woman, from Tuileries!" a pock-marked crone cried out. "It's her, the one who escaped!"

"Who? Who is it? Someone asked. A small crowd

within the crowd had formed.

Honneure tried to back away, but a hand grasped her skirt. "The bastard whore!" the scarred woman exclaimed. Honneure screamed as another pair of hands tore at her, ripping her bodice.

"No!"

"Get her! Don't let her get away!"

Searing pain shot through Honneure's head as someone pulled her hair. She saw a great handful of it come away.

"Leave me alone!"

Hands dragged at her, pulling her down. She was losing footing. A fist connected with her nose and blood splashed.

"No!"

Honneure screamed in denial.

But she could not save herself.

She was going to die . . .

ISBN# 097436391X
Gold Imprint
US $6.99 / CDN $9.99
Historical Fiction
Available Now
www.helenrosburg.com

Blaze of Lightning, Roar of Thunder

Helen A. Rosburg

Louisa Rodriguez was out on the desert gathering fuel when the scalp hunters came, massacred her family and all the people of her village, shot her in the head and left her for dead. Regaining consciousness, she buried the people she had loved, and when she was done she stripped off her bloody clothes and walked naked into the mountains. Where she was reborn.

When horse wrangler Ring Crossman came across the half-wild woman in the western wilderness, she would not tell him her name. So he gave her one. Blaze, for the lightning like streak of white in her long, black hair where a bullet had creased her skull. He gave her his heart, too, although he knew there was no room in her life for anything but revenge.

Vengeance consumed Bane as well. His life was devoted to finding the man who raped his Apache mother and fathered him. Then The Bringer of Thunder, as he was called by his people, crossed trails with the only human being whose thirst for a man's blood was as great as his own. And when they discovered they stalked the same prey, the destructive power of the storm they unleashed consumed all around them. Including themselves.

ISBN#1932815643
Silver Imprint / Historical Fiction
US $9.99 / CDN $13.95
December 2006
www.helenrosburg.com

SUMMER OF FIRE
LINDA JACOBS

It is 1988, and Yellowstone Park is on fire.

Among the thousands of summer warriors battling to save America's crown jewel, is single mother Clare Chance. Having just watched her best friend, a fellow Texas firefighter, die in a roof collapse, she has fled to Montana to try and put the memory behind her. She's not the only one fighting personal demons as well as the fiery dragon threatening to consume the park.

There's Chris Deering, a Vietnam veteran helicopter pilot, seeking his next adrenaline high and a good time that doesn't include his wife, and Ranger Steve Haywood, a man scarred by the loss of his wife and baby in a plane crash. They rally 'round Clare when tragedy strikes yet again, and she loses a young soldier to a firestorm.

Three flawed, wounded people; one horrific blaze. Its tentacles are encircling the park, coming ever closer, threatening to cut them off. The landmark Old Faithful Inn and Park Headquarters at Mammoth are under siege, and now there's a helicopter down, missing, somewhere in the path of the conflagration. And Clare's daughter is on it...

ISBN#1932815295
Gold Imprint
Available Now
US $6.99 / CDN $9.99
www.readlindajacobs.com

THE HINTERLANDS

The year is 1896. In the vast network of the Niger Delta waterways, where palm oil and blood flow from the hinterlands, the ancient Kingdom of Benin is under siege. Legendary trader and leopard hunter Brendan Donivan battles to protect his adopted homeland's sacred civilization from the colonial expansion of the British, while balancing his commerce with the whiteman's world. Life is not exactly easy. And it's about to get worse.

Enter Elle Bowie, New York anthropologist. She says she's come to study clitoridectomy. She claims the crazy Texan traveling with her, the one whose jungle attire consists wholly of a Stetson, boots, and a gun, is her husband. But Brendan suspects there's a lot more to the lovely lady's story than she's letting on.

Brendan, of course, is right. Elle has a lot more on her private agenda than the sexual surgical practices of the Benin women. And she's about to get herself into a bigger adventure than she'd planned on.

Because Mateus, descendant of Portuguese soldiers, who's supposed to be her guide, is a traitorous gnome. The majestic and brutal General Ologboshere, in command of thousands of warriors, has taken an unhealthy shine to her. A passel of bumbling British consular appointees are screwing things up for everybody. There's a war in the wings . . . you get the picture. But the worst, the absolute worst, is that super-feminist Elle is falling in love. With a guy who wears a skirt, no less.

And although he dwells in Benin, land of ritualistic human sacrifice and juju religion, a land about to run red with blood . . . although the lives and loves of many hang in the balance in The Hinterlands . . . Brendan's grinning.

ISBN#1932815112
Silver Imprint
US $9.99 / CDN $13.95
Historical Fiction
www.karenmercury.com

*For more information
about other great titles from
Medallion Press, visit*

www.medallionpress.com